SEVEN HOLES IN ENGLAND

Phil Arnold

USA ▪ Canada ▪ UK ▪ Ireland

Note for Librarians: A cataloguing record for this book is available from Library and Archives Canada at www.collectionscanada.ca/amicus/index-e.html
ISBN 1-4251-1472-5

Printed in Victoria, BC, Canada. Printed on paper with minimum 30% recycled fibre. Trafford's print shop runs on "green energy" from solar, wind and other environmentally-friendly power sources.

TRAFFORD™
PUBLISHING

Offices in Canada, USA, Ireland and UK

Book sales for North America and international:
Trafford Publishing, 6E–2333 Government St.,
Victoria, BC V8T 4P4 CANADA
phone 250 383 6864 (toll-free 1 888 232 4444)
fax 250 383 6804; email to orders@trafford.com
Book sales in Europe:
Trafford Publishing (UK) Limited, 9 Park End Street, 2nd Floor
Oxford, UK OX1 1HH UNITED KINGDOM
phone +44 (0)1865 722 113 (local rate 0845 230 9601)
facsimile +44 (0)1865 722 868; info.uk@trafford.com
Order online at:
trafford.com/06-3231

10 9 8 7 6 5 4 3 2

CHAPTER ONE

"You bin in the army?" Lawrence asked, after searching my papers with a crinkled look of distaste on his face.

I shook my head and returned his glare.

"Not at all?" he asked persistently, staring at me.

"I've been in the air force," I said.

"You could be shot or worse," he said.

"What could be worse than being shot?"

"If they catch you, you'll find out pretty damned quick."

"So I've got the job then?" I asked.

"You are the only one to apply so far. I keep telling you it's dangerous. You'll need an army background to do the job."

"I was a sergeant in the air force police," I protested.

"These people play for keeps. We need a man who thinks as they do. I don't think you will last a week."

"You said I was the only applicant. You've got no choice."

Lawrence chewed his lip, and the wispy moustache below his podgy nose quivered as he thought about it. He was watching and weighing me up at the same time.

"We might consider you," he said after awhile.

Three days later I received a letter from Lawrence telling me to report to a place in Oxford Street, London. The envelope also contained a railway warrant and five, ten pound notes.

The next day I found the place after walking for awhile. I climbed three flights of stairs to where a man was sitting at his typewriter. After eyeing my threadbare suit his gaze dropped to the slip of paper I was offering.

"Ah yes," he said, defrosting a little. "Mr Cox, will you go through the door?" he asked, pointing to a glass door and then returning to his typewriter.

I entered the room and walked up to a desk where Lawrence was sitting, then waited as he finished phoning. He swung around on a deep-seated chair and shot a quick look at me as he waved me to a stiff-backed chair in front of the desk.

"Do have a seat, Mr Cox," he said.

I slid onto the hard wooden seat and waited for him to start.

"For the last time, I ask you to reconsider if you are capable of doing the job we want of you. Do you understand?" he asked.

"I think I do," I replied, squirming on the seat as the coldness of the wood permeated my thin trousers.

"And do you also understand that once we employ you to do the job we will disclaim all knowledge and responsibility if you are caught by the opposition?"

"I understand that too."

Lawrence handed me a couple of pages of printed material, pointing to the bottom of the page.

"Sign there on the dotted line," he said, giving me a ballpoint pen.

I scrawled my signature on the form without reading it, and handed it back to him.

"Now we have it in black and white, I can now reveal what in fact the job consists of," he said, sliding the paper into the desk drawer. "We have it on good authority that somewhere in the country there are piles of illegal arms dumps. We have proof that these dumps were made by the IRA. We also know that there are seven in number and, to a certain extent, what they contain."

"Semtex and other arms I suppose," I said, still squirming.

"*Exactly*. The trouble is where are these dumps? That is what we want to know."

"And that is where I come in?"

"You got it in one. For this information we are willing to pay you twenty thousand pounds, plus the unlimited use of our resources where applicable."

"Can I have something on account?"

Lawrence broke into a thin smile and handed me an envelope.

"I've seen to that," he said. "There is a cheque for two thousand pounds. You'll get other payments as you progress."

"Where do I start?" I questioned, pocketing the cheque.

"Here you are," he said, giving me a small map. "The only bit of information we possess is in here. Trouble is it's very sketchy. Only a small help I'm afraid."

I took the scrap of coloured paper and unfolded it. On it

was a small area of south Buckinghamshire with a tiny dot representing something in the middle of a small wood.

"You're right it's nothing," I agreed, "but it's a start I suppose. What do I do now?"

"You report to an address I will give you, where they will equip you with the means of saving your life."

"You mean firearms?"

"I mean exactly that. We have a big arsenal, so you can pick your own weapon."

Lawrence handed me another printed page on which were directions to where I had to go. He held out his hand.

"I'll wish you the best because you will need all the luck you can get."

I gripped his hand and was surprised at the strength that lay in so elderly a man.

Using a thousand pounds of my money, I purchased a second-hand car and set out on the first leg of my journey.

The address on the paper proved to be a rundown building that was a front for the hive of industry that really went on. Several rooms belied its real purpose in life, which was to counter the threat of terrorism exercised by different groups of dissenters.

Pretty female clerks marched back and forth carrying wads of papers, for all the world making it seem like life in any normal office. Even the routine of the clerks was false because in the basement, which never saw daylight, other things were happening. Groups congregated in little rooms where they were taught the various niceties of self-defence against an antagonist with murder in mind, or soundproof rooms with never a hint of weapons being used or fired.

"Mr Cox," a grey-haired man called, startling me.

I nodded in answer, and allowed him to lightly pull my coat sleeve with me in tow rubbernecking at every sight and sound we encountered. At last we came to a solid looking, iron-banded wooden cupboard with several heavy padlocks hanging down from black painted hasps. The man produced a shiny key and turned it in the slot of one of the locks, pulled it open and released the hasp to drop down. When he opened the cupboard, he reached in and drew out a short barrelled, Smith and Wesson .38 calibre pistol.

"Try this," he said, putting the gun into my hand. "It might suit you, or do you have a preference?"

"No," I said, and gripped the butt hard. The gun felt smooth to the touch and settled nicely into my palm. "This'll do for now."

For the next hour I practised with the weapon, firing off quickly at a target more than thirty yards away. I was pleased to find most of my shots were within inches of where I had aimed.

"Very good," my companion said, after examining the target. "It's obvious you know how to look after yourself."

Later, just as it crossed from morning to afternoon, I swung the steering wheel to the left and went up a small incline to a roundabout at the crest of the hill. Below me, the motorway snaked away into the distance, carrying with it three lines of flowing traffic that disappeared into a thin mist on the top of a distant rise.

For a few miles I watched for a signpost showing the name of my destination, and when it came I was surprised to find it pointed to a church. For awhile, as the engine ticked over in front of me and the seconds slid by, I stared hard at the building trying to imagine the place being a hotbed of IRA activity - the thought seemed ridiculous. I was about to go when I saw a movement at the side of the churchyard. There was a flash of colour and a woman appeared.

I stayed my hand from putting the car into gear, and stopped the engine by turning the key. I got out and standing by the car door shouted across to her.

"I'm looking for a small piece of woodland," I said as she peeped around the corner of a brick pier. "This is Coney End Church isn't it? On the map there is a small wood and it is shown as quite near here."

She stepped into a shaft of sunlight and stood there looking at me. She was a small mousey woman with stringy brown hair that curled around her scalp like rope skeins.

"No such place," she declared, toying with a bulbous necklace that was hanging from her scrawny neck.

"It's on the map, a Coney Wood," I protested, holding out the scrap of map. "Here, look you can see for yourself."

She replied by just standing there looking at me. I was fast running out of patience with the woman. I was about to press her further when a soft voice sounded nearby and a man stepped into my line of vision.

"Can I help you?" he asked, showing a set of snow white teeth in a smile that looked like a permanent fixture.

"I was just asking the lady..." I began then stopped when his head shook from side to side.

"She's a bit simple I'm afraid," he explained. "I'm the vicar of the parish. She helps in the church, a sort of helpmate if you know what I mean."

The woman shifted her position and vanished from sight behind the pier as the vicar spoke over a spare shoulder.

"Will you water the plants in the vestry, Hilda?" he said then waited as the woman's shuffling footsteps faded into the background. "Poor soul," he said, turning to me with a smile still on his lips. "She lost her mother a little while ago, which added a lot of worry to her mental condition."

"I'm sure it did," I grated, thinning my lips with impatience. "I'm looking for an area of woodland near this village and I saw her standing there so I enquired whether she knew of it."

"I heard what she said and she is right," he replied. "There is no place known as Coney Wood, not now."

"Not now?" I echoed. "So there *was* a place of that name?"

"Certainly, but ten years ago a developer bought the site and cleared it of trees and brushwood. After that a builder took it over and built an estate of houses and other buildings on the ground, so the wood doesn't exist any more."

I blew a hot breath of annoyance at the news, so with great effort gathered together a grimace of a smile.

"Thanks for the information, vicar," I said, preparing to slide into the front seat of the car again. "Looks like I'm on the wrong track."

The church bell rang out the hour of three into the quiet afternoon air, the strident ringing cutting out all sound until the final bell faded away. I reached for the key to turn on the ignition and it was then an afterthought occurred to me.

"By the way, vicar, who was the builder of the housing estate?"

He shrugged his shoulders as he bent down to answer through the half-open window.

"Some firm called Patrick Murphy. An Irish company I believe. We had a few Irish labourers who lived in a couple of caravans in the wood before it went. I remember them well because they used to get drunk in the village pub on pay nights and sing Irish songs. We couldn't understand them because they sang and talked in Irish all the time."

"Did you see them when they had finished the work?"

"See them?"

"Yes, I mean when the houses were finished."

"No, they just seemed to vanish one morning before we were up, took their things with them as well. I heard a couple of them bought one of the houses and lived in it for awhile, but they also disappeared and weren't seen again."

CHAPTER TWO

Bingo! The elation shot through me like a bolt of electricity. 'Wheeew!' I shouted inside, 'pay dirt without even trying'. In the first instance, success, and then some - I was on my way to the twenty thousand. The feeling of happiness lasted all the way to my destination, where I stopped and beheld the sight of eight houses constructed in a semicircle around a small square.

Where the hell am I going from here? I wondered, looking at the scene in front of me. They all looked normal, just bricks and mortar with grey tiles and red brick chimney stacks that were so alike they reminded me of toytown.

I scratched my head and breathed out a sigh, realising that the work of unravelling it all was about to begin. That in itself was a wild thought because there I was in enemy country with not a single idea with which to console myself, and to add to the agony, I didn't have the slightest notion where to start.

I glanced through the car window and tried to imagine where the arms dump was situated. Under a garage or buried beneath a ton of earth in someone's garden? It wasn't hard to picture it; wrapped in plastic sheets to keep out the damp or in lined boxes where the weapons were kept in greased wrappers ready to emerge into daylight - with what in mind? That was another thing that puzzled me. What were they intending to do? Start another war, revolution, local unrest? They would need a bigger arsenal than this to have any effect on a country the size of the UK, plus the resources it could find in an emergency. A hive of buzzing bees swarmed in my mind, flitting from one idea to another.

I was taken by surprise when I saw the face of a child peering at me through the windscreen. For a few moments I returned the stare without moving, and the child, a girl, looked at me without blinking, plainly fascinated by my presence and the fact that I was the only one in sight. The friendly approach, I thought, and crooked my mouth in a smile – nothing happened. The girl still stared at me and I started to shift uncomfortably in my seat, trying to avoid her eyes, but then I had some success when I bumped my head on the steering wheel as I bent down. The eyes screwed up in ecstasy and the girl's face wrinkled in a grin.

Sensing a breakthrough, I wound down the window.

"Hello," I said as the child continued to stare at me, "you from around here, darling?"

"My mum said I shouldn't talk to strangers," the girl said, backing away.

That put me in a quandary. On one hand I had to find out a little about the area and on the other I had to be seen to agree with the child about not talking to strangers, to put her at her ease.

"Good girl," I said sweetly. "Your mother is right to tell you so. What's your name, love?"

"Sara," she replied, then jerked her head around as a faint cry sounded from one of the nearest houses. "Got to go now, me mum is calling me," she said, then skipped away down the small incline and was lost through a brown, painted garden gate.

I decided to give up then. There was nothing to do except go back to square one and start again, so that is what I did. Within a few seconds I was on the phone dialling the number Lawrence had given me before I left the office in Oxford Street. After listening to the burr burr that buzzed in my ear seven times, the dulcet tones of the overweight official came over the wire.

"Hello," he said sweetly, "how may I help you?"

"That bit of map you gave me is no use whatsoever," I said, without introduction. "Where'd you get it anyway?"

"Oh, it's you," he said in answer. "I was wondering when you would call me, Mr Cox." He sighed into the mouthpiece. "You're not the only one we employ you know. It was not the piece of map that was important, it was the way the information was acquired," he went on. "The man who collected the info also collected a bullet in the back. We cremated him two weeks ago, so his contribution is vital."

"Maybe so," I allowed. "I'm sorry to hear of it. Too bad it's all been for nothing."

"*Nothing*," Lawrence bellowed into my ear. "I don't get you. What do you mean *nothing*? We have it on good authority that the information we gave you is correct and reliable. We wouldn't have given it to you if it wasn't."

I gave him a quick run through of the events that had happened in the village, and waited for his reaction.

"Gone?" he said, almost in a whisper. "But how can a wood vanish into the blue? There must be something left, a few trees perhaps, bushes, hedgerows – something?"

"Nothing... Nothing but concrete and bricks everywhere," I insisted, spluttering with the effort. "They cleared away the lot."

"So the map is no good?"

"That's what I've been saying for the past few minutes. They don't exist any more."

Lawrence was quiet for a moment as the statement circled his brain. I could hear his steady breathing on the other end of the wire. I could almost see his train of thoughts queuing up for space in the gateway of his mind. I steeled myself because I knew what was coming.

"We'll have to start from scratch," he said at last. "Go back to the place and make some enquiries."

"I suppose you mean *me*. *I'll* have to start from scratch as you put it."

"Well, we are paying you a large sum aren't we? Anyway, you have the edge over everybody else inasmuch as you know the lie of the land, and that is an advantage where any new body is concerned, isn't it?"

"I suppose so," I conceded dryly, "and talking about money, I need another financial transfusion."

"Can't help you there, I'm afraid," he said in a sorrowful voice. "We have our budgets and must stick to them. Your monthly cheque will be credited to your account as agreed."

That is when he rang off, leaving me with a buzz of

disconnection in my ear and a knot of cold frustration in my breast.

"Bastard!" I yelled, swearing at the receiver and dropping it on its rest.

Mentally I calculated how much I had remaining in my pocket then stepped from the phone box into the shadow of an overhanging oak tree. Pausing for a moment, I looked both ways trying to get my bearings.

The village consisted of two rows of cottages, one on either side of a narrow, tree lined road that curled through it like a prostrate snake. At the beginning of the twist was the church with its pigeon pocked spire rising out of a forest of gravestones that littered the foot of the building. In the centre of the building was a big clock face with the hands pointing to seven thirty, below which was a massive oaken door with a glass-encased light extending outwards on a metal rod.

I swung my gaze in the other direction and caught sight of a white painted construction with exposed, black wooden timbers, and a sign hanging down, swinging slowly in the soft evening breeze. It was a pub - the only one in Coney End. I made for it without hesitation, certain in the knowledge that if there was any life in the village most of it would be concentrated there.

When I pushed open the door with the word 'Lounge' inscribed in the woodwork, I heard the gentle murmur of soft conversation that stopped when I stepped into the room. The bar was brightly lit, highly polished and surrounded by a row of padded barstools that sprouted like mushrooms in front of it. Each one was anchored to the floor by a shining circle of metal, which gleamed and reflected the spotlights buried in the ceiling above. A man and woman stood behind the bar, no longer talking but staring at the suddenness of my entrance.

The only other person in the bar was a man with a small goatee beard. He had stopped in the act of drinking a glass of beer that was now suspended halfway to his lips, no doubt as a result of my sudden appearance. He was watching me through steel rimmed glasses that made his eyes protrude behind thick glass lenses – an effect that was startling, to say the least.

"Evening all," I said, striding in.

"Evening," returned the man at the table.

Before him on the table was a pork-pie hat together with a black cane that was lying beside it. A brown leather briefcase rested against the legs of his chair and snuffling at the heel of one of his shoes was a small mongrel dog. As I approached, the dog growled softly in its throat, but was quickly hushed to silence when the man tapped it with the edge of his shoe. The glass was then returned to the table and the eyes finished their appraisal by shifting to another direction.

"Evening," echoed the man behind the counter.

He waited expectantly as I stared at the hand pumps.

"Bitter," I said, staring back at him as he fixed me with a look. "Make it a pint."

An awkward silence fell and an atmosphere was building. The woman broke it.

"Quite nice now after that little shower we had."

She had a blue rinse in her hair, the effect being spoiled by the fact that it looked as though it had been applied in a hurry and was streaky. Her skin was patchy with yellow spots amid the stain of grainy suntan on her neck and the flesh of her hands. Gold rings glittered at her throat and on the fingers of each hand.

The pint came up frothy and clear, and as the man accepted the ten pound note I offered, I sipped the liquid.

"That's better," I said, pretending to relish the beer as the man returned with my change. "There's nothing like a good drop of bitter I always say."

He looked at me and dropped the coins onto the counter.

"It's not as bad as some I could name," he said, straightening up a soggy beer mat.

After awhile, when the clock on the wall pointed to nine and I was about to order my third pint, the door opened to admit another man. The newcomer came in and sat at the table with the first man. He began to talk in a low whisper, all the while making signs with his hands as if to emphasise each sentence with a positive stamp.

Glancing around slowly, I took in the whole picture of the two men, trying hard not to appear as if I was interested in them. I paid for my beer and sat on one of the stools nursing my glass. The bar had a mirror at the rear of the parade of spirit optics and now and again I caught sight of them as they spoke together, all the time glancing up to see if I had heard what they were saying. They suddenly stopped talking and sat there looking at the dog that was whimpering under the table. The man with the thick glasses patted the dog on the head, which made it stand up, its tail wagging with delight.

"Not now, Chum," he said with a laugh, "later, later."

The men continued to sit together engaged in quiet conversation for another few minutes, then the man who had just arrived got to his feet and left – leaving thick glasses and me. The barman brought me the couple of ham sandwiches I had ordered and I sat chewing them with my back to the door. Suddenly the man at the table removed his glasses, put them on the table before him and looked across the room at my back.

"Mr Cox," he said softly, and waited as I stiffened with surprise. "Mr Cox, my name is George Brewer."

I swung around, almost choking on my sandwich, and looked at him intently.

"How do you know my name?" I demanded, swallowing a crust with some difficulty.

"We have a mutual friend in London," he replied, with a smile, "a friend by the name of Lawrence."

CHAPTER THREE

He pointed to the vacant chair beside him.

"Why don't you come over here?" he said quietly. "We've got plenty to discuss."

"We certainly have, Brewer," I agreed, getting over my initial shock.

I slid off the stool and settled in the chair.

"Just call me George," Brewer said, moving the hat and cane.

"Well, George, you tell me why Lawrence has sent you here and why he didn't tell me today when I phoned him."

"He only got wind of a plot to eliminate you a little while ago. He sent me to warn you to be on your guard. They know about you and why you were sent here."

"Now isn't that charming? I'm on the receiving end of an attempt on my life and I'm only into the first day's work."

"They play for keeps as you must have heard."

The glasses were now full on me as he returned them to the bridge of his nose.

"I guessed that, George," I grated, returning his stare.

"They don't pay you twenty grand for nothing and, just out of curiosity, who was that other guy you were talking to just now?"

"I was coming to that," he said. "He got in touch with head office and offered to sell some information to us for a price."

"What information, about what?"

"About where the arms dumps are located no less."

"How on earth did he manage to get in contact with Lawrence, and for that matter, how does he know about us?"

Brewer gave a sharp laugh that caused his glasses to jump up and down on his nose.

"The IRA knows all about us and our work," he said, fingering his glass. "I'm rather surprised they know about you already though, but that shows just how efficient they are. They're not just a bunch of ignorant Paddies you know. They are a well-organised army equipped with the best of modern arms as well as a completely capable spy network whose job it is to find out about the opposition and eradicate it. They do this with the utmost efficiency because only last month they shot one of our chaps."

"I heard about that," I said. "They cremated him two weeks ago."

"Yes they did," Brewer said quietly, "but did you know you are his replacement?"

"Now that you mention it, no," I replied, feeling uncomfortable and getting the idea I was being used.

The hairs on the back of my neck began to rise in sympathy with the feeling, sending small shock waves through my system.

"That man, Mason by name, wants a million quid for telling us the location of the dumps," Brewer continued, stroking his beard.

I nearly choked with surprise.

"*A million quid*, and I'm just getting a measly twenty thousand for doing the same thing," I said, pushing the sandwich plate to one side.

"Yes, but I'm thinking he'll have to go into hiding 'cause the million won't do him much good with a couple of bullets in his head, will it?"

I shook my head to acknowledge the fact.

"Well, are they going to use him?" I asked, fully convinced I was out of a job that I wasn't sure I liked anyway. "It seems to me it will be cheap at the price he's asking rather than risking us to do the job."

Brewer looked at me coyly and winked.

"He's not the first to want to come over to our side," he said, "and I don't think he'll be the last. A million is a lot of money, as another of the IRA informers found out – to his cost. He was discovered floating in the Thames minus his head and limbs. They are taking a big risk in betraying their terrorist taskmasters. Once you are in the IRA it's for life."

"Supposing he comes up with the goods," I said. "The authorities can get rid of the arms dumps with one swoop. It'll be worth it for them to pay the money."

"I'm thinking they will, but to be on the safe side they are employing us to find out something as well."

"Yes, if I don't get killed in the meantime," I said. "What about you, haven't they had a go at you yet?"

"Oh yeah, a few times, but I've been lucky. You learn to see them coming, so you take evasive action."

"Yeah, I bet."

I looked at the dog beneath the table, snuffling at Brewer's shoes.

"What about the dog, do you always take it with you on an assignment or is this just your idea of taking it for walkies?"

Brewer laughed at this and, reaching down, patted the mongrel's head.

"Sounds like a good idea at that," he said, watching the dog wag its tail furiously. "No, I take him along because it appears abnormal to see a spy on duty trailing a mongrel dog, and while they are working it out I'm doing a bunk – simple!"

"What about your glasses? Seems to me they must be a bit of a handicap under the circumstances. I mean, are your eyes that bad that you need such thick lenses?"

"Another part of my defensive ploy," he replied. "I use everything to confuse them."

And me as well, I thought, trying to work it all out and not succeeding too well.

"Do you need them?" I said aloud.

"The glasses? Nah, my eyes are as good as yours."

"Then how do you manage to look through them with those big windows? Don't they make you see double?"

"That's the secret; they are split into two. The bottom half is just false lenses. That is the part I look through. The top half is magnified and it makes my eyes stand out like boiled eggs."

I was about to ask him to explain it all again, but a little voice within me warned against it and I gave it up. I decided to veer onto another tack.

"Another thing puzzling me, mate, is how you knew I would be in here tonight, I mean, you were in here waiting for me."

"In Coney End everyone ends up either here or in the church. It being evening, it's a fair bet it will be the pub, so here I am. I had also lined up a meeting with Mason, so I killed two birds with one stone so to speak."

When the barman returned, I dropped my voice a couple of semitones lower and spoke softly so he couldn't hear.

"What about this bit of a map I've got in my pocket? I've been to the site, but no wood exists, just a lot of houses where it used to be," I whispered.

"I know about the map, and it *is* strange that it points to a piece of land that doesn't exist any more. We obtained it from the man who was killed recently. It is the only clue we have in tracing the arms dumps, so hang on to it."

It was at this moment that the dog began to bark as two people, a man and a woman, entered the room. Brewer quickly silenced it by pushing it with the heel of his shoe then waited as the newcomers sat on the barstools.

"I've got to get back," he said out of the corner of his mouth. "When I see him tomorrow, I'll let our mutual friend know what has been going on. Perhaps he can give you a bit more to go on, but I doubt it. He only has the information we supply and you already know that."

He trailed out through the doorway followed by the dog dragging on its lead, leaving me with a thousand unexplained questions buzzing around in my head.

On my way home to my London flat it began to rain and it was soon beating against the windscreen. The wipers were hard put to clear it for awhile, and several trails of miniature waterfalls were forcefully rushing down the glass. I cursed as a drip splashed onto my head, warning me of a hole in the roof, then another and another as the downpour increased.

By the time I reached my front door the side of my jacket was a dark patch of wet cloth that saturated my shirt beneath. I entered the building feeling cold and miserable, and after stripping and drinking a hot cup of coffee in front of a blazing gas fire, I crashed out on the nearby settee and went straight to sleep.

CHAPTER FOUR

A warm shaft of sunlight shone across my face bringing me to consciousness, and I sat up wet with sweat. The fire on the wall was belting out the calories and the room was like an oven. With an effort I turned off the gas tap and watched the red glow die away into blackness, crackling as the cold invaded the firebrick surround.

Over a cup of steaming coffee I read the front page of the morning newspaper, and ate a slice of toast and marmalade as the pangs of hunger echoed through my empty belly like the rattle of a firing machine gun. I leafed through the remaining pages of the paper and put it down beside me, spilling marmalade on it from between two slices of squeezed together toast. I swore, as the marmalade seemed to stick to everything it touched, and licked all my fingers and one wrist to dispel the stuff.

Later, I dressed quickly, putting on a clean shirt and tie, which cheered me up no end as the laundered cotton touched my skin. I fingered my closely shaved chin and combed my hair sideways to disguise the fact that I was going ever so slightly bald on the crown of my head. I surveyed the end product of my attempt at ablutions and scrubbed my teeth with the side of an index finger. My toothbrush lay at the bottom of the toilet bowl where I had dropped it the day before.

A nice soft breeze was blowing as I let myself out of the house, and the smell of a new day with sunshine attached was in the air. When I began to cross the road, from the corner of my eye I noticed a black vehicle parked a couple of hundred yards away. When I was about ten yards from the kerb, I heard the sound of a screaming engine rising in pitch, and I turned my head to ascertain the cause of the noise. For the few blinks of a surprised eye I was rooted to the surface of the tarmac road, unable to move and mentally handcuffed by the suddenness of the movement. I stared fascinated at the sight of over a ton of shifting metal making a beeline for me.

From then on a feeling of being in the wrong place at the wrong time struck me, and with a superhuman effort, which belied my body weight as well as my surprise, I dived for the safety of the kerb and pavement, sprawling on my knees just as the metal monster roared past me, spewing black exhaust smoke. The evil looking bumper, gleaming with metal malevolence, sliced the area that I had so suddenly vacated, then shot by with a screaming shriek of burning rubber and whirring wheels.

"Fucking bastard!" I hurled after the flying car as it rattled into a side street and disappeared.

I rubbed a pair of skinned knees and got to my feet just as an old lady reached me.

"I saw that," she said indignantly. "Bloody drivers these days, you can't trust 'em on the roads no matter what."

So saying, she snorted again to show her anger, and without more ado continued on her way. I compressed my lips in pain and surprise when she walked away with hardly a backwards glance. I was glad of the sympathy and managed to smile sweetly at her departing figure, although the grazes were stinging like crazy. I developed a limp in both legs, which seemed to equal out each other to a funny plod; something that had the baffling ability to shift the pain to one leg just as the other was about to touch ground.

The grating voice of Lawrence dug like a gimlet into the soundbox of my ear, and to escape the aural assault I held the instrument a couple of inches away from my lobe.

"Brewer was just on the blower," he said, burping his breakfast deep into my eardrum so that I was glad of the two-inch cushion of air. "He mentioned a certain person called Mason, and I want you to follow it up with immediate effect. Brewer will be looking into it from another angle. When he is ready he will contact you, so there is no need to worry about it if you don't hear from him for awhile – clear?"

I mumbled a 'yes' into the receiver and was about to relay all that had happened that morning when I realised the phone was dead. The bastard had rung off without warning.

I made my way back to where I had left my car and, with a sigh of annoyance at the phone call, slid behind the wheel. As well as cutting me off at the vital moment, Lawrence had also forgotten to give me details about Mason, leaving me high and dry as to his whereabouts. I was also in the dark about how to deal with the man and what to offer – the million quid, for example. What authority had I to offer the man anything? In the back of my mind was the suspicion that Lawrence had deliberately held back the information, with what in mind God only knows.

It was not the first time he had withheld such knowledge. I wondered why he thought it essential to tell me so little. My greenness could be a deciding factor, I thought then my musing turned to Brewer. Maybe I can contact him and get the low-down on Mason, but how do I get in touch with him? Why, the phone, naturally, but I don't have his number do I? Well, use the phone book to find him, you fool!

Very soon I was back at the phone box calling the operator and wanting to know the number of a George Brewer, who lived somewhere in London. Naturally she wanted to know the address of the subscriber, but I couldn't supply one because I didn't know it. I left the phone box feeling like a fool and, after thinking quite hard, headed for the only place of free information; the local library.

I never realised how many Brewers there were in London until then. Page after page passed before my eyes and thousands of telephone numbers danced before my widened gaze as I fanned them into a solid mass before me. It was unbelievable how many George Brewers there were as well – pages and pages stretching from east to west in a wall of agonising number columns that seemed to coagulate into a thick stew of numbered hundreds and thousands. I gave it up and resigned myself to finding him through sheer luck. There was nothing for it but to go back to Coney End and see if I could find a lead from there.

Very soon the familiar landscape of the village, with the church spire thrusting upwards from the huddled group of cottages, came into view. The strange thing was the lack of human agency on the streets, and that morning was no exception. No doubt it was due to the fact that the surrounding countryside was all farmland and the people were employed on the farms. No, I corrected myself, for three small children were playing on a swing on a piece of wasteland at a fork in the road, their yells of delight seeming strangely out of place in the sombre air of the otherwise deserted village.

Not so the pub though. The car park of The Wishing Well was half full and even from that distance the sound of taped music floated to me on the breeze. It was mixed with the occasional raucous bellow of laughter of a local male resident as he merrily and loudly drank through his lunch hour. What's good for them is also good for me, I decided, and slowly nosed the bonnet of the car towards the source of the music, passing deserted cottages and a little post office-cum-general store that was hidden behind a well-spread oak tree - also deserted.

After parking the car on a shifting carpet of gravel, which sprayed up with an alarming rattle against the underside of the car floor, I went down a small flight of three stone steps and entered the pub by the side door. As I stepped inside, the noise grew louder and the music more tinny. Wreaths of tobacco smoke hanging like clouds in the still air of the pub parted to one side like writhing fingers as I walked down a small passageway to the bar in the front of the building.

Two surprises awaited me when I opened the door, both in the shape of two familiar faces. One was peering through thick, milk bottle bottom lenses at my sudden entrance, the other with the frightened features of the informer, Mason.

CHAPTER FIVE

For the passing of a few seconds we stared at each other, shock plainly hitting the three of us with equal degree, so that the slience began to build up to a charged pitch. Brewer broke the ice by giggling, and the moment of surprise was over and the situation eased.

"Just the man we were talking about," he said, casting a look at his companion, who was still eyeballing me. "Mr Mason here," he said, swinging towards me, "was just saying what's going to happen to his offer now that I've been transferred. I've just got through telling him that you are taking over from me and are authorised to continue in my place."

I strode over and occupied another chair at the same table. I looked straight into the hard gaze of the informer, noting the florid face of a man who was sweating slightly on his upper lip, and of the evasive way he had of avoiding my direct look by lowering his eyelashes.

"Lawrence never said anything about the million quid," I said, looking from one to the other. "He never even gave me time to tell him about the car that nearly ran me down outside my house this morning. Deliberately, I might add."

Brewer appeared unmoved, as did Mason, but they did exchange a knowing glance, which seemed to suggest such an incident had happened before.

"That'll be Sweeney," Mason said to Brewer. To me he said, "That is one fucking fine man you'd better avoid 'cause he is the hit man of the army, a hard, no nonsense, died in the wool bastard who thinks it's his mission on earth to kill Ireland's enemies – no fooling."

"Thanks for telling me," I said. "I'll give him a wide berth."

Brewer spoke up then, fixing me with a stare, glasses glinting with reflected light.

"I've put Mason here in the picture. He knows we need the information and we are willing to pay for it. He also knows we will need proof that he knows where the dumps are located before we authorise payment."

"And what do we do first, Brewer?" I asked. "And what do we do when we find out where they are?"

"We will leave that little problem hanging, shall we? Right now, Mason has elected to take us to one site to provide the proof we need to continue the agreement."

"OK," I said, rubbing my hands together, "when do we start?"

"Not so fast," Mason said, hard eyed and stern faced. "I want some guarantees first."

"Like what?" I asked, equally as hard.

"Like… giving me a deposit as a guarantee of good faith."

I laughed loudly at him and shook my head.

"You are one big fool if you think we have that sort of money on us, mate. A *deposit* – what do you think this is you're dealing with, Marks and Spencer? If you have any sense you can see that." I got up, meaning to go. "Come on, Brewer, let's go," I said, hoping Mason would swallow the hook. "It's no good talking to the small fry. We are only wasting our time."

"Hold on!" Mason cried, catching hold of my arm. "I didn't mean exactly that. I know you ain't got that sort of money with you. You'd be a fool to carry it, but I must have some form of assurance that I will be paid."

"And you will be," Brewer interjected, before I had a chance to reply. "Lawrence will see to it I can promise you."

"Lawrence means nothing to me," Mason returned, with a sneer. "I've met countless government lackeys whose word means no more to me than the hot air it takes to make 'em. They say something and when it comes to the crunch, deny they ever said it." He breathed in a lungful of smoky air and dispelled it with flared nostrils. "No," he said at last, "I know I've got to deal with someone and it looks like being you two."

"At last you've got it, Mason," I declared, sitting down again. "We can give you no guarantees, but we are ethical. You keep your side of the bargain and we'll keep ours."

"Perhaps we can get down to talking about visiting the site to see if you really know what you are saying," Brewer said, now that it was calm again.

"We can go to the site, sure, and we can look at the area where it is situated, no problem with that I'll tell you, but that is all we can do," Mason said quietly, "then the rest is up to you."

"When can we see these dumps and what they contain?" I asked.

"You can see the site anytime you give me some form of monetary guarantee. I must have something to ensure I get the cash."

"I already told you we can't do that," I said, becoming irritated at the insistence of the man. "So what have we got now – stalemate?"

Brewer suddenly had an idea.

"Look, I will get a post-dated cheque from Lawrence for a hundred thousand pounds on the understanding that when we see the arms it will be honoured."

"And that's another thing," Mason said. "You can't see the arms straight away only see where they are stored."

Now Brewer's big lenses with strange coloured eyeballs were turned on Mason.

"Can't see them," he echoed in a high tone, "but, we *must* see them. How do we know if they are there if we don't see them?"

Mason shrugged his shoulders and raised his eyebrows.

"We must be very careful," he said, staring into the glasses. "The army are not fools; they know the dump can be found and broken into. That is why they provide a means of destroying the contents to ensure the arms cache will not fall into the wrong hands."

Mason now had our full attention and he knew it. For the space of a few seconds he fell silent and waited for our inevitable question.

"What do you mean *destroy*?" I enquired, dry mouthed.

"You know, blow it up," he answered quietly. "Listen to this. The people who built the dumps also constructed a form of booby trap designed to go off if the wrong person tries to gain access. This is well known to me and other members of the army – we know how to disarm the bomb."

"I see," I said thoughtfully. "So the bastards have set up a trap for the unwary. If they try to get in, up it goes."

Mason nodded.

"So you see you will need me, not only to show you the place, but to make the booby trap safe," he grated.

"Well, that's another reason to use my idea of a post-dated cheque," Brewer said with gusto. "Lawrence will authorise it when I tell him what it's for."

"What about the other nine hundred thousand smackers?" Mason asked.

"What about the other arms dumps?" Brewer counteracted intently.

Mason's face turned red with the pressure of temper, and for a moment I thought he was going to strike Brewer.

"The agreement was that I show you where *one* is, not the lot," he said, gritting his teeth in a tight line.

"Did I say that, mate? I'm afraid you're wrong in thinking the boss will pay you for just one. We need the others as well. Seven dumps, one million quid; simple arithmetic."

"Simple is right, like you think I am. There's no difference between any of you. To hear you is to hear your boss, Lawrence. A deal is a deal..." He paused, breathing hard. "Do I get the cheque or not?" Mason insisted, gazing hard at Brewer.

"That part of the deal hasn't changed. We've got to make sure about the location in any case."

Mason sighed and relaxed, and I had the feeling he was about to give in. He slumped back in his chair and passed a thin hand over his brow.

"I can't tell you about the other six because I don't know them," he muttered in a strained voice. "I only found out the location of one by accident. The advice was given to me instead of another member. Only a few of the followers get the whole picture and they are high up officials who have proved themselves beyond reproach. Those responsible for the bombing campaign in England are the army elite, who will never surrender until they get what they want – a united island of Ireland, nothing less."

"Thanks for the lesson in politics," Brewer snapped, "but this is *now*. What're you going to do about it?"

"What can I do but comply?" Mason said, with a trace of misery in his voice. "You have me over a barrel because I need the money to clear out."

"Then when can we see the site?"

Mason picked his lip and frowned in concentration.

"It's Tuesday now," he said thoughtfully. "Make it Friday, yes, Friday is the day because I have to make some other kind of arrangements now that we have a deal." His face brightened into a smile of relief now that it was settled. "You gents don't realise the sacrifices I'm making telling you all this. I'm giving up a lot to co-operate with you, and you know it. I'm a patriot, but I'm a realistic one. Trouble is others don't see it that way."

"My heart bleeds for you," Brewer said, acid dripping from his tongue.

"Then I'll see you Friday at nine in the morning, here in Coney End. Come prepared for a long journey and don't be late 'cause I won't wait long."

Mason stood up, nodded to the two of us and disappeared through the doorway.

"Do you think we've got something at last?" I asked a quiet Brewer as he sat fingering his glass.

"Maybe," Brewer answered, his tongue licking a trace of beer froth sticking to his fair moustache hair. "Anyway, we'll know Friday won't we?"

We didn't know Friday or Saturday either because Mason was incapable of telling us anything.

As we stood in the car park of the Wishing Well pub cursing him for his lateness, we had little knowledge of his whereabouts or his condition. After waiting until noon, we finally decided he wasn't going to show up and ruefully made our way back to the Smoke, complaining bitterly.

"Back to square one," Brewer sighed, leaning back to pat the dog in the rear of the car. "I really thought we had him. For awhile I thought our luck had changed."

"And it did – for awhile," I said, agreeing. "He's one big slippery customer and we took him for granted."

After awhile the conversation lagged and we drove into the outskirts of London in silence, immersed in our own thoughts. After dropping him at the corner of his road, I drove back to my flat totally convinced we had seen the last of Mr Mason. We had, although not in the way I had imagined.

After having a quiet to boring weekend watching TV and catching up on my reading, I contacted Lawrence on the Monday, hoping he would give me another lead to follow.

"You can forget Mason," he rasped in my ear.

My mouth dropped a couple of inches when he continued.

"Yesterday he was found with massive injuries at the foot of a high-rise building. They said it was suicide because of his apparent contrition in betraying the IRA, but we know better don't we? Taking into consideration the number of 'accidents' that have happened in the past couple of years, the likelihood of it being accidental is completely laughable I'm sure."

I recovered my senses enough to croak into the receiver.

"But he was alive last week. We spoke to him, me and Brewer, last Tuesday. He never looked like he was about to take his own life."

"You aren't listening to me, Cox. I said it *wasn't* suicide because it bears all the hallmarks of Sweeney's specialist hand."

"I've almost suffered at the hands of this man, Sweeney. Only last week he almost ran me down outside my flat. You never mentioned it," I said, feeling hurt at the omission.

"It'll go on your record report and you will be rewarded financially, I suppose."

That cheered me up no end. Like lightning, I mentally calculated how many near misses I was destined to be involved in during my time in Lawrence's employ. The thought was happy and the future enriching, I was hoping.

"How much will I get?" I enquired, still thinking of money.

"Not a lot if you're not around to collect it."

I gulped, nearly swallowing my tongue, which got in the way of my spluttered reply.

"Wha-what's that you say?" I said, trying not to cough.

"I had a note pushed through my letter box this morning. On it was written these few words, *Mason now, Cox later.*"

CHAPTER FIVE

For a few seconds I could not believe my ears, and Lawrence's heavy breathing gushed into my sound box like the steady rise and fall of crashing surf.

"You heard what I said?" he asked after awhile.

"Yes, but it's slow in registering. Me next, eh?"

"That's what the note said. Short and to the point."

"Perhaps it's the work of a crank. Somebody who-"

"I don't think so. Too much of a coincidence," Lawrence interrupted. He sighed, a long drawn out sound that beat into my ear like a suppressed hurricane. "It looks authentic all right. Seems like you're a marked man," he said, ending his statement with a wheezy cough.

"Can you give me some sort of idea what Sweeney looks like?"

"Yes, he's stocky, has a close cropped head that closely resembles a bullet. He's about six two, with a scar just above his left eye. I shouldn't draw too much support from the description because he uses a lot of disguises."

"Sounds like a pretty nasty sort of a guy. Typical picture of an archetypal villain, who will stop at nothing."

"He is, but he's not alone, not by a long chalk."

"You mean there are others?"

"Yes, of both sexes, so watch yourself at all times."

"This is beginning to get a little alarming."

"Remember I told you it was dangerous in the first place."

That is where we left it. I slammed the phone box door in disgust and headed homewards, filled with the knowledge that I had bitten off more than I could possibly chew – a distinct extra worry that was becoming more burdensome with each passing second. Now I was studying each passer-by with a suspicious eye, looking for the scar above the left eye and the bullet-shaped head that went with it.

When I arrived home I found an envelope lying on the mat, and after slitting it open with the bread knife, I studied the contents with interest.

Meet me this afternoon, two o'clock outside Woolworths.
Jeannie

Now the plot is beginning to twist, I mused. Another character had entered the scene and to make matters more intriguing it was a woman, or so the note claimed. I recalled that Sweeney used disguises, so now he was dressed as a woman? Not so easy for him, I decided, as he was over six feet tall, and how many big women do you see in the course of a day? Mind you, you do see some, I also thought, but they stand out, not in a crowd, but in front of Woolworths where the note said she would be. Anyway, in a public place like in front of Woolworths, who would be so silly as to attempt murder? I decided to go and find out because I was not about to sit around and let him find me.

I found myself on the other side of the road from Woolworths, studying each female who went in and out of the building. I tried to hide behind a telegraph pole that was too thin to conceal me, getting puzzled looks from passers-by and ducking back when I thought I had been seen. I grinned as a man stopped and stared at me, trying to look as though I was something to do with the phone company and was about to climb the pole. I looked at him then the pole, and was about to tell him to piss off when, out of the corner of my eye, I saw the figure of a woman standing by one of the door pillars. I treated the man to a broad smile, and shrugging my shoulders to denote I didn't know what, stepped off the pavement and crossed the road.

As I got near, I noticed that the person had a shapely body and a pair of equally shapely legs to go with it. I decided that if it was Sweeney he must be quite a fellow.

"Jeannie?" I enquired, as two eyes of azure blue turned on me.

"Mr Cox?" she asked with one of those disarming smiles you can't help but enjoy.

"I got your note this morning, so here I am."

She had clear facial skin with just the slightest trace of powder and lipstick. Her nose was small with a delicate face surrounded by a circlet of light brown hair, which added charm to the picture.

"Can we go somewhere and talk?" she asked, casting those big blue eyes at my welcoming smile.

I stepped aside and allowed her to lead the way to a small tea room next door to Woolworths. It was one of those self-service places and, after paying at the till at the end of a queue of people, we carried our teas over to an empty table and spread out on the upholstered chairs. I lounged back on one and waited expectantly for her to explain, which she did almost immediately.

"As you must be aware by now, I'm connected with the IRA."

I nodded, so she continued.

"I have been for a number of years. I love my country and want to see a united Ireland, but having said that, I don't want it at any cost. Not at the expense of human lives of innocent women and children. That is why I've decided to come over to your side to help you."

"And when did you make this decision?" I asked, watching her closely.

"It's been on my mind for a long time," she answered quietly.

"It's not motivated by financial gain?"

"Of course not!" she replied hotly. "I'm not another Mason."

"So you know him?"

"We all know him. He's out to sell the secret of the arms dumps regardless of whom he hurts."

"Did you know he was found dead at the bottom of a tower block on Sunday?"

I was still studying her, so the look of surprise could have

42

been feigned, not so the blanch that changed her cheeks to white.

"No, I didn't know, so they carried out the threat."

"Who, Sweeney?"

"Maybe, probably they'd use him to execute Mason."

"So it *was* Sweeney who did the killing?"

"Him or Harvey. Another hit man on whom they can rely."

"Harvey? A new name. Have they got two hit men?"

"*Two* men?" she said incredulously. "They've got a dozen who will be only too pleased to cause mayhem on the English mainland, men and women alike."

That was thought-provoking I realised, and let the woman's revelation circle my brain. If it was true, we were up against a bigger force than we had at first thought. If it *is* true, I said to myself again, only this time it seemed less of a novelty than before. She began to grow in ethical status every time she opened her mouth, and I breathed a thankful sigh of relief that I did not have a partisan woman patriot with which to deal.

"What's really in it for you?" I suddenly asked, watching her face to catch any sign of deceit.

"Nothing but the knowledge that others will not be harmed because of an obsession."

"You call patriotism an obsession?"

"It is when you use guns to obtain your ends."

"Do you know the location of any of the arms dumps?" I asked.

"I know the one where Mason was taking you."

"Whereabouts are the arms buried?"

"They're not buried, but rather the opposite, if you think of it in that way."

She paused to sip her tea.

"What do you mean? They're up in a tree somewhere?"

Her face creased into a smile at my attempt at humour, and her lips twitched slightly as a laugh escaped from them.

"What's so funny?" I asked, taken aback.

"*You* are, Mr Cox. You're so obvious it's hilarious."

"Does it show up that much?" I asked in a rueful voice.

"Of course it does, but I was expecting the question, so it doesn't count. Now, the next one before I run out of answers."

All right, I breathed to myself, now for the big one.

"If I asked you, would you take me to it?"

"Yes, I believe I would," she replied, looking straight at me.

CHAPTER SIX

For a minute I couldn't believe my ears or my luck. I was about to ask her to repeat her answer, but when I ran through the words inside me I resisted the temptation and instead smiled the sweetest smile I could muster. She was not slow in copying my effort and smiled back, showing a set of perfect teeth and the tip of a delicate pink tongue.

"Where do you live? I'll give you a lift," I offered, thinking the meeting was at an end now that she had seen fit to help me.

"There is a condition attached to my offer of help," she announced in the middle of my act of self-congratulation.

I inwardly jerked to a standstill and waited for the crunch.

"Did you want something else?" I asked with an innocent face.

"Something else? What do you mean? You've given me nothing."

"Nothing," I repeated, "nothing? But you are a member

of an illegal organisation. I've given you your freedom, and you say you've had *nothing*."

She gave me a strange look and stood up to go.

"You looked like a man I could trust, but it seems I was wrong in my judgement. Sorry I bothered you, Mr Cox."

Something came over me and I grabbed the sleeve of her jacket.

"Sorry I said what I said," I apologised. "I lost my head for a minute. Please don't go."

She hesitated, looking down at me. I tried to be the picture of the contrition I felt, pleading with my eyes and the strength of my hand, which was gripping her sleeve in a tight fist.

"Well… all right," she said, slowly and reluctantly. "We'll let it pass this time, but if you want my co-operation in this affair to the full I'd advise you to curb your tongue."

"I will, I will," I assured her, eager now that she had relented. "I can't apologise more intensely."

"Now, that's better," she said, smiling again. "For awhile I thought I had misjudged you. It's not often I get the opportunity to size someone up, but you interest me."

Inwardly I glowed to a fine ember at this boost to my morale. For a brief moment there I thought I'd lost her, and strangely that notion was now uppermost in my mind as I gazed at the woman. It seemed to me there was a lot to her, and as she returned my study with a look of her own, I resolved to follow my instincts and play along. This now promised a new form of relationship, as the first preliminaries were over and the second stage of our association had begun.

"I'm flattered," I said, preening inside, "and from the lips of so pretty a woman it must be praise indeed."

"Now who's the flatterer?" she asked, regarding me shrewdly through eyes gleaming with merriment.

"I am I suppose," I said, then changed the subject to our earlier discussion. "I don't want to appear ungrateful when you say you don't want paying for telling us the location of the arms dump, but it is vital we get the information right away. You see, we don't know when they will strike again – or where, come to that."

"I'll put you out of your misery by saying I'll take you to see this particular one tomorrow," she said, raising the cup to her lips. "Shall we say 10 a.m. tomorrow morning?"

I nodded in agreement, unable to answer because of the excitement I felt and the elation I was enjoying.

We headed east in the glow of a soft summer morning. We were travelling at 50mph along an almost deserted road with the tarmac rolling away behind us, leaving a small dust cloud in our wake, and the road stretching out before us. Inside the car I was hunched behind the wheel watching the road unwind and mentally committing the direction to memory. Jeannie was studying the pages of a coloured road map.

"Not far to the turn-off," she said, pointing to the map and turning to me. "About another half mile, you'll see the sign well before we reach it."

When the sign slowly grew in size until it went by, I swung the wheel sideways and drove the car up the slope of a small hill to a signpost pointing to my left.

"Over there," she said, pointing to a small dirt road and indicating it on the map. "Up there about four miles and then it's a side road to our destination."

After about fifteen minutes we entered another track overgrown with weeds, and squealed to a stop by the side of a paint-peeling gate that straddled a disused path going under the gate and into a wall of wild undergrowth.

"This is it," she announced, getting out and approaching the gate, "but we need a tractor to break through that lot."

I turned off the engine and stood by her looking at the gate. It was attached to two, thick timber posts and was supported at one end by a pair of rusty hinges and held at the other by a rust-encrusted metal chain and iron padlock. Over an unknown period, the chain had worn a deep groove into the rotten timber post and caused the gate to settle into the ground where it lay almost disintegrated.

"We'll need a key to open the lock," Jeannie said, bending down and inspecting it, "and by the looks of it, a hacksaw as well to free the chain."

After gazing at the chain and padlock for awhile, I suddenly stepped forwards and pushed her to one side.

"I think I have the answer," I said, aiming a kick at the corner of the gate.

The wooden construction fell in a heap at my feet; a bundle of rotten wood and rusting iron. Before us was a wall of head-high weeds and interwoven brambles that threatened to block our passage and tear us to pieces if we tried to penetrate it. In answer to this problem I turned the car around and reversed into the middle of the jungle of weeds, flattening it and tearing a small pathway through the meshing leaves and clawing thorns. Next we entered a field of almost the same design, but spaced out. Thick growth of wild rye grass and other indefinable weeds

48

speared upwards, with the occasional barren patch of chalky ground mixed with small pieces of flint appearing without warning.

Getting out of the car, we skirted the nettle spears and downy growths of thistle fingers waiting to sting us, and, jumping the small outcrops of weeds where possible, eventually stopped at a clump of stunted thorn bushes. There we paused to catch our breath, then looked at each other.

"Is it much farther?" I enquired, wiping the sheen of sweat from my brow.

"Look around the corner of the bushes," she replied, nodding.

Wondering, I peered around the edge of a tendril of bramble thorns and beheld the sight of a partially ruined, stunted windmill dominating the skyline, and the seashore in the background.

"Well, I'll be..." I cried in surprise. "A bloody windmill!"

I parted the bushes still farther and stood there drinking in the sight of the windmill, filled with excitement now that the secret of the arms dump was about to be revealed. As we drew near we could see the building was in a sorry state because the main brick structure had collapsed, causing the wooden roof to fail and cave in on itself. The ground was littered with bricks and rubble, and the remains of the rotten wooden sails were mixed with the piles. Standing a few feet away from the base of the windmill, Jeannie pointed to a rusty square plate let into the brickwork about three feet from the ground. The four feet square, iron plate seemed to be almost a part of the structure, the only giveaway a keyhole that, judging by the size of it, indicated that the key to open the door was massive indeed.

"There it is," Jeannie said looking at me. "Now what do you propose to do?"

What indeed? Now that the thing was staring me in the face and I realised it was all finally there, I was devoid of any idea about what to do next. By rights, I should report the fact that I had discovered the location of the arms dump, and leave it for the appropriate department to deal with it. That was the proper course of action to take and I knew it, but what if the girl was lying or was incorrect in her knowledge of the place where the arms were situated? Far better I make sure the arms were there if I didn't want it to be a wasted journey.

"We'll need a key to get in if we are to see if the arms are there," I said, stepping forwards and tapping the plate with extended fingers. "I wonder how long this plate has been here. The iron is thick with rust, so maybe we can prise it open with an iron bar."

"If you do you will activate the security arrangements. The place will go up and so will the armaments inside," she said over my shoulder.

"So it's true, there is a booby trap. Mason told us about it. We thought he was lying to make it seem like it was more difficult, so he would appear indispensable."

"I assure you he wasn't untruthful; the place is wired to explode. Maybe since it was done the bomb has deteriorated, but who's going to find out, you?"

"Where is the booby trap? Is the key somehow involved?"

She shook her head.

"From what I've heard, there is an inner door that is spring-loaded to start the detonator. You have just one minute to open this door and do the necessary to stop the process."

"Can you stop it?"

"Yes, I think I can. We were shown the method."

"Will you do it for me?"

Jeannie stepped back from the building and stood looking at me. There was a certain coyness about her now and I sensed as much when she spoke.

"You remember that I said I had a condition to my offer of help?" she said, looking slightly to one side. "We were in the tea shop when I said it."

"I vaguely recall it," I muttered, wondering where this was leading. "What condition are you thinking of?"

For a moment Jeannie was silent, and the void made in the silence was occupied by the twittering of a flock of birds flying overhead.

"I was thinking of turning over the arms to the British Government on condition that you will free a compatriot of mine," she said at last. "This friend, a woman, was wrongly convicted of planting a bomb in a recent bombing campaign in London, and she is serving a twenty-year sentence, but is innocent of the charge."

"I can't promise that," I said in a huff. I was in a hurry and she was trying to delay things by imposing an impossible condition. "You'll have to take it up with others who have the authority to deal with it."

She sniffed in derision, and a tiny blaze of stubbornness lit a flame in the fierceness of her stare.

"Nevertheless, that is the condition," she said grimly. "Now it is up to you to honour your part of the bargain."

"And if I don't?"

"Then I will withdraw my offer."

"But I know where it is now," I said, laughing in triumph. "You can hardly stop me reporting it to my boss."

"I will though, I promise you."

I was still laughing when I saw the automatic pistol gripped in her right hand and the look of determination directed at me by her steely gaze. My laugh became shallow and faded away.

"So now we really know whose side you are on," I said, eyeing the gun. "Would you use that weapon on me?"

"If I have to. It seems you're not taking me seriously. This gun will convince you otherwise."

"OK," I conceded, "let's say you have a valid point and that your friend was wrongly imprisoned. This is something for the politicians to iron out, not me."

"That's your last word?" she asked.

When I nodded, she silently waved me away from the door with the automatic.

"What're you going to do?" I asked, wide-eyed, and then surprised when she produced a big metal key and put it into the keyhole.

"Just a minute," I said, alarm in my voice. "I thought you said the door is wired."

"That's right," she agreed, "so you'd better be ready to start running now. Remember you only have one minute before it blows up."

"This is downright dangerous. Won't you reconsider?"

"No," she answered.

With a squeak that irritated the nerves, she turned the key and gripped the edge of the plate with the tips of her fingers. Her nails dug into the cracks, seeking any weakness in the rust coating between the two surfaces, and finding none she attacked it with the butt of her gun. I moved to prevent her, and my shadow struck the base of the brick wall, so she swung around pointing the gun at me. I smiled sheepishly and moved away, holding my hands up to indicate that I had the message. She stood back and gave the door a look of frustration.

"Doesn't look like it's going to move," I said in a helpful way, but inwardly feeling relieved. "Why don't you leave it until later and let the experts open it?"

In answer, she picked up a rusty six-inch nail and, using the pistol as a hammer, drove the iron spike into the gap between the bricks and the plate door. For awhile, as the metal nail tried to penetrate between the surfaces, we both watched the progress, one willing it to do it, the other wishing like hell it wouldn't. Above, a warm sun shone down on the scene, and the animal stillness caused by the hammer blows of metal on metal seemed to hold its breath in an agony of suspense and wonder at the disturbance. Suddenly the door parted company from the surrounding bricks and opened to a crack of two inches or more.

At Jeannie's yell of triumph my heart sank and I got ready to run, all the while trying to glimpse what she was doing. I had to admire her show of courage though. As I chanced whether I had the notion of rushing her or wrestling the gun from her, she dropped the gun and was struggling to pull the door open. Now realising she meant to go through with the threat, I teetered to my feet ready for instant flight, but reluctant to run because in the back of my mind's eye was the thought that she was a mere woman and I a dominant male. The notion didn't last long either when the door opened with the creak of rusty hinges and yawned wide.

"You'd better run for it," she said, and then stepped through the doorway into a narrow opening where I could see another door. "Once I set the detonator going," she said over her shoulder, "it's irreversible, so you have got to get out now."

I still hesitated even though my hair started to rise with the suspense. I watched her calmly open the second plate door and reach inside. The seconds began to tick away as she worked, and a feeling of helpless tension invaded my breast, beginning to bring out a stream of fresh sweat that trickled from the end of my nose. Suddenly she shot out of the hole and streaked by me.

"Come on you bloody fool," she shouted. "The thing is going to blow at any time!"

For a split second I was taken by surprise by the abruptness of her move and stood rooted to the spot. When the sheer danger of my presence there registered, I twisted about and hared after her departing figure, desperately counting the remaining seconds. Ahead of me she reached a mound of earth and stones, and disappeared from sight behind the hill, leaving me still in flight, leaping the clumps of coarse grass and tearing weeds, and mentally calculating how long I had before the explosion. Fifty-three... fifty-four... fifty-five... fifty-six... I counted and jumped into the pit beside the woman, who was crouching down as low as she could, hands tightly clasped over her ears, head resting on the earth. Fifty-seven... fifty-eight... fifty-nine... sixty... I hugged the ground and waited for the bang. Sixty-one... sixty-two... sixty-three... sixty-four... The seconds piled up with extra time added to the minute, so my spirits soared with them.

I lifted my head above the mound line and stared at the shape of the windmill, which was still dominating the skyline. I reached over and prodded her in the ribs.

"It looks like your bomb has let you down, sweetheart," I jeered.

She lifted her head from the earth and turned a troubled face to me.

"I can't understand it," she cried unhappily. "I must've done something wrong."

"So you must have, darling," I said, laughing at her.

Then the windmill disintegrated with a massive roar.

CHAPTER SEVEN

The explosion tore at the ears, and the fierceness of the blast vibrated through the surface of the ground. The tremor radiated outwards and finished with a violent echo that rocked and reverberated through the countryside in furious series. With it came the wind. The blast conjured up a hurricane of powerful air that blasted through the vegetation, bending branch and bough alike in its passage outwards. After the explosion and wind came the rain. The masses of material blown upwards and outwards with the force of the blast peppered the countryside with disintegrated bricks and pulverised timber, while other objects mixed in the rain hurtled downwards to join the litter on the ground. One such object hit the earth mound above my head and slid down the shifting soil where it lay at my feet, blackened and smoking. I reached over and picked up the hot object, recognising that I held the butt of a rifle in my hands. I dropped it onto the bed of the pit and stood up to get a better view of the scene.

The windmill had vanished, that was for sure. The circle of bricks that constituted the wall bulk, the squat shape of the lower building that housed the arsenal, the mound of rubble at the foot, even the lengths of timber sails – all gone. Nothing remained but a smoking pit crowned by a large pall of dust, which was settling on everything in the vicinity.

I slowly climbed out of the pit and retraced my steps, followed closely by the woman. Everywhere the ground was littered with the results of the explosion and I stepped over it all as it lay intermingled with the tall grasses and weeds. I stopped on the edge of the crater watching the lazy curl of dirty grey smoke rising up from it, noting that there was nothing remotely like a gun left in the pit. My head still rang from the effects of the explosion and I shook it rapidly to clear it. Jeannie joined me on the lip of the hole, gazing at her handiwork with an expressionless face.

"Proud of your work?" I asked, through gritted teeth. "Your paymasters will pat you on the head and give you a medal for this."

"I'm not concerned with them," she flashed, spots of anger heightening the colour of her cheeks. "I told you of my reason for the destruction of the dump. Indirectly, you are responsible for it as much as I."

"*Me!*" I fumed. "What a bloody cheek. I did all I could to prevent you from blowing it. You are to blame and nobody else."

She stepped back and stared at me. Her eyes were blazing with fury and her chest rose and fell in quick succession. Her teeth ground together in a firm line and her lips bared in anger.

"Be careful, Mr Cox," she hissed. "I still have a lot of influential friends. You'd be wise to think about that."

"Not now you haven't," I said, pointing to the hole. "Not after that abhorrent deed you don't 'cause you are coming with me to do some explaining."

"You wouldn't dare. I'm a citizen of the Irish Republic."

"Come on," I yelled.

I made a grab for her and she replied by taking a swing at me. I ducked and stumbled on the edge of the crater, falling to my knees. I straightened myself to gaze into the business end of the automatic.

"I was forgetting that you had the gun," I said ruefully. "Now what?"

"Now I'm leaving, so don't try to stop me."

"Oh I won't, duckie, I'll just wait until later when you are least expecting it."

"You'll have to find me first and that will be hard," she sneered. She prepared to leave, backing away and still covering me with the gun. "I'll take the car, so you will have to walk for a bit. You'll enjoy the walk though I'm sure." She backed farther still, laughing like she was enjoying it. "Goodbye and good luck," she hurled over her shoulder as she turned away and broke into a run.

I was halfway across the ground in pursuit when the tyres of the car spun in a furious grab at the undergrowth. The vehicle jerked across fallen branches and meshing weed stems, screaming the engine acceleration and sliding wheels as it cleared the greenery and raced away, leaving me cursing at my forgetfulness in leaving the key in the ignition. To the tune of the car's engine dying away in the distance, I started to walk, muttering threats under my breath and dreading the distance I had to go before I could get some sort of transport. I had a bit of luck, however. When the track ran out and a minor country road came into view, a solitary car appeared and I ran out into the middle of the road to flag it down. The driver of the vehicle, an old guy, was taken by surprise and braked sharply, stopping a yard from me, tyres screaming. The man lowered the window in haste and leaned out yelling at me.

"What the hell do yer think yer doin?" he shouted heatedly. "Get outta the way or I'll run yer down, yer fool!"

"My wife's having a baby," I lied, trying to look distressed. "I've got to get to a doctor quickly."

His expression changed and so did his manner. He leaned over and clicked open the passenger door.

"Quick, get in," he yelled. "I know where there is a doctor."

He raced the car to a local hospital and left me in the entrance hall where I promptly walked through a couple of corridors before letting myself out by the back door. From there I hailed a passing taxi and within ten minutes was relaxing in a comfortable seat, in a train back to London.

Lawrence's tone was a little caustic, to say the least, when I told him what had happened.

"Weren't you expecting something of that nature to happen?" he snapped after I had told all. "You let that opportunity slip through your fingers like a gifted amateur. Now we have to pick up the threads and begin again. You really *must* be a little bit more professional you know if you are to succeed in this job."

I choked and was unable to talk. Of course he took the

moment of silence as an admission of guilt, and continued his tirade.

"We had one arms dump in our hands and you let it slip through your fingers. The altercations will be immense in Whitehall. My job will be on the line I can tell you."

"I-I-I," I stammered, still unable to get it out.

He still didn't get it. His voice dropped to a note of compassion, which dripped thick drops of patronage like the dripping of a blob of melting jelly.

"We mustn't dwell too much on past differences though. Heaven knows we are only human after all. We have our weaknesses after all, don't we?"

Before I could reply he changed the subject.

"Brewer will contact you before long. In the meantime, maybe your lady friend will get in touch with you again with another offer. If she does, which I am sure she will do, cultivate the advance, even encourage it, her being such a nice bit of crumpet as you inferred. That is all, goodbye."

He left me with a feeling of hopeless rage and a burning desire to get my fingers around his neck in a stranglehold. After the events of the previous two days I was in no hurry to lay myself open to more of the same.

When I arrived home I took out the revolver with which I had been issued and inspected it. The gun was still shining with newness, the metal gleaming as it lay in my palm. I thoughtfully weighed it in my hand, loaded the cartridge chamber from a full box that had accompanied it and replaced it in a shoulder holster. I got into the harness and pushed the holster into position in my armpit, relishing the feel of the weapon and the power it represented.

The sky was overcast the next morning, so I wrapped myself in the protective folds of a raincoat and stepped outside just as the first drops of rain hit the pavement. With hurried footsteps I walked the distance to the phone box and, as the raindrops lashed down on the metal top, I arranged to meet Brewer later that morning.

Brewer showed surprise when I told him about the discovery and destruction of the arms dump.

"Bloody hell! A woman you say?" he said, raising his eyebrows.

"And ready to do anything to free her friend."

"Sounds like it too. I'll bet she was a worthy opponent when it comes right down to it. Perhaps she should join her friend in jail. We can't leave it to chance. If she is dangerous we'll have to take her out."

Strangely, the thought of killing Jeannie seemed to worry me more than a little, even with the knowledge that she was prepared to shoot me, or was she? The incident at the mill could have produced a reaction even a placid person would find abnormal, with abnormal results.

Brewer was talking again and I shook the idea from my mind.

"Seems to me, she knows a lot more than you think. I'd like to find out what position she currently holds in the IRA and if her rating is in the top echelon. Apart from that, what are her feelings with regard to the recent spate of bombings in London?" Brewer's glasses glinted in the light and the bulbous eyes were on me. "Do you think she will contact you again? The chief says it is our only hope if we are to find out where the other dumps are."

"She might," I said thoughtfully, picking my lip. "She wanted to get her mate out of jail. That is why she went through with the last lot. She might do just that if we dangle a big enough carrot."

"You mean let the other bird go?"

"Why not?" I said, winking. "We've got her description in a hundred different ways. There'd be no problem in picking her up again."

"That's true. She's a marked woman in that respect."

"What we gonna do, arrange a jail break or something?"

"Nothing so corny. They'd smell a rat and that's for sure."

"Just let her walk out with our blessing?"

"In a manner of speaking, yes." Brewer nodded. "We'll let it be known that she was the victim of British justice and other facts have come to light, making her conviction unsafe. Result – another hearing through which she'll get bail. From there it's not a big step to the republic."

"Who's responsible for this idea? As if I didn't know."

"Lawrence, naturally, he has that sort of mind."

We did make contact within the week, although not in the manner we had been discussing.

One of the places I nearly always frequented was a local bank where I regularly drew out a sum of money to last me the week. In that building was a lift, and I was using it to reach another floor to consult an official with regard to investing some of the money I was getting from Lawrence. It was on the third floor that a thickset man got into the lift and stood to one side of me as the doors closed. It was one of those self-service lifts you operated yourself, and the door had only just closed when I felt something prod the small of my back as a voice snarled into my ear.

"Don't make a move, don't make a sound. You do an' I'll kill you. You understand?"

I nodded and stiffened in surprise. I was about to ask him who he was and what he was after, but the gun next to my spine felt really menacing, so I bit back the enquiry and raised my arms.

"Lower your arms and listen to me," the gruff voice ordered.

"You know whom I represent. You might know who I am. If it had been Sweeney you'd be dead by now, but he's a hothead."

He coughed in my ear and mint fumes stung my nose. I realised that I had just met Harvey.

"Now, we can do it the easy way or the hard way. It's your choice."

"What do you mean?" I asked huskily.

The lift jerked to a stop at the fourth floor and the doors started to open. The floor outside was bare of any life and my assailant pressed the button to go downwards. I stood there in two minds whether to make a break for it at another floor or go with the gunman as he wished, hoping he would give me an opportunity to escape later. The chance of me trying to tackle him by force was decided by the presence of the gun still pressed into my back.

On the second floor a man entered and stood to one side, ignoring us by gazing fixedly ahead of him, and we descended to the ground floor in silence.

"Now we'll go to the front door where we will go through the doorway without any trouble," Harvey whispered in my ear. "Once outside we will proceed to a car parked just down the road. You are again warned that if there is any sign of you gaining or trying to gain attention or cause trouble in any way whatsoever, you will be shot. Is that clear?"

I nodded in a numb way and stared ahead of me as I allowed the man to propel me through the bank and outside into the street where he jerked my head sideways to indicate I was to go that way, followed closely by the man who had concealed the gun in his pocket. Ahead of me, a figure got out of the car and pulled the rear door open, then stood waiting for us to draw near. Harvey jerked his head at the car then to me, and I slid onto the back seat with him sitting next to me watching me closely, the gun now exposed and pointing at me.

"Don't bother to memorise the way," he said gruffly, popping a round sweet into his mouth. "We very seldom use the same address twice."

The smell of mint invaded the air of the car as he sucked the sweet.

It was somewhere in South London that the car pulled up outside a rundown, three storey terraced house. After the men had looked in all directions, I was ushered up several stone steps, pushed through a thick wooden front door and seated on a wooden kitchen chair.

"Now," said the gunman from a chair he had placed opposite me, "we want some answers to a couple of important questions. What happened at the windmill?"

"Windmill?" I asked, in a show of pretence. "What windmill are you on about?"

I regretted it immediately because Harvey hit me on the side of my jaw with the gun and leaned back as the blood trickled out of the corner of my mouth. I coughed and screwed up my eyes in pain. The other man, a thin faced, sallow skinned person with darting eyes and a hooked nose, giggled at the sight of the blood. He was leaning against the wall and the sound echoed through the partially empty room.

Harvey silenced him with a look and turned to me again.

"I'll ask you again, only this time give it some thought 'cause I'll start on the other side of your face if you answer wrong. Now, what happened at the mill?"

"It was blown up," I answered thickly.

"By Jeannie Grant?"

"Is that her name? She never told me."

"*I'll* ask the questions. Why did she do it?"

"Because I wouldn't give her the guarantee her friend would be freed. I said only the government had that power."

"So she blew the mill up because you refused?"

"I expect so. I don't remember too much 'cause it happened too fast."

He blew a hot breath of annoyance and raised the gun in a threatening manner.

"You'd fucking well better start remembering fast if you want to stay healthy, mate. Fox was in the self same spot like you are in now and he is pushing up the daisies. We can do the same to you, make no mistake about it," he said menacingly.

"Fox being the British agent who was killed recently?"

"You mean you didn't know?"

"I knew someone was killed. I didn't know his name."

"Right, now we are getting off the track. Did she give you the name of the friend who is in prison?"

"No, the only names she ever mentioned were yours and Sweeney."

My jaw was still aching with the treatment handed out by my captor, and when I explored my lower gum I was able to rock a loose tooth about with the tip of my tongue.

"Now," Harvey continued, "do you know the locations of any more arms dumps?"

"I don't personally. I can't speak for Brewer or Lawrence."

"So you say Jeannie didn't reveal any details about others there might be?"

"That's what I'm saying 'cause it's the truth. She never mentioned other sites and as for telling me where they are, I don't think she would."

Harvey studied my face for awhile, and with screwed up eyes beholding me with puzzlement, voiced his uncertainty.

"It strikes me you know a lot about someone you've only just met," he said. "You seem to have had more than just a casual conversation, I'd say." He turned to the other man who was watching the proceedings with interest. "Wouldn't you say that, Brough? Wouldn't you say just that?" he said sarcastically.

Brough giggled with amusement; a high falsetto sound that made him sound effeminate.

"Maybe he has carnal knowledge of the lady," he said.

He giggled some more and then ceased when Harvey spoke again.

"Now, that's a strong possibility, Mr Cox. Is there something going on between you and Jeannie?" he asked, looking at me.

I smiled at the idea, an action that caused me to wince with the pain in my jaw. The prospect doesn't seem entirely without some sort of foundation as far as I am concerned because I have been attracted to her from the first time I saw her, I mused. I wasn't about to give the gunmen the opportunity to laugh at me, so I chose my words carefully.

"She's a stranger to me. I only met her briefly before we went to the mill,"

I said.

"What do you know about Coney End?" Harvey questioned, in a subdued voice.

"Nothing. I was given a piece of map of a certain area that has now been built on. I went there on a couple of occasions where I met Brewer and Mason, the last being when we saw Mason for the final time. He was found later that week at the foot of a high-rise building – dead. He was going to give us the location of the windmill dump, the one Jeannie blew up."

"OK," Harvey said, casting an eye on Brough. "We know it all now don't we, Brough?"

In reply, Brough pushed himself from the wall and, with a quick leer, put his hand inside his coat and brought to light an evil looking hypodermic needle and a bottle of colourless liquid. While I watched, Harvey crept up behind me and when Brough tipped up the bottle to fill the needle, he put an arm around my neck to restrain me. The last I saw of the pair at that time was Brough shoving the needle into my arm and both of them standing and looking down at me as I lost consciousness.

CHAPTER EIGHT

I awoke, which was fortunate for me, in the back seat of my own car parked in front of the building housing my flat. The car had been returned to me after the woman had taken it, probably by Jeannie herself, but I opened my eyes to see the familiar sight of the road in which I lived spread out before me.

I got out of the car with shaking legs and spinning head, and made my way to the front door where I leaned up against the door frame and waited for my brain to settle. Slowly the world stopped revolving and with an effort I fished the door key out of my side pocket and fell inside.

For awhile I sat on the floor collecting my thoughts and wondering why Harvey had let me go. This caused me pain and I shook my head to clear the remains of the drug from my brain. I wondered how long I had been out and whether it was the same day on which I'd started out. The questions piled up like an unclimbed mountain that stared back at me without giving any answers. I gave up at that juncture and staggered into the living room, spreading out on the settee and going to sleep.

When I awoke, I thought about reporting the whole incident to Lawrence and was about to go out when a knock came on the front door. In readiness to ward off any more kidnapping attempts, I snatched the revolver from its holster in the bureau drawer and, holding it before me, opened the door. Two azure blue eyes gazed into mine and a disarming smile crooked two lips into a line of red-lipped welcome.

"Hello," she said softly, looking deep into my eyes. "I thought I'd better come around to apologise for taking your car and making you walk. You looked so fierce back at the mill that for awhile I was frightened of what you might do, so I grabbed the nearest thing to get out of it and that was your car."

"Well, I'm relieved it is only that," I said, opening the door wide. "Won't you come in for awhile as I've got something to tell you? That is if you don't already know."

She entered with a puzzled expression on her face and, once inside, turned around to face me.

"I'll be willing to bet you are about to tell me that you have been contacted by others in the army, am I right?"

I stood amazed at how correct she was proving to be.

"And am I right in saying that this contact is named Harvey?"

"Too right you are," I said.

I told her all about what had happened earlier, not forgetting the final part where I had woken up in the car she had returned.

"They're getting bolder," she said. "I'm only sorry I can't do anything to help you. The only thing for you to do is to withdraw from it all. Forget about the arms dumps and what happened at the mill. Tell Lawrence to go to hell and stuff his job."

"I can't do that; I'll lose a lot of money."

"Better that than lose your life. They are dedicated men you are playing with. If you get in the way of their deal they will eliminate you, make no mistake about it."

"Don't worry, I will be expecting it next time," I vowed, stuffing the gun into my pocket. "I owe Mr Harvey a slug on the jaw, and that other creep, Brough, the one with the needle..."

I fingered the bruise on my face and circled the inside of my mouth with my tongue, feeling the loose tooth. Jeannie shuddered at the mention of the name, Brough.

"Now, there is one man who makes my skin crawl," she said in disgust. "He's like a snake that slithers on its belly to get what it wants, and when he's got it will crow about it to everyone. He's sick in the mind, which I'm convinced affects his body. He is sickly and unwholesome – urgh!" she ended, shuddering again and shaking her head, seemingly to put him out of her mind.

I made coffee and we drank it sitting before the fire. The closeness of her body to mine sent curious sensations of pleasure through me, causing me to feel a happiness I'd not known for years. Now and again I felt her eyes on me as she secretly studied me - wondering what? I was prompted to ask myself what she was really there for. Was she only there to find out what I was supposed to know? Was her surprise at hearing that I had suffered at the hands of Harvey just a ploy to get in with me again and find out if I knew about other arms dumps? I decided to pump her before she had a chance to do it to me.

"Harvey tried to make me reveal whether I knew where the other dumps were," I said, looking closely at her reactions. "I told him no, but he seemed to disbelieve it."

She swung around to face me at this, interest plainly written on her features.

"And *do* you know where there are any more?" she asked, in a whisper.

For a moment I thought of lying to her to lead her into a trap, but that depended on whether she intended to pass on the information to another, namely Harvey, or keep it to herself. I had to make sure.

"Lawrence did say there were others," I replied carefully.

"But did he tell you where they were?" she persisted.

"I can't tell you whether I know or not. I've signed a paper, something about the Official Secrets Act."

"Surely you can tell *me*, a friend. Look how I showed you the location of the windmill. That must prove to you that I am genuine."

"Must I reveal anything to you?" I said, peering intently at her. "Anyway, why the interest?"

"I've already told you my interest lies in the person who's rotting away in an English prison. She's innocent, and that's why I'm doing my damnedest to get her released."

"Do you know where the other dumps are?" I asked suddenly, hoping to catch her off guard.

"Me?" she said in surprise. "Now, what makes you think

I've got information on the dumps? That one at the mill was a one-off. Everybody knew where it was."

"Except me. I had to employ you to show me where it was."

"Only to help my friend in prison," she said, flustered.

"Hmm," I murmured. "Why did you really come here?"

"I told you, to apologise. Must I repeat it again?"

"Oh, come on. When you left me at the mill you had no intention of coming back and you know it. What or whom changed your mind?"

"All right, I'll come clean with you. I had another reason to see you again and that is, I still think we can come to some arrangement."

"With regard to what?"

"A certain person in prison."

"Not *her* again! Why don't you give it a rest? She's inside because she committed a crime, and that's where she'll stay until the judiciary think otherwise."

"That's typical of Lawrence, but I didn't consider it of you," she flashed, with blazing eyes. "I thought I had met a man who understood us. Seems I was wrong."

"Understand? Don't you mean naivety? You think you can come here and get me to help you on the pretext that you want to apologise for taking my car. You think I'm that easy to predict?"

"You're right, Mr Cox, I did come here with that in mind and I want to apologise for it too." She arose to go, red-faced with suppressed anger. "I keep making the mistake of lumping you in the same category as my compatriots. Another apology, only this one is sincere. I'll not make it again."

In silence she walked to the front door and even managed a weak smile as she stepped outside.

Even though I had got something off my chest with regard to coming off second best at the windmill, I still felt a curious kind of affinity with the woman, and for awhile the feeling stopped me from going to sleep that night. It was past two in the morning when I finally dropped off, even so, I felt refreshed by the sleep and when I awoke, instantly got out of bed and ate a hearty breakfast.

I was just on my last cup of coffee when a hammering sounded on the front door. Brewer stood squinting up at me when I opened the door while the dog, which was always at his heels, cocked its leg up against my door frame.

"I'm hotfoot from Lawrence," he said, nudging the dog with the tip of a shining black toe.

The dog ignored him, however, and continued to squirt a stream of greeny-grey urine at the woodwork. After dripping in a series of drops, the urine began to run away down the slope of the pathway to a crack between the paving stones where it stopped and disappeared from sight. For a minute we looked on in silence, the stillness broken only by the background of passing traffic and pedestrians. A distant motor horn broke the spell.

"Good thing it only wants to piss. I hate clearing up dogs' mess," I grated.

Once inside, Brewer lost no time in coming to the point. After pushing the dog out of sight behind the settee, he searched in his pocket and produced a letter, which he handed to me. Giving him a puzzled look, I hooked a finger under the sealed flap and tore the envelope open, bringing to light a sheet of notepaper and a Yale key. After giving the key a look, I unfolded the paper and read the short message from Lawrence.

The key is for the lock-up at Waterloo Station. We think it is a dropping point for the IRA, so keep an eye on it - the key I mean. The key was found on Fox. The number on the key is the number on the left-luggage box.

The note was signed with a scrawled, Lawrence.

"We'll take it in turns to watch the box," Brewer said as I folded the paper. "If someone turns up or leaves something in the box, we follow them and get in touch with the other as soon as possible, OK?"

I nodded thoughtfully, studying the note.

"How did Fox get the key? Did someone give it to him or did he steal it? You only get one or two keys, so if two, how did he get one of them?"

Brewer was also having the same thoughts.

"That bothered me for awhile until I suddenly remembered you can get another cut for next to nothing. The next question is if it was given then who gave it?"

"If we knew that we wouldn't have to watch the box, we'd just pull in somebody who's in the know then bring out the rubber hose and go to work."

"Do you think Jeannie had a hand in it? Maybe she tried to persuade Fox to help her, and to show good faith gave him a key to the box. Perhaps she used her womanly wiles on him like she did on you."

I gave him a look to say the gibe had registered, and returned the note to its envelope.

"When do we keep the box under surveillance?" I asked, stuffing the note into my pocket.

Brewer's bulbous eyes regarded me for an instant before blinking.

"If you ask me, there's not been anyone there to watch it since Foxy bought it, so a few more hours won't go amiss. How about tomorrow at ten? We'll watch it in the daylight hours 'cause I'm thinking no one will visit it at night. Anyway, why should Lawrence have it all his own way and work in the daylight and not us?"

I shrugged and agreed with a smile.

"If it is OK with you I'll take the first watch," I said, listening to the dog scratching behind the settee. "And that's another thing, mate. Do you take your dog on jobs like these?"

"Oh, I take him everywhere. He'd pine like mad if I left him behind. He's as much a government dog as I'm a government man. I'm even thinking of putting in a time sheet for him in the future."

I laughed at the prospect of employing a dog, and roared with laughter anew as the dog somehow sensed we were talking about it and thumped its tail on the carpet.

The next day, just as the first passengers of the day waited to board trains from Waterloo to their respective destinations, I stood to one side of the main concourse, one eye on the steady stream of people entering the station and the other on a row of metal containers lining a white, painted concrete wall a short distance away. I had been there since daybreak, and the strain of watching the people go by in search of their trains, coupled with the constant scrutiny of anyone approaching the metal boxes, was beginning to take its toll.

I was about to head for a café and a welcome cup of hot coffee when I noticed a thin faced man dressed in a dark suit and wearing a pulled down trilby hat. He was standing in front of the containers frantically searching his pockets. I was glued to the scene with interest, and as he had found the key he stepped forwards with arm extended, key gripped between his fingers and opened another left luggage container several feet from the suspected one. Seeing this, my heart sank to my knees and with a sigh of despair I turned about and headed for the café and my hot cup of coffee.

During the day I returned several times to the place outside the ladies toilet and, after getting a few curious stares from various females using the convenience, shifted my position to twenty yards nearer the boxes. Sometime in the afternoon, as I was lounging against a wall, I felt a hand on my shoulder and the thick glasses of Brewer glinted in the artificial light, staring up at me. Immediately I looked down in alarm and just managed to step aside as the dog cocked its leg.

"Nothing to report," I said, returning his gaze and then staring about me.

The station was crowded with people hurrying in all directions. The trains arrived and departed with their quota of hastening passengers. The whistles shrilled, warning each influx of humanity that the train was about to depart, and a myriad feet beat a rapid tattoo on the platform surface, many breaking into a run as the train began to move. A succession of slamming doors followed and the whine of the diesel engine rose to the accompanying clang of moving carriages as the train snaked away from the platform. The procedure was reversed when another train arrived at the platform and the passengers hurried away through the huge halls of Waterloo Station.

"Perhaps they've seen you looking, hoping you will tire. They have your description, so they might just be on to you."

"If that is the case, they will have your description as well, so what are we doing here?"

"We could adopt a disguise couldn't we?" Brewer ventured.

"Yeah, if this was November the fifth I could go as the guy."

"I'm not joking," Brewer said, a little irritated by my show of pique. "I often change my appearance by using this subterfuge. Maybe this is why I've come this far without mishap."

"What about the dog? How do you disguise it?" I asked, sniffing.

"When the time comes he'll hide away somewhere."

I wasn't prepared to follow this line to its obvious conclusion because the dog was pricking up its ears and by the looks of him was dying to give me a demonstration.

"If you like, Monty will show you what I mean," Brewer said eagerly, raising a hand to signal the dog that was watching him just as eagerly.

We watched the box for a week, Brewer in a tight fitting blouse and skirt and me in a workman's overalls complete with a shovel I had managed to stick to after its owner had stopped for lunch. The dog, in a curious way, seemed to sense what we had in mind and did a disappearing act for as long as we were present, only reappearing when we moved to go.

We naturally altered position every so often, especially after getting curious stares from the station staff as they passed by. On one occasion, after a porter stopped to examine us suspiciously, I grabbed the shovel and started to dig with it. Brewer, on the other hand, looked like he was soliciting, so to him they paid no heed, even winked at him as he supposedly plied his trade. He played the part so well that I had a slight suspicion he'd done it before.

On the Saturday we had a bit of luck. After deciding that we should work together and not in shifts as was proposed in the beginning, we were engaged in taking up our positions at 9.a.m when, out of the corner of my eye, I caught a movement in front of the boxes. Right there before our eyes was a woman in the act of opening up the watched container. We separated immediately as planned, one to follow the suspect for awhile, the other to take over should the subject begin to cotton on and take evasive action.

After nodding to me, Brewer sidled off and was soon lost to view amongst the crowds hurrying towards the many exits. On the other hand, I kept the woman in my sights by pretending to examine the wall against which I'd previously been leaning, all the while casting seemingly innocent looks about me in the process. It was in one of those casual glances that I saw the woman remove an object from the box and, almost in the same movement, insert another package into the metal container, too quickly for me to see what it was no matter how I screwed my head around to make it out. She gave me one glance to see if I had noticed anything and, when I showed no interest in her movements, shut the door of the container and prepared to go.

To convince her of my disinterest, I attacked the wall with the blade of my shovel and, as she walked by, scraped up an imaginary pile of rubbish. She hardly gave me a glance now, but quickened her pace to the exits, the package held firmly under one arm. In pursuit I thankfully discarded the shovel and, with a certain amount of caution that included dodging behind steel columns and various objects, made my way out of the station post-haste.

Outside I signalled to a waiting Brewer who, with clicking high heels and a wobbling false bust, set out in hot pursuit, followed by a mongrel dog that insisted on examining and drenching each and every post they passed.

CHAPTER NINE

The woman made a tortuous circle of the neighbourhood around Waterloo, presumably to throw off any pursuers. Just when I thought she was never going to get to the nitty-gritty of delivering the package, she set out in a different direction altogether, ending up in a street of well-kept houses with cars and trees lining the edge of the pavement. She walked to about halfway down where she stopped at a white painted building and stood at the entrance to a small drive, whilst looking in all directions. After awhile she seemed to be satisfied because the only other person to be seen was a woman with a dog passing by on the other side of the road. As she turned to walk up the driveway, I waved to Brewer to indicate I was taking over the watch, and he vanished out of sight behind some trees.

I mentally surveyed the house from a distance and decided to wait for cover of darkness before making any move to close in. I retraced my footsteps and soon found Brewer standing on the corner waiting for me.

"It looks like we've found one of their safe houses," I said, coming to a halt. "I don't know how many there are, so I suggest we call in the military before they have a chance to escape."

"If we do that we'll never get the rest of them and the location of the arms dumps will vanish with them."

"Are you suggesting we tackle them by ourselves?"

"We don't know for sure how many there are," Brewer countered, pulling the dog away from a tree. "I'm saying we can watch the house for any sign of a gang. If that be the case, we'll ask for assistance, if not we'll tackle the occupants by ourselves. Whatever we do we've got to keep everything under wraps. This is a politically sensitive subject as Lawrence will tell you, so now it's up to us."

"I only hope you know what you are doing, mate, 'cause all I have is this gun, which is nothing if they've got machine guns to back them up."

"I could get you something bigger if you want. All I have to do is contact the arms stores."

"You mean the place in the car park? What are you going to get, a trench mortar?"

"No, but I could get you a couple of hand grenades or plastic explosive."

Brewer was completely serious and I looked at him with misbelieve.

"Chrissakes!" I said, trying hard to contain myself. "I thought we wanted information from them not to start a war. What do you think I am, SAS?"

Brewer ignored me and peered around the tree trunk. He had on a brown wig that persisted in curling down on his forehead no matter how much he readjusted it. Now a stray sprig of hair fell forwards onto his face and with a gesture of annoyance he brushed it aside. Beside him, the dog's tail wagged furiously when it saw this happen for it thought the gesture was a signal, and began to bark and pull the lead. I shot out a suppressed yell of despair as Brewer yanked on the lead. Suddenly he stopped pulling and hissed a warning.

"Here she comes again."

Across the road the woman had emerged from the house and was opening the gate to the road.

"Get back," I said through clenched teeth, and then tried to hide myself behind the six-inch tree trunk.

Behind me, Brewer had managed to quieten the dog by lifting it to his chest, and was in the process of hiding behind me there, shoulder against shoulder, to present as small an object as possible. We waited behind the tree with beating hearts and baited breath for her to pass us by, but she didn't because after closing the gate and looking about her she turned the other way and disappeared out of sight up the road.

"Jesus Christ!" I blazed. "Why don't you keep that dog under control? You almost blew it, you and that pooch."

Brewer blushed under his foundation and held the dog close to his chest. He had a crestfallen look on his rouged face, which gave him the appearance of a smacked child. He had disposed of the glasses in the interest of his disguise, so it was easy for the dog to lick his face in sympathy. This it did, and soon the dog's tongue was covered in cosmetics. They looked so pathetic I caved in and smiled.

"OK, let's not argue. We must go into that house when it's dark, even if we've only got a couple of pea-shooters. They won't be expecting anything anyway, so the element of surprise will be with us."

We walked about for a couple of hours and by the time we got back to the road it was past eleven. Even so, we used a lot of caution and crept up the road on tiptoe, dodging behind the nearest tree when we thought we heard a noise.

"You go around one side and I'll take the other," I whispered. "Keep the dog quiet, please," I added, gripping the gate and pushing it open.

The gate emitted a high squeak of rusty hinges and I cringed inside, waiting for the expected uproar. The seconds ticked by interminably as we stood like statues, frozen in mid-stride, ears pricked and hearts thumping like mad.

"Come on," I hissed, stepping onto the drive.

Still creeping forwards, we separated at the end of the driveway and I slid around the corner of a brick-built porch, feeling my way along a short passage that lay between the house and a detached garage. With feathered footsteps, I crept through an arch of flowers then stopped and stared at a lighted cloakroom window, my heart thumping.

Ahead of me I heard the noise of shuffling feet, and the silhouette of a woman loomed up before me. I grabbed her in an encircling hold, ready to silence her with a quick thump in the face.

"I wish you had chosen another disguise," I complained. "It gets confusing."

We waited for about two hours for the light to go off. We had gone into a crouch on the pathway, now and again glancing up at the light.

"I think they've gone to bed and left it on," Brewer said in a whisper. "Maybe we can try around the back of the house, where I saw some French windows as I was passing. Let's try there."

Slinking around the back, we arrived at the French windows and stood examining them. The frames were old and warped with peeling paint and missing putty. Between the doors was a gap of about a quarter of an inch, just enough to allow the blade of a knife to slide between. The trouble was we didn't have a knife, so improvised with a comb that Brewer brought to light from his handbag. There was a catch on the inside, one of those wrap-around things, and I easily pushed it upwards, put my shoulder against the frame and pushed. The bloody thing was bolted on the inside. I chewed my lip with suppressed rage, pushed again and one of the panes of glass fell inwards. We froze again, only this time I also prayed and waited, face screwed up in agony.

Nothing happened, not even a creak of shifting timbers. Reassured, I reached into the room and felt around for the bolt, wincing as the fastening gave a little squeak. Another stop for reaction then I stepped into the room, followed closely by Brewer and the dog. Gliding on carpet and bumping gently into various items of furniture, we found a door that opened into a passage that, in turn, ended at the foot of a flight of stairs. That is where I pulled out my gun and started upwards.

The moon helped us by throwing a bar of light through a small landing window and, with creaking stairs and pounding hearts, we gained the landing and stood outside a bedroom door hardly daring to breathe. I pointed my gun at another bedroom door to indicate that Brewer should go in there then gripped the handle of the first door. It opened soundlessly and I stood in the gloom listening for breathing or any movement.

Nothing - not even the creak of a spring. I felt along the wall in a search for the light switch. I found it and, holding the gun in a tight grip, switched it on. The room was empty and I heaved a sigh of relief.

My thoughts returned to Brewer and I quickly slipped outside again and there he was.

"Nothing," he hissed, and pointed to a third room. "Come on, they must be in there."

I gave him a nod and held my gun tighter in my palm. Instead of masking our footfalls by creeping along, we both ran at the door and burst through it, followed closely by a madly barking dog. We waved our guns, ready for anything. I stood and groaned to myself as the light went on. I turned to Brewer, who was also staring around disbelievingly.

"The bloody place is empty," I said in despair.

"But it can't be," he protested. "What about the parcel, where is that? Why did she try to cover her trail so well, and the light, why did she leave it on?"

I shrugged in reply and stuffed my revolver into my coat pocket. I was as confused as he was, and the woman's movements were a mystery to me.

"Perhaps she was on to us," I said.

The room was furnished with a double bed, a small bedside table, a lamp with a plastic shade, a chair with a padded seat and back, a polished wardrobe and a double-barrelled shotgun, which was hidden inside the wardrobe.

"Jesus Christ!" I said, astonished. "They must be expecting a bit of opposition. Imagine what they can do with this."

I broke the gun open and extracted the cartridges, putting them into my pocket. I closed the gun again and replaced it in its original position. Searching further, I found a box of cartridges on the top shelf and a small diary with a list of names on the first few pages. Brewer was looking over my shoulder as I turned the pages and he whistled with surprise when he read the first names on the list.

"Do you recognise any of them?" I asked.

"A couple," he answered, taking the diary. "Wonder what they are doing in here."

"Your guess is as good as mine. Anyway, I think we should take it with us just in case it's important. They might come back soon, so I think we should evaporate."

He snapped off the light and, with the dog bringing up the rear as usual, we closed the bedroom door and descended the stairs, pausing only to replace the glass. We were about to depart when the front door banged as someone opened it.

The noise of the opening door cracked like a pistol shot in the darkness of the house. I grabbed for the French window at the same moment as Brewer, with the result that we collided and fell backwards.

"Come on, let's scarper," I whispered in blind panic.

I pulled the window open causing the glass pane to dislodge again, although that time the glass flew outwards and smashed to pieces on the garden path. We barged through the opening, scattering curtains and fixings in our flight. Crunching on broken glass, we hurled ourselves across the lawn and into the blackness of a thicket hedge, hoping against hope that whoever they were hadn't seen where we had gone.

In the house the light came on and a figure shook the curtains vigorously, but did not reveal their identity. I was crouching in the thickest part of the hedge with Brewer alongside me. The dog was somewhere in front of the hedge digging up the flower bed while barking with excitement. For awhile, as a hush came over the house and it remained dark, I thought our luck was in and they had given up. The seconds ticked by and extended into minutes, my heart began to slow to a crawl and I relaxed inwardly.

Suddenly things started to happen. Brewer swore at the dog when it barked again, the curtains parted as the light went on and a figure stepped through the opening making straight for the dog. Against the square of light from the window I saw a big bulk loom up about twenty paces away and stand there nursing the shotgun, which was pointing directly at me. A deep voice came at us out of the gloom.

"I know you are in there, so come out now while you still have the chance."

A metallic click followed closely by another came in the stillness of the night. We didn't move a hair, hardly daring to breathe. The next warning rang ominously into the air.

"I have a shotgun here. I'll give you just five seconds before I start to fire."

The voice started to count, and when it reached four Brewer wriggled out of the hedge and stood before the man. I realised he was doing the right thing and, following suit, I stood before the gunman wondering whether to pull my own piece and take a chance on him seeing me do it or bluff it out. I chose the latter.

"All right, guv," I whined, adopting a servile voice, "it's a fair cop, we only wanted to give the place a once over to see if it was worth our while coming back. Call the cops an' we'll take our medicine."

The shotgun waved towards the house and the gunman growled.

"Raise your hands and make towards the house. Make any funny moves and I'll kill you."

He got behind us and waited as we trooped across the lawn back to the house, watching intently as we progressed through the French windows and into the back room. Another man was waiting in the room and was immediately joined by the woman we had been following. The man with the shotgun stepped into the light and was revealed as big and beefy with a close cropped head. Oo-er, I groaned to myself, this has got to be Sweeney. I was right.

"They must've followed me here from the pick-up, Sweeney. I thought I might be followed, but the dog fooled me into thinking I was safe 'cause they looked so ordinary," the woman said.

Sweeney walked over to her and cracked her in the face with a bunched fist.

"That will make sure you are more careful in future, Maureen, we can't have failures if we are to keep everything under wraps. If this happens again we'll send you back to answer to the boss. Do you understand?"

Maureen nodded tearfully and held her jaw in her hand while the second man stood back looking on, not interfering in any way. He was a tall thin man, ruddy of complexion with hard eyes that stared at the woman. He had black hair and sported a gold ring in one ear. Seeing how the land lay, I resolved to continue my impression of a burglar to the fullest because somehow I had the feeling we would be next.

"Look 'ere, guv," I said in the same voice as before. "We're willing to take our punishment as I said before. Call the law like I said."

I was looking at Sweeney when I said it and he held me in a vicious glare as he raised the wooden butt of the shotgun and poked me in the stomach with it.

"Shut your fucking mouth, Cox," he spat at me. "Nobody is fooled by your play acting, so don't bother to convince us otherwise."

Brewer piped up as the dog growled in sympathy with me.

"You don't think we were foolish enough to try this type of operation without some kind of back-up do you?" he said as I bent over with pain. "Right now there are upwards of a dozen fully armed men outside ready to rush you at our signal. If you want to avoid any unnecessary bloodshed I'd give up if I were you. You are heavily outnumbered in any case."

Sweeney laughed hoarsely at Brewer's attempt to seize the initiative, and stepped forwards to do the same to him as he had me. Instantly the dog showed its teeth in a growl, pointing his nose threateningly at Sweeney.

"Keep it quiet or I'll silence it," Sweeney said, with menace thick on his tongue. "You don't think we're falling for that one, Brewer, do you?" he sneered. "We had a good look around outside like we always do before we came in."

"Then why did you miss us, mate? We managed to find you, so why can't others do likewise?"

Sweeney chewed on this for awhile with a troubled look on his face that belied his attempt to pooh-pooh the possibility. He peered at the other man and jerked his head to the accompanying jeering laugh of Brewer, who had seen the signal. Meanwhile, I straightened up with difficulty and, with pain scything through my vitals, looked around me. Something occurred to me other than that I inwardly cursed myself for forgetting. In my pocket was my gun, which Sweeney had forgotten to take, but so too were the cartridges I had unloaded from the shotgun whilst we were upstairs. I resolved to take my life into my own hands and take a chance.

In full view of Sweeney and the other two, I slipped my hand into my right pocket and, with Sweeney's shouted warning ringing in my ears, I pulled my gun out expecting to feel the thud of shotgun pellets tearing into my body. Sweeney pulled the trigger and to my utter relief nothing happened. He tried again with the second one, but the same thing happened. I breathed in a huge breath and pointed my gun at Sweeney. He couldn't believe it and was still working the breech. He broke open the gun and stared at the chamber in disbelief.

"Looking for these, Sweeney," I asked, plunging my hand into my pocket and producing the two cartridges. "I took 'em out a little while ago."

I jerked my gun up and down at the shotgun and he dropped it to his feet and raised his hands, all the while treating me to a look of extreme malevolence. The other man also put his hands in the air, as did the woman. Keeping them all in my sights, I walked up to the huge bulk of Sweeney and looked up at him. He met my gaze with eyes reduced to slits and lips set in a curled-up sneer.

"Sweeney," I said, raising the gun until it was waist height, "you are one big hell of a man, and vicious too."

I then hit him across the cheek with the barrel of the gun. He wilted in pain, blood running from his mouth, eyes blazing with hatred. When he spat in my face I hit him again, only that time the gun bounced off the side of his head. As I watched, he slid down the flowered wallpaper and tilted sideways, out cold to the world.

Brewer shouted a warning. I turned swiftly to see the other man disappearing through the open doorway and I snapped off a shot that buried itself in the door frame a split second after he went by. Brewer held his gun on the woman as I hurled myself behind the door and slid slowly around the woodwork, peering closely into the darkened passageway. Immediately a bullet dug into the wall just above my head, bringing down a rain of plaster that showered me like falling confetti. In reply, I loosed off a round in the general direction of the other's gun flash and ducked as the gunman returned the compliment.

We exchanged fire several times, and the night was ringing with the sound of shot after shot, until I ran out of ammo. I was thinking fast as was the other man I imagined. After I ceased firing he stood up from his position at the foot of the stairs, coming towards me. He had counted my shots and was advancing down the passageway at great speed. I heard the slide of his shoes on the carpet as he inched nearer, now sure that I had come to the end of my ammunition supply.

I remembered the shotgun and grabbed at it. Desperately, I raked in my pocket and, finding the shotgun rounds, slammed them into the chamber just as he decided to make his move. I closed the breech as he came into view aiming his gun. Two gun blasts crashed out together, and in the close confines of the building the noise deafened me momentarily. His bullet tore a hole in the sleeve of my overalls and spun away into the air before burying itself in the ceiling. The shotgun charge blew a hole the size of a saucer in the belly of the man. He at once shot back with the force of the blast, and draped himself over the banister where he slowly buckled at the knees.

Within a short time my tightened nerves began to ease in my chest and I rested my forehead against the door frame. The coolness of the wood was a balm to my aching head and, for a time, I held it there, revelling in the relief it gave me. I lifted my head to see the crumpled form of the dead gunman lying in a heap at the bottom of the stairs. I let the shotgun slip from my fingers and sat down on the floor close to the unconscious Sweeney, who was slumped nearby.

After the tremendous amount of gunshots we had exchanged, the peace afterwards seemed like heaven. I was enjoying the feel of it until the dog licked my face. I screwed up my face as its acrid breath entered my nose.

"God!" I exclaimed, shaking my head and holding my nose. "What's this dog been eating? Its breath stinks to high heaven."

CHAPTER TEN

"What're we going to do about these two?" Brewer asked as I pushed the dog away. "If we leave them here they'll only go back to what they were. I think we should hand them over to the police, but then a lot of awkward questions will be asked, so we've got to let them go."

"Bullshit," I swore. "They'll only do the same thing. If we take 'em out of circulation right now we'll have less bother in the search for the other arms dumps, but If we let 'em go it will end up the same way. Either we win or they do, it's as simple as that."

I chewed my lip as I finished talking.

"You're right," the girl broke in. "You'll have to kill us all if you want to succeed, and that will take some doing I can tell you because there are thousands of us all ready to die for our country."

"Shut up, you murdering bitch," Brewer said vehemently, pushing the woman against the wall. "I know your kind, blowing women and children to pieces to further your cause.

You're nothing but a lot of butchers who will stop at nothing to get what you want."

The woman fell silent at this outburst from Brewer, and with downcast head studied the floor. Beside me, Sweeney began to stir, reminding me of my apparent lack of gun support. I bent down and retrieved the shotgun just as he opened his eyes.

"Well, well, back in the land of the conscious," I said, holding the gun so that he could see directly down the barrels.

"Next time I get you in my sights I'll pull the trigger, and it'll be loaded," he mumbled, through thickened lips.

"There'll be no next time," I returned, motioning him upwards, "not for you anyway. Maybe in about twenty or thirty years the death penalty will be reintroduced and then they will hang bastards like you, but now the only thing you can look forward to is a cage where you can do no more harm."

Sweeney regained his feet shakily and stood there swaying. I stepped back with the shotgun still on him, ready to fire if he made the slightest wrong move. My ribs still ached from the dig in my stomach. Sweeney glared at me from his superior height and looked at the shotgun wishing, no doubt, it was unloaded like it had been before. That is when I realised the rest of the shotgun shells were upstairs.

"Keep an eye on him while I creep upstairs," I said to Brewer. "Watch him though as he's liable to try something."

After I handed the shotgun to Brewer I mounted the stairs, passing the lifeless body of the other man and then going into the bedroom where I rummaged through the wardrobe looking for the box of ammo. I reached up to get the box and was about to go when a piece of paper caught my eye. It was a page from the diary we had found earlier and it appeared to have fallen from it. I was about to read something scrawled on it, but was prevented from doing so when the sound of the shotgun being fired boomed through the house.

I raced from the room immediately, just in time to see Sweeney and the woman pull the front door open. Sweeney saw me at the head of the stairs, levelled the shotgun at me and pressed the trigger. It was all done in a split second, so the chances of avoiding the charge were practically nil. The hammer struck a spent cartridge, which was fortunate for me, and an irate Sweeney threw the weapon down in disgust.

"We'll meet again, Cox," were the words that floated up to me as he went through the doorway.

I took the stairs in two goes and, pulling out my pistol at the same time, shot through the open doorway into the front garden. The sound of running footsteps met my ears and I fired at a couple of fleeting shadows against the night sky, but the footsteps continued until they died away in the distance. I retraced my footsteps and, with an anxious heart, entered the house again to see the huddled form of Brewer lying on the floor. I carefully lifted his head and he opened his eyes painfully. Blood was seeping from a wound in his shoulder where the slugs had hit him and he was lying in a widening pool that was saturating his wig to a reddened hue.

"Easy," I said as he moved his head. "Just lie there until I can get help."

His head turned to one side and I followed his painful gaze to see the dog lying on the floor licking a wound to his leg.

"He caught it as well as me," Brewer explained, looking up at me. "Will he be all right?"

His eyes were bright with concern at the dog's misfortune and he had a small tear in the corner of one eye.

""Of course he will," I assured him, looking at the dog as the reddened tongue continued licking. "It's only a flesh wound, so you stop worrying, mate."

"The girl jumped me! I was forgetting her," he said, pain etched across his face. "Sweeney got the gun and shot me as Monty went for him. I couldn't help it."

I made him comfortable on the floor with curtains for a pillow and blankets from the bed upstairs to keep him warm. Fortunately I found a phone box less than two hundred yards away. Within half an hour a small van and attendants, which Lawrence had ordered, were carrying him and the dead gunman away. As they sped away I stood at the door watching the van grow smaller, then I looked down and realised I was still clutching the small slip of paper, which I had forgotten in the excitement of the recent events.

The light of early morning was growing in the sky as I turned on my heel and held the paper before me. It was torn at one corner as though roughly detached from the diary, and on it was one single word – *Towers* – and nothing else. The back was blank, so no joy there. I reversed it and mouthed the word,

Towers, Tower of London? Was it the name of a place or perhaps a person? The word was a puzzle that's for sure. I pulled the front door shut and headed for home and a welcome shower, still muttering the word.

It was well into the day when I finally arrived at the flat.

I stepped into the warm needles of water and let the liquid wash out the aches and pains of my body. On examination, I found a number of bruises, but no lasting damage to my skin. I found my appetite though, and wolfed down a couple of doorstep sandwiches before I lowered myself down onto my bed and went straight to sleep.

They took Brewer to an out-of-the-way nursing home in the Kent countryside and when I arrived he had just been through surgery on his shoulder. He was awake after the operation and bandaged from neck to armpit. He wore a pair of headphones over his ears, listening to the radio, and when he saw me enter the room he pulled them off.

"Trust you to get all this comfort and attention," I said with a laugh. "How's the shoulder?"

"It's OK, so is the service. They've given me a couple of needles to dull the pain."

"You look different without the glasses and also the wig," I said, sitting down on a bedside chair. "And how's the dog?"

"He's all right as well, just a small wound in his leg. He'll be out of commission for a few weeks, but that will give him a rest." Brewer dug under his pillow and produced the diary. "I studied this earlier and apart from a couple of names on the first few pages the rest of them are strangers to me. Further through the book though, I found another name on a page that was partly torn out." He handed the book to me open at the name and pointed to the tear. "There must have been other words," he said.

"Well, I'll be..." I said with amazement, and produced

the torn out page. "I found this just before you were shot. Someone must have torn it out and then lost it."

The first word, the one left in the diary, was Brinkley, and when I added the other word it read as Brinkley Towers.

"Sounds like some country mansion," said Brewer, studying the writing. "Maybe it's where one of the dumps is located."

"What, in one of those big houses?" I mused, half to myself. "Yes! What better cover for them than the residence of a perfectly respectable country gentleman?"

"The thought is irresistible," Brewer said, matching my mood. "All we have to do is find out where it is and visit them."

"That's if it is a house of course," I said, running a hand over my chin and feeling a bit of beard I'd missed. "It could be a fun park or hotel. The alternatives are enormous."

Brewer fell quiet at this, digesting the possibilities and what they meant. I ran through a mental list of all the places I knew beginning with the name Brinkley, and came up with precisely nothing. Towers on the other hand presented several alternatives, some of which I dismissed out of hand as unrealistic. However, there was one that seemed to fit the bill when I rolled it around in my mind for a time; a Brinkley Towers Caravan Park somewhere in the Midlands or thereabouts. It's in the book, so I'll look it up, I thought.

"Looks like it's up to you for a little while," Brewer was saying, "but be extra careful of Sweeney now he's had a chance to see you. Give him an opportunity and he'll take it, so if you've a chance to put him away, take it."

I left Brewer surrounded by doctors and nurses, protesting as they began to examine him. Once outside I made for the nearest bar and ordered a whisky and soda, and a phone book.

"Good boy!" Lawrence exclaimed as I related all that had happened the previous night. "Now we are beginning to fight them back. It's good to hear they are getting some of their own medicine at long last. I'm only sorry we didn't find you long ago. Keep this up and we'll see if we can employ you on a permanent basis."

I brushed aside his compliments by mentioning a subject he had difficulty in broaching – money.

"I'd like to take this opportunity to remind you that I haven't had my weekly cheque yet. When I started you promised me I'd-"

"Yes, yes, we'll sort that out in due course," he interrupted, tut-tutting in my ear. "Now you must follow up that lead you have. I'm sure we are getting there, but it will take time. Until then we must carry on until we prevail. Keep in touch and send me that diary with the torn page. Bye."

The phone went dead and, as usual, I swore at him after the event then sipped the whisky until it was gone. The spirit was warm in my stomach as I left the pub and made for the place where I had left my car.

After being on the M1 for two hours, I braked to a stop outside a long caravan and got out. A sign advertised the sale and rental of caravans and a smaller sign hung below it said, OFFICE. I rapped on the door with my knuckles and waited as heavy footsteps sounded inside. The door inched open a foot and a bald head emerged into the open air. He regarded me from behind thick rimmed glasses while his eyes, like two brown eggs, darted from me to my car and back again.

"Yes?" he said with raised eyebrows that overhung the plastic frames like garden hedges.

"I'm looking for a caravan," I said, casting an eye around the outside of the office. "Something like this, but a bit smaller."

"To rent or buy?" he grated, still watching me, but plainly interested.

"Probably purchase if the price is within my range. Can I come in?"

He nodded and led the way inside to a low counter and a chair resting beside it. He jerked his head in the direction of the chair and waited as I sat down.

"We have several vans," he said, handing me a coloured brochure, "all prices. Give me some idea of your requirements so we can fix a price."

I pointed to a caravan on the second page and looked up.

"Now, something like that is what I want."

"We have two of those in the park. Would you like to see them? We close in half an hour, but there is time."

I nodded with pretended eagerness and he led me through another doorway into the park where he stood surveying upwards of a hundred caravans parked in rows on either side of us. After consulting a sheaf of papers he went down one of the rows and stopped at the door of a silver-sided caravan, producing a key hanging from a bunch attached to his belt. We walked about inside examining the facilities, with him extolling the excellence of the caravan without end.

"Lovely," I enthused then hit him with a question that was burning the tip of my tongue. "Is this place Brinkley Towers? I've been recommended by a friend who bought a caravan recently."

"It changed hands and the name more than a dozen years ago," he said, watching me intently with the brown eggs. "Who's your friend?"

I swallowed with difficulty and thought fast.

"Somehow I forget his name," I said lamely, biting my tongue at the gaffe. I drew a large breath and looked at my watch. "Is it that time?" I said, feigning concern. "I really must go."

As I left, he stood on the steps of the caravan wearing a puzzled look as he watched me drive away. I inwardly cursed at the loss of precious time, and put my foot down on the accelerator until the engine blared in protest. I chewed my lip in annoyance until the lights of London appeared over the horizon.

I levered my body from the front seat and staggered up to the front door. I was about to go through my pockets for the key when the door opened and there stood Jeannie, regarding my surprise with a wide smile. I stepped back to look at the number of the house.

"Pardon me, but I thought this was my flat," I said, slipping by her and into the passage.

She dangled a key in front of my face and laughed as I stared at it twisting and turning in her grip.

"These keys are easy to get," she said, lowering it to her side. Her mood suddenly changed to one of unease. "I've got something to tell you that is of vital importance to you. It could mean your life if you make one mistake," she said.

Her face was a picture of concern and it dashed my retort of anger into one of curiosity.

"My life, you say?" I echoed, shutting the door with a bang. "Tell me more."

Jeannie paused for a minute before whispering through tightened lips.

"They consider you a serious threat to the organisation, so much so that they are willing to risk throwing all their weight behind the effort of getting rid of you."

"And how do they propose to do it?"

"They are going to put a bomb under your car."

CHAPTER ELEVEN

"Whoops!" I said on hearing the news. "Now they are getting personal. I shall have to watch my step or get a new car."

"I wouldn't treat it so lightly," Jeannie said, with concern in her eyes. "They mean what they say. You are their number one adversary. They've got to carry out the threat or lose face in the eyes of their followers, so be careful."

"I will, I promise you," I said, leading the way into the lounge. "Can I get you a cup of coffee?" I asked as she sat down on the settee, then I bent down to look into her eyes. "And thanks for warning me."

I smiled and brushed her lips with mine. A small blush of colour suddenly highlighted her cheeks and she dropped her gaze with embarrassment. She fiddled with her hands, which were lying in her lap, and now and again seemed to lapse into a faraway look. I handed her a steaming cup of coffee and sat down beside her. She set the cup down on a nearby coffee table and agitatedly turned to look at me, worry written all over her face.

"You must be wondering why I warned you instead of

leaving it to the army. I told you of my feelings before, so there is no need to go into that again. I hate the loss of life, especially children."

"That's why you warned me is it?"

Her head dropped and her words came to me as if from deep within her soul.

"Every day we were taught that the English were bad. That topic of conversation was never far away from the lips of the Republicans, and even as children the IRA pounded it into our brains until we knew it by heart. They weeded us out and took the fanatics under their wings to wait for adulthood and the chance of joining the movement. That's how a lot of us were drafted into their ranks, even as we were still in school playing games, so it was just another game to us and it was appealing because they always waved the Irish flag to convince us."

"So they brainwashed you, you're saying – from childhood?"

"In a manner of speaking yes, but in a crafty way. Most times you grew out of Republicanism with adulthood, but not in my case. I grew up with a burning hatred of the English and all they stood for. I was a dedicated soldier of the army from the word go. Nobody was more loyal to the cause than me, and that's how it remained until the bombings started. I was sickened by the bloodshed that seemed to happen every day. I didn't bargain for children to suffer for our cause, so bit by bit the shine of the holy crusade to crush our oppressors tarnished. As a result, my friends in the movement became distant. My friend Ellen also felt this way, but she was nabbed after a job that went wrong."

"This is your friend in prison?" I asked.

"Yes, she is serving a sentence of fifteen years for bomb making, only the charge is not deserved 'cause she didn't know what was going on. They used her, knowing she wanted out, but when they were caught she was drawn into the net. She protested her innocence, but they didn't believe her."

Her azure eyes brimmed over with tears and I held her hand with sympathy. It was cold and trembling. She turned to look at me and my heart softened into jelly. I took her into my arms and held her close against my breast, feeling the beat of her heart begin to increase as my arms tightened. I kissed her then, tenderly and warmly, with her face tilted to meet my lips, avid in her search for love. Warm lips pressed with passion and tenderness, which seemed to gain in strength and desire as feelings advanced. It was a touching of souls and kindred spirits, reaching out and consuming a moment of love, passion and desire. Her skin was a delight to touch and reflected my warmth going out to her.

The kiss deepened into a fiery embrace and we drew closer in want. Her breasts were perfect and the nipples stiffened to meet my questing lips. She arched her neck in ecstasy, eyes tightly closed to hold the feeling, the thrill, the delight. The flesh of her body moved in pure joy against me, the tender touch of her tongue on mine, a mixture of excitement and desire. The inhalation of our breaths was a delight as they mingled, and within us the desire to explore new dreams of happiness drew us to seek new heights of ecstasy. We touched the acme of excellence as our bodies joined together in unison of loving desire.

I realised her body was beautiful, and in my headlong

search for perfect love I found her before me, gathered in my arms and willing to share her delights. She responded to my whispered words of tenderness with a warmth and passion that knew no bounds. Her kisses were fire and her caresses unfettered. When we lay together naked in each other's arms and the spent force of unbridled love was an unforgettable ache, we revelled in the touch of cooling flesh and slowing hearts that beat as one within us, secure in the knowledge that we had discovered something lasting and fine in the measure of our lives.

We dressed after making love and laughed together with each article of clothing an object of amusement. I held her bra to my chest to see if it fitted me and she replied in kind by donning my trousers and staggering around the room in them with the bottoms rolled up. We laughed in merriment and kissed again and again. It seemed I couldn't get enough of her and vice versa. We clung to each other at every opportunity and our eyes met in love, our hands clasped in togetherness.

When we paused for breath and my ardour subsided enough to think of other things, the threat Jeannie had mentioned came to the fore. Her colour paled and the joy ceased to show. In its place was the familiar edge of anxiety, which clouded her eyes and face in its misery.

"In the light of knowing what they are doing, I think it is up to me to make the first move," I said, through gritted teeth.

A frown ridged her forehead.

"What do you mean make the first move?" she asked, concerned.

"You know, take the fight to them. Knock 'em off balance

before they have a chance to do it to me. For one thing, I could hide the car, and another, I could continue searching for the dumps as before."

"Have you any more information on them?"

"Nothing, but what was in the diary I found."

I then lapsed into telling her all about what had taken place at the house in Waterloo and of finding the diary and the missing page.

"Brinkley Towers," I said firmly. "I went to a place up north, but it was wrong; a caravan park in the Midlands. A waste of time, but I had to find out."

"Brinkley Towers is a farm," she said so suddenly I jumped in surprise.

"So you've heard of it then?"

"Of course. It's a farm on the edge of the New Forest in Hampshire. Harvey owns it."

"So that's it! That's where the bastard buries himself when he's not working. Thanks for telling me, Jeannie, you don't know how much you've helped me."

Jeannie's face blanched when I revealed my intention of paying the terrorist a visit. To her the prospect of confronting Harvey was dangerous as she was at pains to point out, especially after falling in love with me.

"To save himself, Harvey will use every trick in the book and then some. The only reason he let you go last time was because pressure was put on him by me – yes, by *me*," she added as I looked at her sharply. "I'm not ashamed to say I felt attracted to you from the start. I threatened to reveal some things I know about him if he hurt you. He only put you to sleep otherwise he would've killed without any compunction."

"Well thanks again, Jeannie, seems I'm forever in your debt. However, I've a job to do and all clues lead to him, so it's only natural for me to start there."

Her shoulders slumped in despair when, after reading my face and seeing the determination there, she realised I wouldn't be put off.

"Then I'm coming with you," she said firmly. "I know Harvey and how he thinks. I've been on the farm, so I know all about it."

I was about to point out that the dangers I would be subjected to would equally be applied to her now that she had changed sides, but I merely smiled and realised her need was for me and me alone, and not for her political reasons. I kissed her on her wonderful lips and held her tenderly in my arms, close to my heart where she clung to me with all the abandonment and fierceness she possessed. I was pleasantly surprised, but gladdened by her commitment, and returned her embraces and wild kisses with caresses and kisses of my own until the world whirled in a mad eddy of dreamy rapture and we ascended into heaven completely as one.

"Darling Jeannie," I whispered. "What a perfect body you have, so smooth, so exquisite that when I'm pressed close to you my mind spins like a roundabout."

She laughed and snuggled closer. Her arms were naked and folded around my neck. I rested my chin on the soft roundness of her forearm and revelled in the touch of naked flesh.

"I have you in my spell," she laughed, drawing closer as my kisses began to arouse her again.

"It's a lovely spell I'm under and I like it."

"Don't talk, just make love, darling Coxy." She pulled slightly apart as a thought occurred to her. "I call you that, but what is your first name Coxy?"

"It's William, Bill Cox or big Cox!"

Her laughter pealed out at this and she fell back into my arms still giggling at the joke.

CHAPTER TWELVE

The light of dawn flooded the sky as we stood in a clump of trees and saw the outline of a farmhouse through a light morning mist. I shivered in the cold and drew my coat closer to my chest, as did Jeannie beside me.

"We've got to cut our way through it," I said, staring at the barbed wire fence that blocked our passage.

She held her finger to her lips to indicate silence, and pointed to a single light that glimmered through the gloom.

"They have a security system alarm that goes off if you make a noise," she whispered in my ear. "They also have a pair of Dobermann dogs that are automatically released when the alarm goes off."

We dropped to our knees and I attacked the barbed wire with a pair of cutters. The barbs were sharp and penetrated my skin quite easily. I cursed as the razor-edged wire drew blood, and sucked my fingers to ease the pain, quietening to a suppressed mutter when Jeannie hissed a warning. Wrapping my handkerchief around my bleeding fingers, I parted the strands of glistening wire and cut a path through it. There were three layers of the stuff and, as we crawled through the coils, the barb endlessly snagged us and our clothes.

Finally we wriggled through the hole and stood gazing about us, ears pricked and senses steeled for any movement. The silence held as we moved away, hardly daring to breathe lest it would activate the alarm, me leading with Jeannie behind. She touched my shoulder and soundlessly pointed to the farmhouse, which appeared as a dark bulk in the half-light.

"Around the back, a small larder window with a dodgy lock," she breathed. "The iron bars can easily be dislodged."

With the utmost in stealth we glided over mown grass and slid around a corner of the building to find the window. I reached out and tested the strength of the bars with fingers curled around an area just above the window sill. There were six bars in number, spaced four inches apart and wet with morning dew. Carefully I increased the pressure on them and felt the bars begin to move. I breathed in and tried again. The bar in the middle moved farther outwards and hung there, free of the wooden bedding. I paused and cocked my ear, listening and breathing slowly. Jeannie tapped me on the back to continue and held out her hand to indicate she was waiting to receive the first bar. I smiled to myself in the shadows and pulled the first bar from its home in the window frame then handed it to my accomplice. She bent down and carefully laid it on the ground then straightened up ready for more.

We progressed rapidly in this manner and within fifteen minutes the bars were placed in a row on the ground. The wooden window frame looked denuded now that its protective coat was gone, ready for the next assault. I tested the strength of the glass with prodding fingers and shook the frame gently. It moved, providing a slit just wide enough to insert the blade of a knife. With care I slowly slid the sliding sash window upwards to its fullest extent and stood there looking at it, breathing a huge sigh of relief.

Once inside, we felt around slowly until we found the door. I cracked it open with a single squeal of rusty hinges, and looked out. We were at the end of a passageway that led to another door. I listened for any sound, but the air was still and thick with quietness. Jeannie's hot breath on my neck showed how close to me she was and, after squeezing her hand, I stepped outside into the corridor.

The next door was stiffer and for a moment I thought it was locked on the other side as it fought my efforts, then it yielded at my insistence and opened. Momentarily as the woodwork moved in a quarter of a circle my actions were slow and I stopped every two inches, ears strained to catch any sound. Bolder now, I trod on hard flooring and entered a large room that in the early morning light I made out to be the kitchen.

"It's only early," Jeannie whispered in my ear. "They won't be up yet. They have a woman who comes in mornings about six. That gives us time to find out who is in the house and how many there are."

I pulled my gun from its holster under my arm and made for the next room, which was the dining room. I glided through, poking the tip of my gun between a pair of sliding doors, and stepped out into the hall with a grandfather clock ticking away in one corner and a wide flight of thickly carpeted stairs that ran upwards and disappeared with a twist to the right. I heard a sound and Jeannie was standing beside me trying to breathe as softly as I was. I waved the gun to show her my intention of mounting the stairs as I put a foot on the first step. She shook her head, however, and pointed to a barely visible light at the side of the third step, and to the other side where another light glimmered.

"Alarm!" she mouthed at me, and I nodded in the half-light to show I understood.

A very faint beam of light crossed the carpet, hardly noticeable to anybody who trod the stairs. If Jeannie had not been there I would have blundered through it, raising the alarm and warning them of my presence. I stuffed the gun into my waistband and clambered onto the banisters where I slithered up the polished rail until I had passed the danger area, then dropping soundlessly onto the carpet, I crouched on all fours, ears cocked.

The silence still held so, encouraged, I straightened up and climbed higher. At the top of the stairs the landing ran away in two directions and I paused in a pool of light coming from a window, unsure of which way to go. That is when the sound of voices suddenly became audible and a door banged at the end of one passage, followed by the swish of soft footfalls as the owner trod through the carpet. I swiftly stepped back into the shadow of the wall and heard the feet shuffle to a stop. A door opened and closed and the sound died away to the noise of running water. A bathroom, I thought, and pushed away from the wall clutching the gun. My footsteps were also deadened by the carpeting then I listened at the bathroom door and heard sounds of splashing water. The sound of music came to my ears and a light clicked on in another bedroom.

Noiselessly I glided over the carpet and held my ear to the woodwork. Other sounds were drowned by the music, so when the door suddenly opened inwards and I nearly fell inside I don't know who was more surprised, me or the woman known as Maureen, the one who had been with Sweeney in the house in Waterloo. For a split second we stared at each other in surprise, rooted to the floor. I recovered first and grabbed her in a vice-like grip then bundled her backwards with the gun poking in her face.

"One peep out of you, darling, and it'll be your last," I snarled, pushing her backwards onto a rumpled bed.

I tied her arms and legs to the bed with her own stockings and gagged her with the pillow case.

"Now, honeybunch, you tell me who else is in the building. Just nod or shake your head."

The eyes stared at me in horror, still unable to fully comprehend.

"Now, who's the one in the bathroom - Harvey?" I said through gritted teeth, and waited as her head nodded. "Anyone else?" She nodded again, eyeing the gun now two inches from her face. "Sweeney," I persisted, "Brough?"

She nodded both times and I knew then I was in for it with all three terrorists present. Something brushed the door and Jeannie was by my side, exchanging glances with Maureen who eyed her malignantly.

"I think Harvey is in the bathroom," I said quietly.

"Then the other two must be on the other landing," Jeannie whispered. "There are two more bedrooms there."

"We'll concentrate on the one in the bathroom first," I

said grimly, watching the woman Maureen who was listening intently. "Meanwhile, you keep an eye on Maureen."

I gave Jeannie a parting wave and slipped out of the room. The bathroom was still occupied as I could hear the sound of bathwater draining away. I steeled myself inside by gritting my teeth together, and settled down to wait. It was full daylight now and a weak red sunrise peered through an end window in a red glow. Soon there were signs of the occupant departing from the bathroom because the light went out and a lock clicked to open.

In a sequence of events the door opened, Harvey emerged in a heavy looking dressing gown, I stepped forwards with my gun raised, he saw me and stopped, then stood stock still with shock written all over his face as I bounced the gun on his right temple. He folded then struggled to reach the door frame for support. I hit him again in the same spot and he crumpled to the floor with a soft bump. I stood there breathing heavily, looking down on the heap of clothes. By rights, to make everything safer, I should shoot Harvey now and only have the other two to deal with, I thought. I raised the gun and levelled it at Harvey's head, squeezing the trigger slowly then I stopped and lowered it to my side, inwardly cursing my reluctance to hit a man while he was down, even though in Harvey's case he rightly deserved it.

I kicked at the fallen man to make sure he was unconscious and looked around for something with which to tie him up. He was a burly man, with plenty of weight to go with his height, so the idea of dragging his bulk to his room had little appeal for me. Instead, I rolled him back into the bathroom and left him stretched out on the floor. Now it was the turn of the other two and I earnestly wished I could be as lucky with them as I had been with Harvey.

I tiptoed to the other side of the landing and listened again. I wondered whether to wait for someone to stir, or to barge in. The second idea appealed to me, but with one precaution; the noise of my entry could wake the other. I decided to go in slowly. I was not prepared for the sight that met my eyes on the other side of the door. The two men were sleeping in a double bed, snoring softly. Sweeney was lying on his right side with Brough close behind him, cuddling him, with one arm thrown around Sweeney's neck. The sight of the two men almost provoked me to laughter until I remembered how they had murdered people in cold blood, and the thought of it chilled me to the core.

I carefully circled the bed and looked for any weapons. There were none, so I guessed they were under the pillows or in their pockets. This being the case, I resolved to wake them up gently, one at a time. I put the barrel of my pistol against the forehead of the sleeping Brough and pushed it hard into his flesh. His eyes flickered and opened, then opened wider, eyes fixed on the gun. I put my finger to my lips to indicate that he should be quiet, and waved the gun sideways to show that I wished him to get out of bed on the other side. He licked his lips nervously and got out, watching me and the gun, then I flicked the bedclothes and waited as Sweeney became conscious. His eyes gazed into space before registering then, muttering a vile oath, he flung back the covers and leapt out of bed, coming to a stop at the sight of the gun held in my hand.

"Just stay right there, Sweeney," I said, threatening him

with the gun. "It will give me the greatest pleasure to shoot you, so don't push me."

I waved them together and they stood there naked and self-conscious before me. I had to laugh at their discomfort and did just that.

"Well, well," I said, standing well away from them, "look at the pair of faggots. I never thought it of you, Sweeney. I took you for a hard man whose only interest is how hard you can hit, and now I find you are sleeping with a man. You're nothing but a pair of poofters."

Sweeney said nothing, but his eyes said it all. His hands were clenched by his sides, giving me the impression he was wishing they were around my neck in a stranglehold.

"Now, I want you both to march out of the room," I said, changing the tone of my voice. "I'll be watching you very carefully, so don't make any wrong moves. Make no mistake, if you do I'll kill you, be sure of that. Now, move slowly out of the room and keep in sight all the time. Right, *move!*"

Out of the room and into the corridor I watched them, and all the way to the bathroom where I kicked the door open to see Harvey just picking himself up off the floor. Soundlessly, I jerked the gun and ushered the three along the corridor and into the woman's room where I waved them back against the wall.

Jeannie stood by me and gave me the woman's automatic pistol.

"I'd be grateful if you would allow me to get some clothes on," Brough pleaded, and then subsided into a malignant stare as I snarled at him.

"Shut your fucking mouth! I'll tell you when you can get

dressed. Now, seeing as you're so eager to start talking, I'll begin with you. Give me the right answers and I'll let you live a bit longer – maybe. Right, where are the rest of the arms dumps?"

Brough jumped visibly with the directness of the question and could only gape with surprise. He exchanged surly looks with the other two men and dropped his eyes to the floor. I sighed and shook my head.

"I'll give you just five seconds to answer and then I'm gonna shoot off one of your fingers," I said, swinging the gun around to him.

He still hung his head sullenly as I looked at my watch. At the end of the time I squeezed the trigger and a shower of blood and finger flesh splashed on the wall behind him. Brough screamed in agony, clutching his shattered finger with the other hand, watched by the others with not a sign of emotion.

"I don't know where they are," he gurgled tearfully, pain etched deep in his face. "They won't tell me."

He began to cry with pain, low sobbing moans that bothered Harvey so much he snarled at the wounded man.

"Shut that row!"

"Oh, so now the *hard man* wants to talk," I sneered, covering him. "You tell me then, where are they?"

"You'll get nothing out of me," Harvey grated. He jerked his head at Brough saying, "He's right. We never told him where they are 'cause of what he is."

"And what is he?"

"A homo, what else? We wouldn't risk telling him. He's just there to make the side up that's all."

Brough's wails had subsided into sniffs as he bemoaned the loss of a fingertip. He was sucking the end of his left index finger and periodically spat out a gob of thick blood.

"Perhaps you can help, with the same inducement," I said to Harvey, narrowing my eyes.

He was about to answer when the dogs began to bark outside as the daily woman let herself into the farmhouse, banging the door behind her.

CHAPTER THIRTEEN

"Ah, shit!" I swore as I heard the door bang shut.

"I'll see to it," Jeannie said. "She knows me, so I'll put her off. I'll keep her downstairs for as long as I can."

I gave her a wink of encouragement as she went, and pointed to the floor whilst holding the others in a hard stare.

"Down on the floor, all of you. On your belly face down, and don't move a hair."

I watched them go to their knees and then prostrate themselves on the carpet - Brough with difficulty. Meanwhile the woman, Maureen, was turning blue without sufficient air filtering through the gag, so I pulled the pillow slip away and issued a warning.

"Not a sound from anyone or I'll gag you all."

I settled down to wait. Time advanced and I heard the clock downstairs chime seven o'clock before Jeannie returned.

"She's gone out to do some shopping," she said. "She will be away for a couple of hours, maybe three, so that should be enough time for you."

"I won't waste any more time," I said, rising from the chair on which I had been sitting. "You first, Sweeney, I'll give you a quick choice. Either you tell me where the nearest dump is or I will kneecap you right now."

I rammed the barrel of the pistol against his right knee joint and pulled back the hammer.

"Now, you murdering bastard," I yelled, "tell me or so help me I'll pull the trigger."

Beneath my touch I felt Sweeney begin to tremble and his breath began to labour as he imagined his kneecap in ruins and being crippled for life. He began to sweat as the seconds progressed. His eyes closed in agony, so I jerked the gun to assimilate the action of firing.

"All right, all right," he bellowed in fright, "but I only know one. We all only know one 'cause they don't trust us with any more."

I pushed again.

"It's the truth, I swear it," he yelled, spittle showering from his mouth. "We swore to keep it from each other, 'cause of security they said."

"Shut your fucking mouth, you traitor," Harvey snarled at him, and visibly wilted as I hit him on the back of the head.

"Now, Sweeney," I said between pursed lips, "give or I'll..."

I left the rest of the threat unsaid as I lifted his head by the back of his hair and banged it down hard.

"What more do yer want from me?" Sweeney wailed, as the blood began to flow from his fractured nose.

"The location, you fool," I yelled. "I want to know where it is. Now, come on!"

I followed this up by picking his head up again, ready to repeat the treatment.

"All right, all right," Sweeney cried, spitting blood clots from his mouth. "The one I know is here at Brinkley, buried beneath the Towers monument two miles from here. It's under flagstones down some stone steps, in a room under the old ruins."

I grabbed him by the scruff of the neck and pulled him upright.

"OK, you're coming with me, chum," I said vehemently, and pushed him onto the bed, adding, "don't move from there if you want to go on living."

The next hour was spent trussing up the other three so tightly it had Brough weeping with the pain in his finger and Harvey cursing Jeannie and me with every foul word he could muster. After running out of breath he contented himself by treating me to a succession of malicious looks that I totally ignored. After tying the final knot, I stood back and surveyed my work. Harvey and Brough were tied to each other with dressing gown belts ending in a slip knot around their necks. Maureen remained fastened to the bed with the gag replaced around her mouth.

I left Jeannie sitting in a chair guarding the trio with the express order to shoot them if they tried to escape. I descended the stairs with Sweeney before me, encouraging him to move forwards with stabs of the gun barrel when he faltered.

About two miles away at the top of a small rise in the ground was an ancient, stone built edifice called Brinkley Towers. Two crumbling towers were all that remained of a fifteenth-century fortress built to forestall frequent attacks from French pirates and other marauders.

I stopped the car on a tarmac road about a hundred yards from the towers and quickly hustled Sweeney out. I jerked him around to face the towers and pushed him in the direction of the ruins with the gun barrel. He stepped towards the towers and pulled up with a howl of pain.

"For Chrissake take it easy," he begged, hopping on one leg. "This ground is covered with sharp stones and I ain't got no shoes on."

And no clothes either, I thought to myself with a grin then pushed him forwards again to the accompaniment of another yell of pain.

"When you deserve it you'll get some clothes on and not before," I grated, "and that includes shoes. Until that time you'll just have to put up with it. Now, *move!*"

I gave him a shove and, with Sweeney hopping and me pushing, we climbed the incline to the ruins. We stopped just short of them, resting on overgrown flagstones, where he sat and cuddled his left foot.

"Which one is it?" I asked, tapping a toe on one of the stones.

"Over there." He indicated with a jerk of his head. "Anyway, you'll need a shovel and pick to lift it up. It's been there for more than twenty years."

"We can use the tools in the car," I said, poking him on the thigh with my shoe.

This proved to be my undoing, for he grabbed my leg with an arm that looped about my knee and brought me crashing down to the ground beside him. Instantly he put an arm around my neck and began to strangle me. The gun was lying out of reach where it had flown, and Sweeney was trying to pull it towards him with his outstretched leg. With his massive arm separating me from my breath by crushing my windpipe, I was in danger of losing consciousness and my mind raced, searching for an opening, while my fingers were tearing at the circle of his arm, desperately seeking a grip on his muscular flesh.

The obvious suddenly came to mind, so I dropped my arm and reached behind me. A piercing scream of agony rent the air as I grabbed his testicles and viciously twisted them sideways. The stranglehold slackened instantly and I gasped in precious air at the same time as I tugged soft flesh and tissue once more. This move was also accompanied by a similar howl of anguish as Sweeney doubled over with pain, clutching his genitals.

I coughed and rubbed my throat as fresh air invaded my lungs. On hands and knees I crawled over to where the gun was lying and retrieved it, turning it on Sweeney, who was still writhing on the ground. He swung a pain-racked face at me with tears still shining on his cheeks, holding his testicles in both hands.

"You bloody swine," he said through gritted teeth, "you nearly castrated me."

"Next time I'll finish the job," I threatened, and motioned him to his feet. "Now we'll go and get the tools so you can get to work."

Painfully, Sweeney got to his feet and, at my insistence, staggered to the car where he loaded himself up with tyre levers, a hammer, chisel and a heavy screwdriver. Muttering to himself he tottered back to one of the flagstones and began to work. After about half an hour of heaving and grunting he straightened up.

"It's impossible. They've been down too long. I need bigger tools to pull 'em up. These tools ain't no use," he said.

"Get on with it," I ordered, watching a passing cyclist eye the naked man with backward glances of astonishment.

"At least get me some clothes, I'm frozen stiff," he begged, rubbing his hands together.

"You work a bit harder and you'll get warmer," I said, waving the gun.

Sweeney snarled an answer and attacked the flagstones with great hammer blows that cracked the corner of the stone. Encouraged, he increased the strokes and the massive lump of rock disintegrated and fell inwards. He stopped, gasping for air, a look of triumph on his features, before falling to his knees and lifting out the heavy pieces.

Before me was a small flight of steps that ran down and disappeared into the darkness below. I gestured with the gun for him to step aside, and leaned over to see more, but the gloom prevented me from doing so.

"OK, down you go, mate, and no tricks," I threatened. "Remember I've got a trigger finger that aches to put a bullet in you, so don't try it."

Down we went through a curtain of hanging spiders' webs and scuttling beetles, down the crumbling, dank dark steps and through fetid air to a heavy looking steel plate set in a solid stretch of wall. It was secured to the wall with six, rusty iron screws. Seeing the screws, I climbed back up for the hammer and screwdriver. I silently handed them to him and stood aside as he worked on the metal screws. He struggled to turn them and barked his hand more than once as the tool slipped. He cursed and sucked his hands as the blood began to flow.

The screws slowly turned outwards until the last one fell and bounced on the packed dirt floor. Sweeney wiped sweat from his chin and levered on the metal plate. To my surprise, and Sweeney's also I suppose, the plate came away easily and he stood it down to one side.

"I only hope I do the right thing," he muttered, reaching in and opening the inner door. "I've only been told how to disarm it, not shown. If I make a mistake we both go up, so you'd better pray I do it right."

The truth is I did say a little prayer when he was fiddling inside. It was also frustrating to see his back as he worked, and not be able to monitor his actions because I had the suspicion he was about to try something big – and he did just that.

"Get out quick, the two chemicals have mixed together," he shouted. "That means we will be killed if we stay here. Get out, *now!*"

I led the way, slithering up the damp slimy steps and out into the daylight where I hared for the car and shelter, firmly convinced Sweeney had activated the explosive mechanism. I crashed the gears in starting the car and gnashed my teeth in rage as I realised Sweeney was heading for the cover of a small wood and I had no chance of recapturing him without a lot of bother.

I squealed to a stop with a rise in the road to give me shelter, and climbed out of the car. I had only just breasted the rise when, in the distance, the two towers of the Brinkley edifice ascended into the air and disappeared in a boiling cloud that instantly enveloped them and the surrounding countryside in a thick pall of dirty black dust. The blast from the explosion reverberated around and rolled away into the distant countryside while the rain of stone particles showered down around me like hailstones. I stood up, watching the billowing black cloud and the scattering weapon remnants covering the ground, knowing full well I'd failed to secure my objective. I sighed and shook my head, realising Sweeney had outfoxed me and was even now on his way back to report to the boss, whoever he was. I clenched my teeth and re-entered the car, turning the wheel in the direction of the farm. I was determined to salvage something, so it was natural to head for it.

A feeling of urgency entered my breast when the farm came into view. The dogs were barking and the place was illuminated from house to barn, but no people emerged as I drove up. I swiftly skirted the outbuildings, gun at the ready, and pulled up at the corner of the farmhouse, ready to fire. The silence hit me like a wall.

I hit the front door with my shoulder and raced up the stairs with the door crashing behind me. The bedroom was empty and the things I had used as bindings were scattered around the floor. The birds had gone and, to my horror, so had Jeannie.

CHAPTER FOURTEEN

I left the farm as I'd found it and started for the forest, passing a small knot of locals who were gazing in wonderment at a pile of rubble that used to be a local landmark. I sped up the motorway with a small worry in the pit of my stomach as I thought of Jeannie and wondered where they'd taken her. I vowed terrible vengeance on them if they were to hurt her.

I drove it from my mind when I arrived home and had a welcome shower. The water streamed over my body and washed the tiredness from it. I dried myself and changed into a clean shirt and trousers before making a couple of ham sandwiches.

Later, calling Lawrence, he gave another rasp of disapproval in my ear when I told him what had taken place at the farm.

"While we appreciate your efforts in locating the second arms dump, another pile of ruins is hardly a help in the fight against the IRA."

"But I found another dump – one less to find in the long run."

"In the long run, certainly, but unhelpful if we are to get convincing proof to intern the terrorists. A lot of shattered gun pieces and burnt cartridge cases are no evidence with which to convict them," he said.

"And what about Jeannie?"

"She's an IRA member. She'll have to take her chances like the rest of them."

"If I get the chance I'm going after her," I spat into the phone, "and the dumps can go to hell."

"You'll find we can sue you for the return of the money we paid you if you refuse," Lawrence said pointedly.

"Ah, bollocks," I swore into the instrument and slammed it down enraged.

Walking home, I racked my brain searching for an answer, but finding none. Looking for a way, but seeing none. I felt low and, finding a pub, I entered and ordered a drink. The alcohol warmed me inside and after awhile I relaxed as it took hold. When I finally left the pub I was feeling a lot more cheerful with four double whiskies and sodas sloshing about in my empty belly. I continued my walk home and for a time Jeannie was absent from my mind. It was then, through the alcoholic daze, I spotted a car on the edge of the pavement with the rear door opening wide. I stepped aside to avoid colliding with a man who had emerged, then felt myself being manhandled roughly. I resisted instantly until I felt something push against my side and a voice hissing at me.

"Don't make me use this. Get into the car and do not make any trouble, Mr Cox."

I was in two minds whether to resist, and raised my arm to protect myself when a thunderbolt crashed against my head and blackness descended.

Through a swirling vortex of slowly clearing grey mist the sounds of human voices came to me as if in a dream. I listened for awhile as they echoed through my brain, trying to decipher the sounds into reason and failing as the exercise only seemed to cause me pain.

I relaxed and opened my eyes to see an expanse of dirty white ceiling above me with a single light bulb dangling down to me on the end of a frayed wire. I blinked in the strength of the lamp and felt the heat from it, although it was four feet above me. My gaze slid to one side and I ever so slightly twisted my head as, in the glare of the light, two shadows came into view. I blinked twice to clear my eyes from the influence of the light force and gradually lifted up one shoulder. I regretted it at once, for a streak of raw pain shot through my head. I closed my eyes to mentally contain the pain and gritted my teeth to drive it away.

I figured out that the voices were about ten feet away and to my left. As far as I could make out there were only two men taking part in the conversation, although others might have been present, but silent. I tried lifting up again and raised my head in the same manner. The shadows appeared again, moving and gesticulating as they tried to make their point. As I stretched farther, the thing on which I was lying gave a creak and the voices stopped. I stiffened and closed my eyes in feigned unconsciousness as one of the shadows rose up and came over to me.

His breath was warm on my face and smelled of coffee. He held my head in his hands roughly as he came close to me. I felt him staring into my face breathing against my cheek. He lifted one of my eyelids between thumb and finger, and looked into it closely.

"I think he's still out," he said, releasing my eyelid. "You must've hit him with some force, Joe. Hope he don't croak it if the boss wants to question him."

"I know just how much they can take," said Joe. "This one is one who takes a little more, so I gave 'im a bit more."

The first man persisted in his anxiety for my welfare.

"You know how the boss is; he don't like it if we make mistakes," he said, with apparent awe. "He'll make us sorry, you mark my words. If he croaks it'll be down to you, Joe, an' not me."

"Go on, feel 'is pulse if you're afraid," Joe scoffed, coming over to me. "Here, let me do it."

I felt him lift my hand and feel my wrist. His fingers dug into my flesh and I tried to breathe normally when his nails pressed hard, almost to penetration. Satisfied, he dropped my hand and I breathed a prayer of thanks to the Almighty as they seemed to accept it. Slowly I let the breath out between tight lips and settled down to wait. Time slipped by and I fell into a dreamless slumber, listening to the drone of their voices. I had no way of knowing the time or how long I had been there, so realising the need for rest I allowed myself to sink into sleep.

I was instantly awake as a door banged and a general raising of voices rang through the air. I pricked my ears up at the onset of the noise, trying to put a name to the voices, but nothing sounded familiar. Someone touched my arm and soft lips briefly brushed my hand. Jeannie, I breathed to myself, and opened my eyes. Her face was close to mine and smiling when she saw my eyes open.

"Darling, are you all right?" she whispered.

I slued my eyes around to watch the opposition and lifted my head when I realised we were alone. After having a good look about me I saw I was in a windowless room, on a single bed, with a square table and two chairs against a far wall where the two men had been sitting. Jeannie was beside the bed bending over me, concern etched on her features in a worry line above her eyebrows. The furrow vanished into smooth skin when she saw I was all right. She took my hand between her fingers and held it to her cheek, keeping it there when my fingertips stroked her flesh.

"So they've got you here too," I said, looking deep into her eyes then looking all around once more. "I suppose this is another of their safe houses," I said, almost to myself. "What're they going to do with us?"

"Kill us, that's for sure," she said. "In your case because they think you're a big threat to their organisation and mine because they think I am a traitor, no matter whether it is justifiable or not. They don't listen to any explanations, so it's no use trying."

"What's the location of this place?"

"Somewhere in London," she muttered in a low voice, "and I'll tell you something else that might be of interest to you."

"What's that?" I queried, feeling the lump on the back of my head.

"It's a bomb factory as well. They manufacture devices from Semtex here. I know because I've seen the explosives they use. It comes here in car loads, even in the pockets of the men themselves. When they are made, the finished product is transported to all parts of the country and secreted away ready for another offensive."

"Got it all figured out haven't they? The hits are big, getting bigger daily with nothing to stop them going to any place anywhere. They'll soon have us over a barrel."

"My sentiments entirely," broke in a third voice coming from the open doorway.

The newcomer, a tall man with grey hair and an iron grey moustache stood there, apparently listening to our conversation.

"Ryan, another member," Jeannie whispered in my ear.

"I hope you are comfortable, Mr Cox," Ryan said, striding over. "Sorry about the bump on the head, but you have a reputation of being awkward, so we were taking no chances."

I offered no thanks for his show of regret, false or not, but ignored him and sat up on the bed eyeing my surroundings with suspicion.

"What is this place and why am I here?" I demanded, after craning my neck in all directions.

Ryan chuckled loudly.

"I've got to admire your nerve, Cox. You've blown up two of our arms dumps, severely injured and maimed one of our operatives, killed another outright and forestalled our movements at every turn. Up to now we found we were able to control Lawrence and his underlings, even predict where they were going to hit us, and take precautionary measures. You are a different kettle of fish, Cox. You've got this irritating ability to strike where we least expect it. That is why we intend to take you out, and for good. Jeannie, your accomplice, will also be killed. Unfortunate in her case, for she was a loyal member of the brigade, but necessary now that she has changed sides."

I sniffed to indicate derision.

"And you think you'll get away with it, even now, as Britain is notching up success after success in dealing with your kind of democracy? The world is in agreement with us in this matter."

"Our struggle against British imperialism concerns us, not the world."

"Terrorism is worldwide as you well know. You're no different from the rest of the murdering scum who kill innocent women and children to gain their ends," I said, angrily.

Ryan coloured up and spoke through compressed lips.

"We cannot hope to convince those who've been indoctrinated by the British ruling classes. The teaching is too deep, too ingrained, so we take up arms to fight our cause because we know we will never succeed politically."

"Then you are finished if you can't do it peacefully."

Ryan shook his head and gave a sigh.

"I have said that we will never win without the gun and the bomb, not if we are to gain a united country. That is why we will fight against all those who oppose us. It is also one of the reasons why you will both be condemned to death."

"Why do you have to include this woman?" I argued, looking at Jeannie. "I almost compelled her to do what she did. She just wanted to help her friend in prison."

"We know all about it and her friend. She has a long history of using the soft approach to a united Ireland and will not accept that our ways are more productive. We were willing to go along with her way of thinking as long as she played a non-active part. When you came on the scene everything changed. She went completely overboard, joining you at the farm completely. She knew what she was getting into and the consequences of her actions. You will both face the court to determine what kind of death you will suffer."

"Am I hearing right? Are you setting up some kind of court to try us?"

"You heard right. We intend to try you for crimes against the Irish people. We did it before in the case of another agent called Fox, who was shot while trying to escape from us. In a further execution, Mason, a traitor to our cause was compelled to throw himself off a high-rise building, and so it goes on. We kill all traitors regardless of their sex."

It was at this moment he was joined by the two other men who had been in the room previously. Joe, the one who had hit me, muttered something into Ryan's ear and stood close by, glaring at me. The other man, a short fat person with a ruddy complexion and big banana-like hands, stood beside him exchanging glances with Jeannie. Ryan smiled a thin smile at me and nodded his head.

"Seems I'm wanted urgently by someone." He waved a hand about himself. "Make full use of our facilities," he invited, breaking into a laugh. "I'll be back to sort you out, don't fret."

All three walked out and locked the formidable wooden door behind them.

"They seem to think they are at war and empowered to form some sort of drumhead court martial to try us," I said, looking at Jeannie with a slight smile.

"Yes, and they mean it too, as has been proved time and time again, so don't dismiss it too lightly, dear. Others have tried before to their cost."

I stood up from the bed and walked around the room, examining the layout. I tested the door for strength and found it strong with no play whatsoever. I pulled at the mortise lock and turned it. The lock was stiff and presented resistance. I inspected the walls for any sign of a crack to indicate the presence of a hidden window. Nothing – the room was a solid cell of four walls and a door from which not even a mouse could escape. We were locked up good and tight, and after deciding so I returned to the bed and sat down on the hard mattress.

"What's this place," I asked Jeannie as she joined me on the bed.

"As I said, it's a bomb factory," she replied. "I've never been allowed to find out where it is exactly. I've always been blindfolded. All I can say is it's somewhere in south-east London, but where… ?" She broke off and shrugged her shoulders in defeat.

"So we'll have to play it their way for a time," I said. "In the meantime we'll do what he invited us to do and make ourselves comfortable."

Suddenly she was in my arms and our lips pressed together, soft at first, but deeper as we held each other, tasting our different lips. We felt the force of each other's love surging out and being greedily accepted by the other. She pulled away out of breath, sucking in lungfuls of air, eyes briefly out of focus with the strength of my kisses.

"My God, darling, you had me going for a moment," she puffed, red in the face. "Let's find a way out of this predicament before we get sidetracked by lovey-dovey."

"OK," I said, yielding to the idea, but not convincingly, "but I prefer making love."

I made a grab for her, but she evaded me by dodging behind the bed. I laughed at her antics and she joined in our merriment by giggling at me. The time went past quickly and easily, enjoying each other's company, laughing and joking at the pretence of love making.

"We've got to approach this problem sensibly," Jeannie giggled, twisting out of my arms. Her features were red with laughing and her blue eyes danced with delight. "We must give it some thought if we're to get out of this kangaroo court set-up," she added.

"I'll plead insanity and throw myself on the mercy of the court," I returned, grabbing and missing.

"You can't be serious, can you?" she giggled, stepping aside.

"What for?" I asked, raising my hands palms upwards. "Listen, this might be the last chance we have of making love, you know that? Mr Ryan seems to have jumped the gun with regard to our guilt and the future looks far from rosy for us in front of this court."

"They'll kill us, there's no doubt about it."

"Surely the hearing is a farce? That is why Ryan pronounced us dead."

"Do you think we can get out of here?"

"What, escape? Highly unlikely, and not from this room anyway. The walls are too thick and the door too solid," I said, shaking my head.

"What're we going to do? I don't want to die, not just yet."

"Nor do I, sweetheart. I'm thinking of asking them to commute the sentences to one of life imprisonment."

Jeannie choked on this and we laughed together for awhile as she tried to regain her breath. Her adorable breasts heaved, and my fascinated eyes feasted on the movement hungrily.

"Come on, now," I coaxed, full of urgency, "let's enjoy what remaining hours we have left in loving each other."

"We can't," Jeannie whispered with a smile, "they might have hidden cameras watching us. It's too embarrassing."

"The dirty perverts!" I exclaimed. "I'll soon fix them."

I jumped onto the bed and reached upwards. Gritting my teeth against the pain of the hot glass, I twisted the bulb in its bayonet cap holder and wrenched it downwards.

CHAPTER FIFTEEN

After Jeannie and I spent several hours making love, the door uttered a squeaking sound and opened to admit the three men. I weighed the possibility of rushing them, but when Ryan produced a wicked looking automatic from his pocket I hurriedly changed my mind.

They stood in the light coming from outside the room and Ryan waved the gun to indicate we should follow him. With Ryan leading and the other two taking up the rear we went from the room and walked along a wide corridor to a brightly lit doorway. Our leader jerked his head to indicate we should enter, and stood aside as we went in. For a moment we stared at the group of people waiting for us, until a hand on my shoulder steered me to a chair facing the assembly.

With Jeannie at my side on another chair, I leaned forwards to see the people; six men and two women in the act of sitting down at a long polished table. Four were familiar faces. Harvey, Sweeney, and Maureen stared right back at me while Brough glared at me, hatred plainly written on his face. I treated him to a long look of contempt, slowly wreathing into a sneer. The other four, a woman and three men, were talking amongst themselves.

One of the newcomers, a balding man with curly grey hair sprouting out just above his ears, held me in a hard look and tapped a sheaf of papers that were lying on the table before him.

"We've brought you here to say you have been found guilty as charged," he announced, circling the tablecloth with the same look. "We've all come to the same verdict, so there is no need to discuss it any more."

This was echoed by the group, who uttered a chorus of murmured approval.

"Well, well," I sneered, "and not a word said in our defence. What kind of court is this supposed to be anyway?"

"You've only been brought here to learn the method of your execution," baldy said, standing the papers up and shuffling them into order whilst tapping them on the table. "This we have decided, and it is death by shooting, sentence to be carried out tomorrow."

I gave a hoarse bellow of laughter on hearing the sentence, which drew a few looks of surprise from the table because they expected us to beg for mercy.

"You'll never win," I said, shaking my head. "Even your own people are against you with your murdering campaign. Very soon they will cast you out, you and all your killers."

"Be that as it may be," baldy said, smothering a yawn, "you'll die tomorrow as we have decreed."

That was that – all over in a matter of minutes. We were made to walk back to our cell and bundled inside so quickly we hardly had time to breathe. The lock turned and the heavy mortise mechanism shot into place leaving a void of silence just broken by the sound of departing footsteps. Even that died away and we were left in a well of noiseless density interrupted by the sigh of our own breathing.

I fingered my emergent beard and racked my brains for an answer, but nothing came. Jeannie's eyes followed my movements eagerly, expecting me to come up with some infallible plan to get us out of danger, and when I collapsed onto the bed her eyes opened with surprise.

"Morning will come quickly, Bill," she said, "and so they will carry out our execution."

"I expect they will," I allowed, gazing up at the light bulb.

Someone had replaced it into the holder and the bulb blazed down power and heat as well as light. I picked my lip, thoughtfully running the outline of an idea through my mind.

"Tell me darling, are they liable to come back for awhile?"

"Maybe," she said, looking at me. "Why?"

"Why would they come back here before morning?" I asked, answering a question with a question.

"To give us something to eat and drink I suppose."

I got to my feet and winked at her.

"I'm beginning to get a little hungry and thirsty aren't you, dear?"

"I suppose so, well, thirsty. Here, what're you working on?"

"Just go over to the door and keep your ears primed for

any sound of someone returning. I want to experiment on something I've been turning over in my mind."

I winked at her a second time, which did nothing but increase her curiosity.

"Let me in on it, will you?" she said in a low voice.

"OK, first of all strip off the bed covers and rip out the wire holding the metal base together."

I saw her look at me sideways, so insisted.

"Yes, there is wire. I saw it earlier today when we were making love."

Whilst she pushed the covers on the floor I walked over to the light switch and with my thumbnail undid the plastic wall plate, exposing the electric wires. Carefully I freed the wires from their plastic holder and pulled them out, still live. Jeannie handed me the wire from the bed and I wound some of it around the metal door handle whilst still retaining the two ends. Memorising where the two ends were, I switched off the light and plunged the room into darkness, praying that I didn't make a mistake, I jammed the two ends into the switch wires, getting a small shock in the process and bringing the overhead light on.

"Hope it works," I said, shaking my hand. "Good job the place is dry or I'd be a hospital case."

We waited for an hour and no one came. We sat on the ruin of the bed and talked of getting away, naturally. Time went by and we calculated it was well past midnight, although we really had no idea whether we were correct.

"It must be late 'cause I'm feeling so tired," Jeannie said, yawning. "Seems like they've gone to bed for the night. Pity we had to ruin the bed," she added ruefully.

It was about twenty minutes after Jeannie had drooped onto my shoulder that a sound filtered through the woodwork of the door and a key rattled in the keyhole. The handle turned and a man stepped into the room. In pretence of sleep, I inwardly cursed the trap I had set, and waited to pounce on whoever it was.

The door flung wide, and amid a flash of electric current and an ever-widening cloud of blue smoke the twitching body of Brough could be seen. His hand was outstretched, gripping a wicked looking dagger that gleamed evilly in the light. His clothing smoked and smelled of burning cloth.

"Looks like his goose is cooked," I said, picking up the dagger.

The other hand that had turned the handle was streaked with electricity burns and his eyes stared sightlessly into space. Brough was stone dead and still managed to scowl.

"No prizes for guessing what he had in mind," Jeannie said, sniffing the smoke. "Seems your trap worked after all, but it was touch and go for awhile."

I nodded and wrinkled my nose up at the smoke smell then tiptoed to the door. I listened for any sound or sign of the others, but all was quiet.

"Whatever he meant to do, he was set on doing it alone," I whispered, and slid like a shadow around the angle of the doorway.

Outside in the corridor I waited for her to catch up.

"You go first as you know the way," I said, out of the corner of my mouth.

The floor was tiled, and masked our footfalls a little. Softly we slid our way along the corridor and past the room where the court had sat. The door was open and it was empty. My nerves strained to catch the slightest sound and in the dark, tense silence of the building a very faint noise could be heard. After a dozen footsteps I made it out to be human voices, and stopped, gripping Jeannie on the shoulder.

"Steady now," I hissed through thinned lips. "We don't want to run into them."

We came to a corner and I peered around the angle of the wall. The passage was in darkness, but the sound of conversation was definitely louder. We were heading into danger and I hesitated before continuing.

"We've got to go this way," she said softly, her lips close to my ear. "There's only one way out and it's this way."

"What about them?" I asked, turning my head and speaking into her ear in turn.

"Nothing for it, we'll have to pass them if we are to get out. The building has but one door and there is always a guard on it. You'll see, if and when we do escape."

We continued to creep forwards, heading for a crack of light that became bigger and brighter as we progressed. The voices were gaining volume and recognition as we neared the bar of light. I stopped short of it, held my breath and looked around the corner. Inside the room three men were playing cards around a table, and the noise was caused by the arguments about the game. The players, thick burly fellows, looked like they were well able to take care of themselves. They snatched at the cards as they were dealt, grumbling amongst themselves as the cards flipped down in front of them. The door masked half the scene as I peered in, but two of them had a good view of the doorway.

I slid into a crouch and, out of sight, inserted a finger underneath the bottom edge of the door. Slowly I exerted pressure and drew the door shut as though it was caught in a draught. It was now just a matter of passing the crack of light and after doing so we paused to breathe again before continuing to the end of the passage where a solid-looking iron door barred our progress.

"The guard is outside," Jeannie mouthed. "This door is built into the wall. He sits in a chair just along a bit. He has a key. Just knock and he will open it, but be careful 'cause he has a gun."

I stood back, nodded to her, breathed in a deep breath and, with the dagger held at the ready, knocked smartly on the iron surface of the door. Almost immediately there came the scrape of a turning key and the door began to open inwards. I stood out of sight to one side and let the man step inside. His yell of surprise was throttled in his throat as I threw an arm around his neck whilst brandishing the knife in front of his eyes with my other hand.

"One yell and you're dead!" I threatened, squeezing his neck.

I made him raise his hands and twisted him roughly around to face me. With the knife waving dangerously near his left eye I patted his pockets and relieved him of his gun.

"Now, sunshine," I said, cocking the gun, "turn around and march the other way, but remember this gun is pointing at your spine, now *move*."

Jeannie pushed the door open and stepped out followed by

the guard and then me. An unexpected surprise met my eyes as we emerged, for we were in a big dusty warehouse. Lofty and wide, it was completely empty of anything except the chair on which the guard had been sitting. Behind it was the building from which we had entered, but to see it you would be fooled into thinking it was the warehouse wall. The iron door was disguised with false bricks stuck to the surface, looking exactly like an unbroken wall. The building was out of sight, hidden from any prying eyes, official or not, a perfect disguise for a bomb factory. I dragged my wondering eyes from the scene and slewed them around the empty warehouse. From outside, the sounds of ships' horns could be heard, as could other noises of passing traffic and human voices.

I ushered the guard over to a pair of wooden double doors and shoved them open with a grunt.

"Well, I'll be…" I said as the daylight streamed in. "London!"

It certainly was! The warehouse was situated by the side of the Thames with Big Ben and the Houses of Parliament in full view. The sight brought a smile of disbelief to my lips.

"For Chrissakes, I don't believe it," I murmured, scanning the river. "There's the seat of parliament, the very heart and centre of the fight against terrorism and all it stands for, and here it lives, in the flesh, a bomb factory less than half a mile away. I just don't credit it."

The guard made a move sideways and I prodded the gun into his ribs.

"Try it, just try it, you bastard, and I'll rid the world of another scumbag," I said savagely.

He treated me to a look of hatred then relaxed his body.

"What're we going to do now," Jeannie asked, "and what are we going to do about *him*?"

I firmed my lips in a pensive way and thought quickly. Up to then we'd had phenomenal luck. The Fates had been kind, but there was no knowing how long the luck was going to last. I was for riding our lucky streak to the limit.

"Listen, Jeannie, I'm going back inside," I said at last.

She protested.

"No, I've made up my mind, it's the best way. We've got them on the run and I think it is up to me to keep 'em at it. Besides, I've got to earn the money the country pays me, Lawrence said so."

I ended up smiling at her as she stood there looking pathetic with worry lines on her face. My heart all but exploded when I gathered her in my arms and kissed her hair and tear-stained cheeks.

"You will be careful, Bill," she breathed into my ear.

"Of course I will," I assured her, holding her close and feeling the warmth of her body, so alive, so vital.

A shuffling of feet reminded me that the guard was nearby and ready to flee if I didn't watch myself. I relaxed my hold on her and stepped back with a smile, casting a look at the man at the same time.

"I'll give you just twenty-four hours to do the job, Bill. After that I'll call in the marines, so you've been warned."

"Right," I said with a wide laugh, "I'll expect a contingent of marines to arrive post-haste tomorrow. Can I depend on it, darling?"

"Yes," she said softly, "and I'll be leading them, so you be there. That's an order, OK?"

"Sure," I said, beckoning the guard with my gun. "Twenty-four hours and the balloon goes up."

I kept her in view all the time she trod the river path to the end of the jetty. Even when she disappeared around the corner of another warehouse I still saw her trim figure in my mind's eye and the delicate way she walked. When the guard moved, he stirred my memory and the reason why I was there. I shook myself from my reverie and ushered him back to the warehouse.

I clicked my fingers and held my hand out. He took out the key and handed it to me. I jerked my head sideways and he went through the warehouse doorway and marched up to the concealed door. I stood to one side ready for anything, but the door swung open into the passage devoid of anyone else. I breathed more easily then and waved the gun from side to side. Without looking at me, the man went in and waited for me as I warned him by pressing the gun into his back. I clicked the door shut and waited for my rapidly beating heart to slow. The guard sensed it and I felt him gather himself to try for an attack. I forestalled any ideas he might have had by grating in his ear.

"Your life hangs by the touch of the trigger, make no mistake about it, mister. I'll kill you with the greatest of pleasure, not because I have to, but I like ridding the world of scum like you."

He laughed to show he wasn't frightened, but it neither succeeded in convincing him nor me because I felt him tremble with the next prod forwards. He responded by going ahead. We reached the card players, still immersed in the game and arguing the toss. Silent mirth spilled to my lips as I readied myself. I edged the guard and myself forwards until we stood in the bar of light falling from the door crack. I waited for the arguing to reach a crescendo when another winner crowed out loud then, gathering myself up, I shoved the man into the room and followed him, levelling the gun at the players.

Pure shock, sudden and paralysing, transfixed the four men gathered around the table. Without exception, they gazed open-mouthed at our entrance and for a time were rooted to the spot. The surprise rapidly cleared though, and a weasel-faced man recovered and made a dive for his gun. I warned him just once by shouting then shot him in the chest as he kept coming. He registered a look of hurt surprise as the heavy slug whanged into him then he slid from the chair sprouting a stream of blood.

"Any more?" I questioned, circling the table with the gun.

A sullen wall of frightened silence met my fierce gaze, punctuated by the agonising groans of the dying terrorist.

"Now we have that settled," I said, waving them backwards, "we'll get down to brass tacks."

I pointed the gun at a fat individual who was beginning to sweat.

"You, fatso, when will the others be back?"

He licked his overfull lips and croaked in reply.

"Very soon. There'll be more guns than you can handle, I'll betcha."

"I didn't ask you that, you fat bastard. You answer what I tell you to answer and no more."

I pointed to another man and watched him squirm as I aimed the gun at him.

"You, you rat-faced lump of shit, *you* tell me."

He visibly shook in his shoes, obviously overwhelmed by the presence of the gun and the direction in which it was pointing.

"Mind that thing don't go off," he said, ogling the weapon.

"It will if you don't do as I say, you gutless bastard," I jeered. "Now, the same question – when will Harvey and the rest of the cut-throats be back?"

"They're due now, all four of 'em. Brough was here with us, but he must've gone outside 'cause–"

"Brough is dead," I interrupted. "You'll see him shortly."

All four gazed at me and then at each other. The groans of the shot man were fading away to a series of sighs. The others edged away from the sounds and the pool of congealed blood on the floor. I nodded towards the open door.

"I want you all to file out of here and go to the room where Jeannie and I were imprisoned. I want you to go slowly, so I can keep you in sight all the time. Anyone who tries to get away will be killed instantly. This is your first and last warning, so think on it carefully."

I walked around the table relieving them of their guns and, after throwing them in the corner of the room, I stood outside waiting for the men to move. Slowly they filed out leaving the dying man on the floor, and moved ahead of me. Their eyes goggled when they saw Brough lying on the floor, and a new spasm of fear passed through them at the thought of the same fate awaiting them.

I picked up the key from where Brough had dropped it and was about to shut the door on them when the sound of the warehouse door being opened came to my ears. Instantly I shot behind the shelter of the open door and waited for the newcomer to draw near. A pattering of quick footsteps followed, then the female terrorist, Maureen, entered the room, gazing at the group and the dead man on the floor. I stepped into view, holding the gun.

"I'm glad to meet you again, Maureen," I said as our eyes met.

"I can't say the same about you," she said, indicating the dead body of Brough with an incline of her head. "This some of your doing?" she asked grimly.

"When I think of what he had planned for Jeannie and me with that knife he carried, the swine deserved all he got," I returned in a short manner. "Be as it may, I'll ask the questions. Now that you are here you might as well tell me where your particular dump is. I know you are one of the trusties, so don't bother to lie."

"Go to hell!" she blazed.

"I probably will, but not just yet," I said, with a shallow smile. "I'll ask you just once more 'cause I'm getting a little bit sick of all your company."

"And you will always get the same reply. You can ask until you're blue in the face, the answer is still no."

I slowly walked over and gripped her dress, ripping it open to the waist. Her face blanched, but she stood there unmoved.

"Let's see what you are like underneath, Maureen," I said, hooking one finger under her bra and breaking the elastic. "Now is your chance to perform for the boys who are waiting to see more." I pushed her to face them and spoke in a theatrical voice. "Maureen is about to act for you boys, in fact she invites one or two of you to take part in a pornographic double act right now. Don't be shy. She'll do anything you ask won't you, Maureen?"

"You wouldn't dare," she said, almost in tears, holding the remnants of her dress to her breasts.

"I wouldn't eh? Come on," I invited the fat man. "Anything goes 'cause Maureen is a bit of a goer. She's done it all before, so don't be shy."

The fat man made a small shuffling noise with his feet and Maureen must have thought he was taking me up on my offer because she gave a little scream and hid behind me. Quick as a flash, I grabbed her and shook her violently until her teeth began to rattle, yelling at her to reveal the name of the dump. She began to moan and the information trilled off her lips.

"It's in a disused underground tunnel off Bank Station," she cried, looking over her shoulder at the fat man. "It's walled up there, about a quarter of a mile from the station."

She collapsed in a heap on the floor amid a flood of tears. I grinned broadly at her misery and patted her shoulder.

"Never mind, Maureen, now that you've got it off your chest you'll feel better for it when doing your time. Of course, the boss won't be very pleased, you telling me where it is. Seems you'll be running for awhile until they catch up with you, but that's the way the cookie crumbles sometimes."

Her face was a mask of tear-stained hatred as she stared at me, in contract to the sheer exhilaration I felt with the whereabouts of the next pile of armaments in my head.

My next movements were almost a joy in the light of what had happened. I gestured the men backwards and, pushing the woman ahead of me, locked the door and threw the key far up the passage. I hustled her forwards up the passage and out through the concealed doorway into the warehouse just in time to see the main double doors begin to slide open. I pulled her back into safety and cracked the door open to see Sweeney and Ryan enter. They were earnestly discussing something as they approached the concealed door. As they came nearer, the sound of arguing was heard mixed with a couple of expletives from both parties. I felt the woman move against me, so issued a warning.

"If you warn them I'll reveal where I got the information about the dump. I'll give you three guesses what they'll do to you."

Maureen shuddered and drew back behind me as we melted into the shadows. I grinned in triumph, knowing I had an enforced ally. We hid in the courtroom and watched as they went by. I heaved a sigh of relief and prepared to slip out through the concealed doorway, then a thought occurred to me and I voiced it to the woman.

"Do you know where Ryan's dump is?"

"No I don't, because it isn't allowed. I only know that he has a bad memory and because of that had it tattooed on the sole of one of his feet."

CHAPTER SIXTEEN

I must have registered surprise, for Maureen even smiled in a vague sort of way. I certainly was, for Ryan having the whereabouts of the arms dump tattooed on his foot spoke acres about the organisation that manufactured him and of the murderous attitude of their followers who carried out their commands no matter what – Maureen included.

"Right, now we have that settled you're coming with me, sweetheart. I can't afford to lose you now that we have another dump."

"I can't come with you," she protested. "Haven't I done enough for you already? If they find out I helped you my life won't be worth a plugged nickel."

My face broke into a happy smile. I had an ace to play and she knew it.

"Perhaps I'll tell them," I threatened.

Her face changed into despair, so I turned the screw further.

"I would, you know, just to see you squirm."

I laughed when her chin fell and a tear gleamed on her eyelash.

"You bastard! You call us ruthless and you show the same qualities yourself. You people ask us to follow the peaceful line then stab us in the back when we do."

"I'm not asking you anything, mate. Your time is almost up, you and your ilk. It's just a matter of outlasting you, that's all."

I pushed her forwards, out through the doorway and towards the double doors. I slid them open and then hurriedly pulled them, much to the surprise of the rest of the gang. From then on it was a matter of who was going to make it into the bomb-making building first – them or me. I was saddled with the reluctant Maureen who, seeing the sort of opposition I was up against, decided to play it smart and show a bit of resistance of her own.

"Help me!" she yelled at the top of her lungs.

She lashed out and caught me on the calf of my leg with a vicious kick, I bellowed in rage and hopped on one foot, dropping the gun in the process. Within seconds I was surrounded by the others and held from the rear in a stranglehold so tight it made me buckle at the knees. One of the men raised a fist ready to crash it into my face, so I squeezed my eyes tight shut ready for the blow.

"Hold it," shouted Ryan, squeezing past the two who held me. "We want to question him first then you can have him."

The restraining arm eased from my neck and I gasped in a lungful of air. I couldn't rub my throat where the arm was because they still had a tight hold on my hands. Instead, I swallowed a gob of spit, which did a little to help the pain. Ryan grabbed hold of my jacket lapels and thrust his face into mine. His eyes were bloodshot and his breath smelled of beer.

"All right, Cox, what's been going on? How did you get free?" he demanded.

Little flecks of spit accompanied the words and I turned my head away to escape the spray. It was at this juncture that Sweeney and Harvey chose to join the crowd. They emerged from the hidden building with the rest of the gang in tow and pushed to the front. Harvey gave everyone a graphic account of what had taken place in the building and pointed an accusing finger at me.

"He killed Brough and one of the guards," he said, staring into my face with darkened features. "He also helped the woman, Jeannie, to escape. She's probably telling them where this place is even now. He's managed to forestall everything we've done in the past twenty years in a matter of weeks. I'm all for shooting him right now in case he does any more damage."

He produced a revolver and levelled it at me, pulling back the hammer as he did so. Ryan knocked the gun upwards and it exploded into the air.

"Where's your brain, Harvey, in your arse? We need him now. Ever hear of a hostage? We'll keep him in case we need him. It's a fair bet Jeannie has spilled the beans to the authorities and they are on their way here right now. If we can't get away by river as we usually do, we'll bargain his life for ours."

"OK," Ryan allowed, "but watch him very closely. He's

a slippery customer and dangerous too. Just give him half a chance and he'll cause untold damage. If you are going to restrain him, do it well 'cause he'll find a way of getting away if I know him."

"Will these do?" a member of the gang asked, holding a pair of handcuffs aloft.

"The very thing," Ryan said with delight. "Now see if he can Houdini his way out of these."

They twisted me around and snapped on the 'cuffs'. I winced as they cut into my flesh, restricting me from avoiding the slap on the side of my face as Harvey turned me to the front again.

"Now let's see you slip outta these bracelets," he said, sneering into my face.

"Now we've got some work to do and it has got to be done quickly if we are to avoid being captured," Ryan said to all and sundry. "First of all we've got to get the equipment out and stack it somewhere out of sight, and don't forget any diagrams of bomb making that will help the enemy." He shouted as the gang began to move away. "And get those already made out first."

I was sitting on the guard's chair as the building was emptied. A man was posted outside to warn of any intervention, and two men were beside me to prevent my escape. Within minutes, bombs, chemicals for experiments, Semtex and other explosives were carried from the building and stacked in the warehouse. The bodies of Brough and the guard were conveyed on the shoulders of two of the men, and every vestige of anything incriminating was removed from the building.

I was ordered to get to my feet and was escorted to the

outside of the warehouse by the two gang members. With one in front and one behind, I was then led down a muddy tow path to a large river cruiser moored against a wooden quayside. I was quickly hustled up a wooden gangway to the deck where I waited as one of them lifted a hatch cover and laid it back on the deck. He jerked his head to indicate I was to enter, and stood back as I climbed in. I pointed to my handcuffs intimating the difficulty I had descending the ladder to the bottom, but I received a push that had me partly scrambling, partly falling to the deck below. I straightened up with difficulty and breathed in as the pain of the fall knifed into my back.

The lid closed above me and I was left in a gloomy darkness, relieved in part by the presence of a small and grimy porthole. Through the dim light I was able to see I was in a sort of locker, with an assortment of wire ropes, oil cans, rusty chains and equally rusty tools. I squinted in the poor light to see a broken file amongst the collection, and a smile eased the pain in my shoulder. Gritting my teeth I crouched into a ball and, with difficulty, brought my arms under my buttocks to the front. The handcuffs were now in front of me and easier to get at. I reached over, gripped the file between my fingers and began working on the area between my wrists.

The file was old and well used. I scraped the skin of my wrists and steeled myself to expect more of the same. The file slipped constantly and very often clattered on the deck. I stopped on each occasion, listening for any noise to indicate I'd been heard. Each time all I heard was hurrying footsteps and the thump of things being dumped in other parts of the boat.

I was about halfway through the handcuffs chain when the lid lifted and a shaft of brilliant daylight held me in its beam. A head broke the light square and eyes peered down at me. I looked up at the face, screwing my eyes together to assimilate light ache. A voice floated down to me, talking to someone else on the deck above.

"He's still lying in the same position," it said, "and even if he gets loose he'll never get out 'cause the hatch is barred on the outside."

The lid thumped down once again, plunging me into the dark and back to the scraping of my file. I gritted my teeth at the pain and licked the abrasions on my flesh. I tasted fresh blood often as the file slipped on the metal. The taste of the rusty file entered my mouth and stung my taste buds. I shuddered and carried on filing then a new noise jarred through the boat. The engines began to throb and the superstructure creaked as they started up. I now knew I had to make my move if I was to escape, so I attacked the handcuffs with renewed vigour. The boat began to rock with the action of the waves and the water hit the hull with a gentle slap. A stiff breeze brought the scent of the river and the smell of Thames water suds chopped up by the propeller wafted down to me.

I filed pell-mell in the dark, cutting more flesh than metal, silently yelling at each slip of the file and occasionally pausing to listen. I sucked my fingers and cursed at the file as it cut into skin then with one mighty grunt of painful rage I raised the handcuffs and brought them down on the bottom rung of the ladder. They parted without any more effort and my hands hung free with a metal ring and chain dangling from each wrist.

I sat there eyeing my surrounding for awhile. The locker was about four feet by six feet and ended up in the prow of the vessel. It had a shelf on either side supporting a clutter of bolts and engine parts. A hacksaw also rested on one of the shelves and I swore at the memory of the filing, long and hard. The beat of the engines increased in tempo as they opened up and the rocking settled down to a rhythm of up and down at each intervention of the waves.

I imagined we were well away from the shore. Jeannie and her force of marines were only to meet with an empty building and not net one of the terrorists. I chewed my lip with annoyance at the thought of the injustice of it all, and promised myself a double haul in the future to make up for it. This cheered me up no end and I stood at the foot of the ladder looking up at the light sifting through the cracks in the locker lid above me. I looked at the old lid again and with rising interest noted it was made of wood. I picked my lip and the hacksaw came to mind. I took it apart and, holding the thin blade, inserted it through one of the cracks then began to saw.

The roar of the engines dulled the sound of my strokes and no gang member came to investigate. I repeated the operation and a small chunk of wood fell past me, as did a flurry of raindrops. I shook off a fringe of rain sticking to my hair, changed my footing to another rung and continued sawing. After about fifteen minutes another piece of wood clattered to the deck below and the rain blew into my face, blinding me. I tore at the thick timber and succeeded in inserting my hand through the hole. I paused for breath then, closing my eyes to the beat of the rain, feeling around above me for the locker bolt. I breathed a silent prayer when my lacerated fingers touched cold iron, and I gripped the bolt and tugged.

I heard a tiny howl as the bolt began to move and, with the sound to encourage me, I increased the pressure. The bolt slipped out of its hasp and I pulled my hand inside. It was impossible to hear anything but the beat of the engines and the hiss of driving rain, so I slowly lifted the lid a bit at a time until it was wide enough to get my head out. Fortunately for me, the lid was hidden behind a windlass, so when I lifted it high and eased it over, the movement was unseen, but not so the wheelhouse. It towered up eight feet in height about twelve feet farther down the deck and when I squinted at it, above the cover of the windlass I saw the shape of two figures through the glass screen.

Through the driving rain I could see the shore gliding by, about eighty yards away at its nearest point. The water was choppy and looked decidedly cold. A light rain mist hovered above the waves and the raindrops pimpled them continuously. I had to make a decision, and I did. With a mighty heave I yanked my body out of the hole and, in a crouching run, made for the rail. Behind me I heard shouts and the crack of a revolver. Running footsteps, dampened by the rain, drummed on the deck as I reached my goal.

I hit the water just as the first of my pursuers skidded to a stop at the rail. The cold waters of the river closed over my head as singing bullets plunged into the waves about me. I dived deep into the oily water, hearing the thrash of the boat's propellers three or four feet away from my body. I kicked for the shore and freedom. I surfaced fifty feet away and was pleased to see the aft end of the boat, with a group of watching men, disappearing into the mist.

With unhurried strokes I swam for the shore and crawled up a stone pebbled beach somewhere in north Kent. I was shivering with the cold and the water ran from my clothes in an evil smelling stream. My teeth started to chatter with the cold numbing my body, and I knew I had to find shelter before I got pneumonia. I staggered up a muddy cliff path, through a wildly thrashing group of bushes and, in the driving rain, ran smack into a wooden garden gate. Blinded by the rain, I undid it and stumbled up the path to a brick porch where I crawled in and sat on the floor, frozen and soaked to the skin. I shivered and then knocked on the door.

In a little, the light came on and the door cracked open.

"Who's that?" a female voice enquired.

I stammered out something and the door opened wider. In the light an old woman was peering intently at me through a pair of metal rimmed glasses.

"Would you like to come in out of the rain?" she asked, pulling her jumper up around her ears.

I lifted my trembling body up then entered the house and breathed a huge sigh of relief as the door closed on the fierce weather.

"Thank you, ma'am," I said, leaning against the wall and dripping raindrops.

"What terrible weather," she said, leading the way into a cosy lounge. "I was about to make a cup of tea. You sit by the fire and I'll get you one."

She waited until I was settled in a comfortable fireside chair and then disappeared into what I supposed was the kitchen. Gradually I stopped shivering in the heat from the coal fire and my clothes started to steam. The smell of the river came off them and I apologised and explained.

"I was in a small boat and it suddenly capsized. I swam to shore, but the boat drifted away." I laughed ruefully. "I won't be going fishing again for a long time I can tell you."

"Fishing in all this rain," she said, shocked. "You look all in." She eyed my clothes. "You can do with some dry things as well."

She fingered her lip as I drank my second cup of scalding tea.

"Tell you what, my husband has a cupboard full of old clothes that he never wears. You can take your pick of them. You look a little taller than him, but about the same otherwise."

Later on, dressed in a sports coat and grey flannels, which smelled strongly of mothballs, I left the woman on the doorstep, holding a bag of sandwiches she had pressed on me. The rain clouds had drifted away and in the dim light of a full August moon I made my way to the distant town.

I hitched a lift on a passing lorry and drifted in and out of sleep as the journey progressed. The driver nudged me awake several hundred yards from my home and I walked to my flat in a sort of dream. In the next few minutes though, I woke up when I discovered the front door hanging open and the carpet soaked with rain. Inside the rooms were a mess. The place had been turned over by someone who had done a good job of searching for something. My mattress had been ripped from top to bottom and other furniture upturned during the search. The only things left untouched were the shower and bath.

I relaxed under the shower needles and dried myself with a curtain that had been torn from the rail. I turned the ruined mattress onto the other side and threw a blanket over myself as I settled down on the bed.

CHAPTER SEVENTEEN

"I can't imagine what they were after," Lawrence coughed into my ear when I related what had been happening. "Perhaps in your dealings with them you took something that belongs to them. I can't bring anything to mind at the moment. Don't worry about your flat though, we have alternative accommodation in the event that something like this happens. I'll get a set of keys to you for a flat we hold in South London. It belonged to Fox, the man who was killed recently, but I know you're not superstitious – you're not are you?"

I mumbled something about being comfortable where I was and why couldn't it be refurbished. Lawrence misinterpreted it as usual and warbled with pleasure in my ear.

"Good work on getting the arms dump from the woman, Maureen. You'll have to contact her again though, if we are to find out precisely where in the tunnel the dump is located."

"Any ideas how I manage to do it?" I asked.

"Do what?"

"Well, contact her. I just got out of the boat by the skin

of my teeth. You're asking me to walk on back into the same situation. To me, that is nothing but stupid if you ask-"

"Cox, you are employed to do just that," Lawrence interrupted. "You are paid well by your employers, the public, to carry out your side of the agreement. This I must insist on. If it means you are to get a few scratches in the process, well, that's all in the game."

"A *few scratches*," I scoffed, visualising the many bruises I had on my face and body. "Listen, I have a collection of bruises that will merit hospitalisation for weeks to come. It's a wonder I'm still in the land of the living."

There was a pause at the other end of the line as Lawrence mentally digested that juicy morsel. He breathed into the receiver in his usual breathless way and coughed once.

"All right," he conceded, much to my surprise. "I'll send the necessary paperwork to your address for an incremental rise. I don't know how I'll justify the increase to my superiors, but if needs be I suppose I must give way."

He muttered into the mouthpiece something about making other cuts in the service and living within the budget then trailed away to silence.

"I need another gun," I said.

"Another firearm?" he replied incredulously. "But we've only just issued you with one."

"Nevertheless, I need one. The other gun was taken from me in the course of my duties. Also I find it useful to wear a bullet proof coat."

"Do you really need one? Those things are cumbersome. Can't you do without one?"

"Listen, Lawrence, I've dodged more lumps of lead in

the past few weeks than you've had hot dinners. My luck's not going to last much longer though, look at Brewer. That's another point; when is he reporting for duty?"

"He was in the task force attacking the bomb factory. The wound is in the process of healing and he is claiming light duties."

"I wish I knew how he manages it," I mumbled quietly.

Lawrence chose to ignore this uttered plea and changed the subject.

"I'll get in touch with the 'car park' and they will issue you with another weapon. Try to hold on to it this time," he pleaded. "The weapons are budgeted to our account and the annual review is subject to close scrutiny."

"Have you any news of Jeannie?"

"Things have happened and moved forwards, you being without any contact with the outside world."

"What do you mean?"

"I mean a *telephone*. We will address this by installing one in the flat you've inherited."

"You're so kind to me, it makes me so humble."

"Don't be facetious, Cox, it doesn't become you."

I swallowed a remark about his parentage.

"I was asking about Jeannie," I insisted.

"As far as I know, she told Brewer she would contact you soon."

We talked for a little while longer then I rang off after Lawrence urged me to do my best to find the rest of the arms dumps. I listened with very little interest and wearily dropped the phone down.

I walked back to my shattered flat and caught sight of my

car standing a little farther up the road. I gripped the handle and was about to enter it when a warning voice in the back of my mind stopped me. Bending down, I looked under the body and found a bomb taped to the underside of the floor and covered in grease to avoid discovery. A couple of wires were connected to it and disappeared upwards through the floor to the ignition switch, I supposed. One turn of the key and up I go. Very disturbing, I mused, and dangerous too.

I straightened up thinking fast. If I call Lawrence he'll know what to do. Probably send around an expert to defuse the bomb. Right now it is a danger to all, being ready to explode at a touch. I sensed a movement behind me as I stood by the car, so I whirled around, prepared for anything. Several yards away was the smiling face of Jeannie, and as she came nearer I returned the smile with one of my own.

"Anything wrong with it?" she questioned, meaning the car.

"Only a bomb stuck to the underneath with tape."

"I was expecting it," she said, looking into my eyes. "What are you going to do about it?"

"Not a lot I can do. Suppose I'll have to get it removed."

"You seem very casual about it." She moved away from the car. "Shall we stand a bit farther away from it?" she suggested.

"It won't go up without the ignition key and I ain't got it."

"Famous last words! Let's leave it shall we?"

I had managed to wedge the front door shut and pushed it open with difficulty to gain access to my flat. Jeannie followed me in and stood aghast on seeing the destruction.

"So they've been here too. Must have been the same time they did the car," she said, picking up an upturned vase and setting it down on the table.

"Made quite a mess too," I said. "I'm wondering what they were searching for. I'm almost sure I've got nothing they want, except…" A sudden thought occurred to me. "I wonder if they were after the map."

"Map, what map?"

Without replying, I ran over to the sideboard, which was resting on its side, and righting it slid it aside to reveal a stretch of coloured wallpaper. I felt it for a moment, running my fingers over the surface of the paper until I found the join. Inserting my fingers, I peeled back the wallpaper and extracted the piece of map fixed to the underside of it with sticky tape.

"What's that," she asked, coming over and standing by my side.

"It's a bit of map Lawrence gave me when I started this job. This must be what they are looking for. I can't think of anything else I've got they would be after."

"You'd better keep it in a safe place or they'll find it. They will be back, I can assure you."

I folded the scrap of map and put it into my inside pocket. Jeannie was watching me and followed my movements.

"I'm thinking, what's in the map to interest them?" she said.

I offered no explanation about the area shown on the map and she didn't pursue it any further.

"Pity about yesterday," I said with sympathy. "The marines got there just that little bit late."

"Yeah, we found an empty place 'cause the birds had flown the coop. They won't be able to use it again though, so that narrows down their area of operations a bit more."

"I've got to find Maureen again to lead us to the third arsenal. I almost got the location from her before I was captured."

I launched into a resume of what had taken place the day before and showed her the cuts on my wrists to prove it.

"Oh, you poor thing, darling," she sympathised, and kissed me on the cheek.

I immediately circled her waist with both arms and pressed my lips to hers. We made love there on the carpet amidst the wreckage of my furniture. Our bodies meshed into an undulating frenzy of perfect love. I kissed her wonderful breasts and the softness of her throat a thousand times, as the sweet sweat of heated passion surged through us without end or reason. Our bodies melted into each other and our desires, ardent and hungry for more. We cling together for an hour like two soaring spirits reaching for the stars, thankfully seeking out and holding the golden reward of precious love. Her breath was a summer rose and the moisture of her mouth the nectar of the gods. In our love we were fine-tuned to each other and our love making knew no bounds. We ended covered in sweat and completely out of breath.

"Whew!" I exclaimed. "Beat that Romeo and Juliet."

I laughed into her ear and uncrossed my entwining legs. Her laughter joined mine and her breath sang into her lungs as I eased my weight off her body.

"My God, I enjoyed that, darling," she said, sitting up.

Our clothes were scattered about us in our mad frenzy

and we went about collecting them and dressing amid the remains of my furniture.

A little later, a messenger arrived at the door and handed me a parcel. After examining it carefully I opened it to find a couple of keys and an address inside – my new home. I managed to salvage most of my furniture and hired a removal man and van to transport it over. I entered my new flat and spread the furniture around the rooms, then wearily got some sleep.

I arose and showered. My beard came off easily with an electric shaver and I slammed the front door shut behind me to search for some breakfast. I ate poached eggs, and lots of toast and marmalade washed down with orange juice, whilst reading the *Mirror*.

The morning rush hour was almost over and the crowds were beginning to thin out. A picture of a train in the newspaper brought back the memory of what I had to concentrate on, and I tapped the table thoughtfully, bringing to mind Bank underground station. I paid for my breakfast and stepped out of the restaurant intent on calling Lawrence to de-bomb my car. He promised to do it that day and I rang off, meaning to head for the nearest pub to wet my whistle.

I pushed the pub door open and was about to order myself a large whisky and soda when a familiar face caught my eye.

"Brewer, by God!" I exclaimed, seeing his reflection in the mirror behind the counter. "What are you doing in this neck of the woods?"

"Looking for you, mate," he returned, squinting through

the thick glasses. "Lawrence told me you have taken over old Fox's digs, so here I am."

"I'm waiting for my car to get de-bugged before I pay the 'car park' a return visit," I said, ordering the drink.

Brewer scratched his beard with a thin hand. His arm was in a sling and the movement showed white bandages.

"How's the arm?"

"Coming along, thanks. A bit stiff in the mornings, but getting better every day." He licked his lips free of beer froth with a small pink tongue, and toyed with the half-full glass. "Good work in getting the bomb factory. We always knew it was somewhere in that area. Trouble was it was so well hidden we passed it by in search after search." He sighed. "Who'd have thought of a building inside another building? A perfect hideaway if ever there was one." He looked at me through the top half of his glasses. "What are you going to do now? Have you any ideas regarding the tunnel dump?"

"So you've got wind of that. Who told you, Lawrence?"

"Certainly, he tells me everything. He says Maureen is the main player in this particular portion of events."

"That's right, or Ryan, whoever we can tie down first."

"You mean the tattoo?"

"Right again, the tattoo." I sipped my drink thinking of that bizarre way of remembering, and laughed out loud. "Just think of it, Brewer, he couldn't remember so he had it tattooed on his foot – and that's another thing to think about" I said, rubbing the smoothness of my shave. "Which foot is it that he has tattooed, his right or his left?"

"Ask Maureen, she forgot to tell you."

"I'll ask her in due course, but she has to guide me to hers first. Trouble is I've no idea where she is, so I've got to find her before I can get going."

"I've heard she is a well known patron of Irish dancing. There is a school of dancing over at Peckham, above Burtons. They specialise in teaching Irish dancing, so maybe they will tell you where she can be reached."

"I'll do just that as soon as I can, mate. Right now I've got to rearm myself at the 'car park'."

I winked and grinned knowingly. He pulled a face and set the glass down.

"I'm making a few enquiries of my own," he said in an undertone. "Right now we have them on the run and if we want to keep 'em at it we've got to increase the pressure until we get to the top."

"The top? Oh, you mean the guy who is running the show," I said, thoughtfully. "That, I'd like to know; the identity of Mr Big, the mastermind of it all. Now that would be some trap if we met *him*, Brewer."

"Yeh," Brewer said, looking into space, "but we know next to nothing about him. He might as well be the invisible man as far as we're concerned. He's kept his identity and reputation clean, so no blame can be attached to him. He can go on for years like this, causing mayhem and suffering all in the name of this organisation." Brewer looked at me and compressed his lips. "Seems to me, he's the linchpin of the organisation. If we can achieve the ultimate in getting to him, the heart of it, we will end all armed resistance here on the mainland."

"Sounds all right, but how do we find out who he is?"

"From informers naturally."

"I thought loyalty couldn't be overcome by mere reward."

"Don't you believe it, mate. Everybody has a price as you must know."

I emptied my glass thinking of those last few words.

After telling Lawrence about the bomb and getting an assurance from him that it would be attended to, I made my way back home to find Jeannie waiting for me on the street corner. She appeared agitated and nervous, and couldn't wait to get inside.

"They've got out an order to kill me," she said, explaining her nervousness. "I'm to be hit because of my involvement in the operation against the bomb factory."

"Well, we all are," I said, hoping to calm her. "Anyway, they were going to shoot us both at the factory and they didn't succeed did they?"

"But this time there is a reward paid for anyone to do it. I'm a marked woman."

"Well, welcome to the club," I said. "My own name must've been scratched on a dozen or so bullets in my time, and so far I've managed to dodge 'em all."

"I'm not used to all this exposing myself to violence. I'm getting to be a nervous wreck."

"You get used to it I'm thinking."

"You do? Pardon me if I beg to differ. I jump at every sound and I'm nervous of every shadow."

"You need a bit of protection. I'll get you a gun to frighten off any would-be assassin."

She melted into my arms then, closing her eyes and returning my kisses.

"Don't rely on me too much," she whispered into my ear. "I'm a bit of a coward and I don't like violence."

"I'm a dab hand at self-preservation," I said, kissing her neck and nuzzling into her shoulder, "so maybe it will rub off on you."

She giggled when my wet tongue touched her skin.

"That tickles," she said, wriggling in my arms.

"It's meant to," I muttered, muffled by the contact.

I nosed into her cleavage and blew a raspberry in the swell of her breasts. I was happy knowing my presence could make her forget her troubles. She fell into the circle of my arms and we made love. For awhile we forgot our cares in our wild abandonment to each other, falling asleep quite naturally afterwards.

CHAPTER EIGHTEEN

The 'car park' was still the same with the usual method of entry guarded by the same man who took me down in the same lift to the bottom floor. At the bottom, the grey haired man took my arm and led me to a room where there were several easy chairs grouped around a big television set. Sitting in two of them were a woman and a bald headed man, who twisted around to see us when we entered the room.

"Two members of our counter-terrorist section, Mary and Dan," grey hair said, introducing us. "Bill Cox, our newest agent. Make yourself at home, Bill."

He went out and left us to it.

"We're just refreshing our memories on a particularly obnoxious pair of terrorists. You might know them as Ryan and Harvey," the bald headed man said, extending a hand of welcome.

"We've heard of your recent brush with them," Mary said, smiling. "Also your elimination of a couple of others, namely Brough and one of their resident firing squad. Congratulations on taking the fight to them."

I grunted, which was supposed to represent my thanks, and shook her hand. It was warm and felt a little clammy, so I quickly dropped it and looked elsewhere.

"Fox was a member of our group," Dan informed me, pointing to a chair beside him, "but they killed him because he was getting too close for their comfort. We know he was on to something important and we also know he wrote a lot of his suspicions down." Dan wiped his brow on a snow-white handkerchief. "His notes went missing of course because we have an informer in our midst. The notes must have been important inasmuch as they might lead us to more of the terrorists, even to the traitor himself."

I listened with interest and watched the screen as more information appeared. It seemed the two killers, Ryan and Harvey, only occupied the middle ground of the army and not the upper echelons as previously thought.

"The supporters number in their hundreds," the TV reporter said in an Oxford accent, "and it is estimated the number of 'sleepers' - those who have joined the community and are waiting for the signal to arise and cause untold chaos - has quadrupled."

Grey tapped me on the shoulder. He handed me another revolver.

"It's the same type, but more powerful; longer distance and heavier hitting power, a truly strong weapon for attacking purposes. Just up your alley, Bill," he declared.

"Thanks er..." I stammered, reaching for his name.

"Douglas – Doug to my friends."

"Well, Doug, mate, now that I'm pretty well established as

you must know, I'm wondering if you can help me by issuing a small lady pistol to a friend of mine. I've promised the-"

"Highly irregular," Doug said, "and against government policy guidelines regarding firearms. I'm afraid it's-"

"Oh, come on, Doug, who's to know? A little .22 calibre handgun for protective reasons. The lady has been threatened and is helping me in the fight."

Later, I left the building with the two guns and boxes of ammunition wrapped in a plastic bag. I dropped them onto the seat beside me and was soon heading south to London and another tilt at the terrorists.

When I arrived I contacted Jeannie and questioned her about Maureen's pastime of Irish dancing and where she was likely to be.

"She does do a lot of dancing over at Peckham as Brewer said, but I don't know about now," Jeannie said, picking her lip. "She has other interests as you know."

"Sure I do," I said, remembering the kick in the shins. "Can you tell me where this dancing school is located?"

"Better than that, I can show you," she said, and grabbed my arm. "It's only a couple of miles from here."

Amid the afternoon traffic in Peckham High Street, we dodged around the after end of a double-decker bus and crossed the street to a big building where we stood looking up at it.

"This is it," Jeannie announced with a nod of her head.

Up above, music could be heard, and a faint tapping of feet on wooden flooring accompanied the music. I shifted to the side a few steps to a set of double fronted doors with thick glass windows and a coat of grey dust. A big brass doorknob poked out from the door and I reached out and tried it. It turned, and the door opened inwards into a thickly carpeted passage running to a glass fronted office with a shiny brass admission counter.

The music was louder now that the traffic noise was excluded and it could be recognised as a piano thumping out a well known melody accompanied by a female voice singing in time to the tune. A flight of stairs carpeted in the same design as the passage confronted us and we were about to mount them when the office came alive as the image of a fat woman with stringy blonde hair filled the office window with her bulk.

"What do you want?" she demanded, breathing on the glass and misting it.

"We're looking for Maureen, she comes here to dance," I said, approaching the glass.

The fat woman shook three chins and screwed up her mouth.

"Maureen? I don't know of any Maureen. You sure you got the right place?" she asked, placing a pair of steel-rimmed spectacles on a button nose.

"Well, she does come here, so I've heard," I insisted. "Can we go upstairs?"

The woman looked hard at me through the glass and began to shake her head. I pretended not to notice her refusal and mounted the stairs.

"I'll not be long, dear," I promised. "It'll only take a minute or so."

I heard her muffled shout directed at me, but I was halfway

up the stairs by that time with Jeannie close behind me. Upstairs we came to another glass-paned door that led into another corridor, and stopped at a notice saying:

GLADYS JONES SCHOOL OF DANCING

PLEASE ENTER

We entered and found ourselves gazing at several lines of sweating people who were dancing to the music. At our interruption, they tailed off into nothing and stood motionless, eyeing us with curiosity. When they stopped, the piano did too and the pianist in turn, a thin figure in a black, tight fitting costume. She held the note until she saw us then paused in mid flow, surprise written all over her face. I was surprised as well, to see the rapidly paling face of Maureen staring back at me.

I sneered at her and mouthed:

"Hello Maureen."

She swallowed and turned her head to the class.

"Rest now everybody," she directed in a husky voice, and as they scattered to a row of wooden chairs at the sides of the dance floor, came over to us. "What do you want?" she asked in a low tone.

"Why *you*, Maureen, or whatever your name is," I answered softly. I looked around the room. "Well, lookee here now at this set-up," I said in a jeering way. "A nice, easy convenient way of hiding away from all the fuss of everyday cares, wouldn't you say, Maureen?"

"I'm not doing anything illegal," she said, dropping her eyes.

"Nothing, but belonging to an organisation whose motto is get what you want regardless of the cost."

I increased the volume of my voice and it attracted several stares.

"I must ask you to lower your voice," she said, in a tone barely above a whisper. "There are children here and they might get alarmed."

"All right," I conceded, "we don't want to frighten the kids." I bent down to her height. "But I must ask you to accompany me to somewhere to discuss a little matter that you know a great deal about, you savvy, Maureen?"

She nodded, still white-faced, and turned around to face the class.

"I'm afraid I've got to call it a day, class," she shouted above the talking. "I've got to go somewhere very important, so we'll have to cut it short. We'll continue the lesson next week as usual."

There were groans all around.

"Sorry about this, we'll have an extra half an hour on Tuesday to make up."

We descended the stairs, went through the double doors and into the street where we waited to cross the busy road full of traffic. We arrived at where I had parked my car and got in, Maureen sitting beside me. I grinned and held her in a humorous glance, which was not quite as light-hearted as it portrayed.

"Where to now, Maureen, or Gladys or any other alias you care to assume?"

"Gladys is my professional name," she said hotly. "My given name is Maureen, so let's stick to that shall we?"

"All right with me, no skin off my nose what you want to be called. All I want are the directions to the arms, so I'll repeat - which way now?"

"You know, I told you where it is; in the tunnel at Bank Station."

"Sure you did, but what tunnel, which way, how far from the station, how far into the tunnel is the cache and, most importantly, has it a self-destruct system like the other two?"

"You'll find out when you open it up won't you?"

"We will, *we* will, darling," I corrected. "You'll be coming along too, so don't make any other arrangements."

She chewed her lip with suppressed rage and subsided into silence. I gave her a cursory glance and returned to my own thoughts. Another thing I found disturbing was the fact that I had to dump her for awhile until the station could be cleared of the public. All trains had to be stopped and the electric supply cut off.

This will take time, I mused, valuable time. Anything could go wrong in the meantime. The opposition will soon know I have Maureen and will take steps to see that she doesn't spill the beans, so it is imperative I stash her safely out of harm's way. The trouble is, where? Jeannie solved the problem by announcing she was going to visit her friend in prison. I grabbed the opportunity to get shot of the female terrorist for awhile.

"We've got to park our friend for awhile until the station

is available, so how about planting her in the nick?" I suggested.

I saw Jeannie shake her head in the rear-view mirror.

"I can't see them accepting her inside without the proper paperwork."

"It'll only be for a couple of days until we can get to the dump." I turned to the silent woman. "You won't mind will you, ducky, seeing as your friends will want to shut your mouth permanently when they find you've told us what we want to know?" I said lightly. "More than likely you'll thank us personally for saving your life won't you, sweetheart?"

"Go to hell," she spat out, eyes blazing.

"Spoken like a true terrorist," I said, laughing and jerking the engine into life.

Some time later, we were gathered in the warden's office at Wandsworth Prison. We sat in some rather stiff wooden chairs, watching him talk on the phone to the minister for prisons.

"Yes, minister," he was saying, fixing us with a look of interest. "I have them here in my office now. They've brought the woman with them." His face drew together in a serious frown and he repeated a previous statement. "I must insist that I receive the necessary authority in writing, minister."

He listened, answering with an occasional grunt as the minister spoke into his ear. He replaced the instrument on its rest and sat there for a minute, seemingly digesting the conversation. His gaze ran from me to Jeannie and then to Maureen who was sitting slightly apart from us.

"Seems it is all right," he said at last. "You must have

some powerful friends to walk in here and demand we take her in."

He nodded at Maureen as he spoke then shrugged a pair of thin shoulders and pressed a button on his desk. A uniformed warder appeared and waited expectantly.

"You'll come back for her as soon as you are ready?" he asked, looking at me.

I nodded once and stood up to leave. He inclined his head to the warder, who clutched Maureen's arm in a firm grip and silently took her out.

"Much obliged for your help, warden," I said, turning to go.

"Tell me something," he said, "who is she, some kind of political prisoner?"

I screwed up my face and winked before going out of the room. I turned once, to see him shaking his head, and broke into a laugh.

The platform of Bank underground station was cold and draughty, and exhibited the indefinable smell of the 'tube'. I studied my wristwatch for the umpteenth time and pulled up the leather collar of my coat, shivering in the cold light of the station. Farther along, two railway officials talked together in low tones, no doubt discussing the cause of their being there. They were to accompany us in our search for the dump and each man clutched a map of the underground system. Apart from them, Jeannie, a somewhat subdued Maureen and me, the platform was deserted

The hands of the station clock reached 4 a.m. and one of the railway employees, a man with white hair parted in the middle of his head, came over to us and pointed to the clock with a nod of his head.

"It's four. The juice has just been switched off. If you will lead on, we will follow you, sir."

"OK, Maureen," I said, taking her arm and leading her to the edge of the platform. "Now it's up to you."

I took her wrists in mine and lowered her down. She hugged the platform edge fearfully. I looked down on her with compressed lips and sat on the edge just above her.

"You sure it's off?" she asked with trembling lips.

I answered her by leaping down astride the gleaming rails and putting one foot on the metal.

"Which way now?" I demanded, watching the fright die in her eyes.

She pointed to the right of the platform and waited as the rest of them jumped down to the track. With Maureen in front, we set out in a line, stepping from sleeper to sleeper to the end of the platform. When we entered the blackness of the tunnel I snapped on a powerful torch and illuminated the snaking lines in a shining light. After awhile the lines branched outwards, disappearing into the darkness as they twisted away. Maureen hesitated at the intersection and we bundled together.

"What's wrong?" I questioned, with an echo resounding all around us.

"I-I can't remember," she stammered, breath frosting the air. "It's been a long time."

"Why did you stop here?" I demanded, flooding her face with light until she screwed up her eyes and covered them with a white hand.

186

"I-I..." she stuttered again, and then cried, "ooer!" when my clenched fist cracked hard against her cheek.

She sat down hard on the track, nursing her jaw with both hands and making snuffling noises.

"Here! I say, just a minute, you can't do that!" one of the officials protested, then collapsed into silence as my torch swung in an arc to pinpoint him.

I reached down and grabbed Maureen by the hair, pulling her to her feet and pushing her onwards. She responded by aiming a vicious kick at my genitals, and missed. I gave her a dig in the back and she staggered forwards another step. It was at this juncture she must have decided to give in because she gave a great sigh of despair and started forwards again.

"That's a good girl, see how much better it is for you if you co-operate?"

"You bastard," floated back to me.

We continued stumbling through the semi-darkness, helped by the occasional light fixed to the tunnel wall. We walked for about an hour through tunnels where clammy walls dripped with scummy water, down a gradient tripping over various objects it was too dark to detect. We clambered onto the rails, balancing on them when the tunnel walls closed in too much for the track to continue. Beads of sweat pimpled my brow despite the cold invading my feet as we sloshed through ankle-deep rainwater and slid through greasy-feeling mud. Maureen slipped and fell several times. Each time I helped her to her feet and felt her viciously shrug off my attentions when I touched her. I ignored her objections and continued to urge her onwards.

I could hear the others labouring for breath at one

particularly difficult obstacle and was tempted to call a halt for awhile. The track stretched ahead out of sight and a pool of brown sluggish water, criss-crossed with miniature waves caused by the constant draught moving along the tunnel, lay before us.

"Does anybody want a rest?" I asked, turning to fix them in the light of the torch.

"I could do with a blow," the white haired official said. He bent over and sat down on one of the metal rails. "How much farther is it?" he asked wearily, wiping the mud from the bottoms of his trousers.

"No one knows except Maureen," I said, shining the light upwards to the tunnel roof, "and she might be leading us around in a circle."

"Oh, Gawd," said the other official.

I studied the water pool and tried to gauge the depth of the water, for the ground dipped, so there was no knowing how far the gradient descended. We rested for awhile until I got to my feet. They followed suit and together we entered the water. It was icy cold and sloshed up to my knees. Ahead of me, Maureen held up her dress and stepped through it slipping and sliding. I righted her several times, once when she fell to her knees and floundered in the water for awhile. She remained silent, however, with not a word of thanks for my help.

Gradually we emerged from the pool and discovered the track again. We were on dry land again and it felt good to leave the freezing water behind. Another intersection appeared, and Maureen stopped to get her bearings. She looked in all directions and finally headed for a branch tunnel that appeared from the gloom without warning. It was old and in the process of disintegration. Piles of dirt and bricks occupied the place where the rails had been removed. A stream of dirty grey water trickled through the rubbish and ran away into the blackness of the tunnel. She entered the mouth of the crumbling tunnel and picked her way over the fallen bricks, then waited until I caught up with her. I directed the torch beam into the dark and lit the way. We walked for about fifty yards and stopped as the tunnel came to an end. We were there, and I breathed a sigh of relief.

"There," Maureen announced, pointing to a section of crumbling wall. "There, behind the bricks. It's only one brick thick and the metal plate is behind them."

I tested the strength of the bricks by attacking one of them with a fallen one, and was instantly rewarded for my efforts when the brick wall crumbled to pieces under the assault and showered down to the ground. Getting Jeannie to hold the torch and illuminate my actions, I held the brick, corner on, and with downwards strokes scratched the surface of the wall support. I got her to shine the torch on the result of the scoring and, with leaping heart, I saw the gleam of raw metal reflected in the torch light – we had found what we were looking for.

Given the condition of the wall, it didn't take long to expose the metal plate, and before the astonished gazes of the officials it stood there naked and formidable.

"Now that you have what you want you can let me loose," Maureen said, backing away.

I ignored her, being too engrossed in attacking the bolts with a screwdriver I had taken with me. She stood back at the edge of the light beam and a frightened look crossed her face as I snatched a glance at her.

"It'll go off if you don't know how to stop it," she said fearfully, casting an eye at the two officials, who were looking edgy themselves.

I turned the first screw and dropped it into the mud. The second and third joined the other in the mud under my shoe. Jeannie stood to one side of me, watching intently.

"Don't worry about her," she said, her eyes shining in the rays of torch light. "I'll disarm it for you."

I grinned and pulled out another screw.

"Let's hope they did not have a change of heart and decided to use another method to detonate it," I said.

"I've got my fingers crossed for you."

"Baby, if I knew it would do me any good I'd cross my eyes."

Even under the strain, her face creased into a smile, and the sight of it made me feel good.

"Is it right what she said?" one of the railway men asked.

"Yes," I answered, grasping the last screw in muddy hands. "It will probably be booby trapped, and dangerous too if we can't disarm it. You can shelter outside the tunnel if you want to."

They nodded, exchanged nervous glances and started to walk down the tunnel to the outside. Maureen, however, was undecided and stood there nervously twisting her hands together.

"Why don't you go too?" I questioned her, trying to exert pressure on the corroded plate. "Your work is finished here.

Jeannie will try to disarm the bomb if there is one, so any time you're ready you can pop off."

Maureen's face was a picture of misery and anxiety. She jumped at every noise. In the half-light she often turned her head to listen to the sounds, and her eyes bulged.

"Do you think they will come here?" she asked with apprehension thick in her voice.

"Who, the IRA?"

She nodded in the gloom, her eyes standing out.

"Maybe they will when they find out you've betrayed them."

"But will they come here *now*?"

I stopped heaving at the plate and turned to study her. Her features were grey and stood out from her face. Her skin was the colour of dirty parchment, emphasising the acute nervousness of her condition. Her eyes stared out at me in terror, and I could see she was on the edge of a nervous breakdown. She started then; not loud at first, but rising up to it - a series of sniffles gaining strength to a fully fledged scream. I twisted and grabbed her arm at the same time she began to cry out. I flexed and gathered muscles in a mighty drive to her jaw and felt her facial bones jar against my knuckles as they connected. I caught her limp body in my arms and gently lowered her to the ground.

Taking up the screwdriver, I drove the blade deep into the crevice surrounding the iron plate and screwed it sideways, exerting pressure as I did so. The corrosion resisted my efforts and stood unyielding. The sweat was rolling off my brow in streams and I constantly wiped it away with my saturated jacket sleeve. I paused to regain my breath and shook my head in despair.

"It's taking a long time," I said, breathing hard and steaming the cold air around me with my hot breath.

Jeannie looked at me in sympathy and kissed me on the cheek. Her face was partly in shadow with black holes where her eyes should have been. We were so close together I could smell the faint traces of face powder on her face. I breathed in a sigh and, gathering myself up, attacked the plate with new vigour, smashing the metal with hammer blows that vibrated my arm and echoed through the tunnel. After a particularly heavy clout that shook me to the armpits, the square of corroded metal showed a line of gleaming metal. I breathed in a welcome lungful of cold air and laughed softly at the result of my efforts.

"You're through," Jeannie said in a quiet voice.

I nodded and wiped a drip of sweat from the tip of my nose.

"Now it comes," I grated, preparing to widen the gap.

I prayed a little then, knowing I was inches away from either penetrating the defences of the arms cache or blowing us and a sizeable chunk of London skywards. With sweaty palms that slid on the wooden handle of the screwdriver, I gripped it and began to gouge the crack wider. The track gleamed ever longer and the plate quivered under my touch. Following the shine of new metal, I inched the plate from its bed in the frame and stood there with the weight of the solid sheet of steel plate resting on my upper thigh. With the corrosion of years sticking firmly to the metal, I felt the full force of the weight, and the edge of the square dug into my thigh. Even so,

I waited for awhile to gather my wilting strength, snatching lungful after lungful of cold, clammy air.

In the distance I heard faint signs of early morning London filtering down from above and the rumble of passing trains thundering overhead. With a final intake of air and a mighty heave I lifted the plate free of my thigh, swung around with it firmly clutched between my extended arms and set it down on the ground, breathing a sigh of relief.

Behind me, Jeannie waited as I lowered the plate to the ground, shining the torch on it to help me. I straightened up, holding her in an expectant gaze, and she turned the torch back inwards, ready to do her part.

CHAPTER NINETEEN

"Now we'll see if our luck is in," I said, standing behind Jeannie as she illuminated the hole.

The inner door could be seen in the gloom and Jeannie touched it to convince herself it was the same design and made of the same material as the others. It was an exact replica of the other two and she shone the light closer to see. I was close to her now and I could feel the tension building up in her as she opened the inner door.

"Steady now," I warned as she reached inside.

Her hands were like white flags darting in and out in the half-light. She pressed her head against the cold hardness of the door frame, breathing in slowly and expelling spears of vaporous air.

"I've got it!" she exclaimed with mounting excitement creeping into her voice, "and it's the same design. There are two bottles of chemicals separated by a rubber tube. When you open the door it activates the upper bottle and the contents run into the tube. If you want to prevent one chemical from coming into contact with the other, you've got to snatch the rubber tubing away before the top chemical can burn through the thin skin of rubber in the tube. You've got about a minute to do this part of the process, but it's not easy 'cause if the rubber is perished it's hard to peel off the tube. It's awkward as well as difficult to reach inside the hole and work around the corner. You can only get your fingers in to do the job."

I waited, hoping the rubber wasn't damaged by age also that Jeannie was in luck. She had her back to me with her arms fully stretched into the dark cavity. She was working blind I realised with a start, with only the feel of her questing fingertips standing between them and oblivion. I swallowed a large lump in my throat and continued to pray.

"I've got something," she announced to the wall, blowing out a speck of dirt that had entered her mouth. "There's a bit of corrosion on the tube, but I've managed to get a bit of the tube off the second bottle. It's stiff, but I'm succeeding."

I didn't want to worry her by telling her we only had thirty seconds or so of the minute remaining. She must have known anyway, but it didn't seem to bother her. Not so myself, for I had time to think and I steeled myself to accept the inevitable, although I continued to pray just in case. The seconds ticked by, the water trickled down the tunnel and the ground about us creaked occasionally. I sweated and jumped, as in the final moments of the minute she backed out of the hole holding the tube aloft in triumph for me to inspect. She tipped it sideways and we both watched the acid pour to the ground and begin to smoke.

"Well, that's the dangerous part over," she said, brushing her hair aside. "Now we can see what the hole has to offer."

I nodded and, avoiding the spilt acid, eased my bulk

between the door frames. Beyond the door was a little ledge with three stone steps leading downwards. Jeannie handed me the torch and I descended the steps into a rectangular chamber. The room, about thirty feet by twelve, was half-full of boxes stacked eight feet high, with a three foot walkway through them to the extreme end. Other parts of the room were occupied by small barrels, steel drums, plastic covered bundles and an assortment of tools. The chamber was dry and well built, the walls being plastered with cement and the floor finished in the same manner.

By the light of the torch I trod the path between the boxes, feeling them as I went by. They were each four feet in length and the wooden tops were secured with two thin bands of metal that circled the box, and a number of wooden screws. I seized a metal bar from the pile of tools and, driving it deep under one of the bands, wrenched the band in half. I quickly did the same to the other one and it snapped off in the middle of the box. The bar had a flat chisel end and it was razor sharp. I dug that end deep into the crack between the box and the top, and levered the wood upwards. With a loud sound of splitting timber the two sections parted and the top fell away to the floor, leaving the bottom half intact and open.

Inside was a flat bed of sawdust and I dug deep into it and felt a heavy plastic wrapped parcel. I dug my fingers deeper into the sawdust and, with a grunt, lifted the parcel into my lit vision. Through the opaqueness of the plastic I could see the shape of two heavily greased AK87 sub-machine guns, both in good condition and ready for action. There were two more in the box and, looking about me, I mentally calculated there were somewhere in the region of five thousand guns stored in the boxes – enough to start a small war. I whistled in surprise at the amount and turned to Jeannie, who had descended into the chamber and was standing close behind me.

"You wouldn't credit it, would you?" I said, swinging the torch around the rest of the room and shining the light on the steel drums. "Now, I wonder what the rest of them contain."

"Does it matter?" she declared. "We've found what we want, so let's leave the rest to the authorities, shall we?"

"Ah, yes, certainly so, but aren't you curious just to know what they hold?"

"I can imagine what they contain, but I'm not about to find out."

"I've got some idea too; explosives I'm thinking."

"You and me both, so let's get out of here before we push our luck too hard."

I laughed then, more with relief than humour. She was right to say let the others deal with it and I was in full agreement with her. I was about to say as much when Maureen made an appearance. She was dishevelled and wore a coat of mud on the side of her face. She also had a bruise on her cheek, which did a lot to emphasise the wildness of her appearance. She was carrying an automatic pistol, which was pointing at my stomach in a way that made me feel decidedly uncomfortable. I raised the iron bar.

"Drop that," she said threateningly.

I let it clatter to the floor with a crash.

"Now it's my turn, you bastard. You wanted to find out where the dump was? You've found it, but a fat lot of good it's going to do you. You want to find out what is in these drums?

197

Well, I'll tell you. It's Semtex, an explosive we use quite a lot, but you won't be worried about that soon I can tell you."

She waved the gun wildly to emphasise her point.

"It was pretty idle and lax of me to leave you alone out there with no one to watch over you, but what I'd like to know is where did you manage to get hold of the gun? I asked. "I am sure it wasn't on you when you left Wandsworth."

"I'm afraid that's my gun," Jeannie said in a rueful voice. "I brought it with me and I've only just noticed it is missing. Sorry about that, Bill."

I shrugged my shoulders in resignation and reassured her with a smile.

"Not your fault, love, if she stole it from you. I'm-"

The rest of the sentence was drowned out by Maureen's bellow of anger as she interrupted.

"Shut your fucking mouth. You won't have any need for it where you two are going anyway," she said, her eyes blazing with rage and hate.

"And where is that?" I questioned, staring at the woman.

My brain was swirling about within me searching for something, anything to shift the initiative from Maureen to myself. Suddenly the obvious hit me. The chamber was lit by my torch and if I was to get to it I could extinguish the light, plunging us all into darkness. The trouble was the torch was four feet away on top of a box. If I could distract Maureen's attention from me for a few seconds I might be able to grab it and flick it off. I waited for an opportunity and it wasn't long in coming.

Maureen was ranting again and in the half-light her face was a mask of grimacing hatred.

"Sure I stole it from you, traitor," she sneered at Jeannie. "Now you can both pay the price of betrayal. You're going to hell where you both belong."

"You going to shoot us?" I asked, moving a foot closer to the light.

"Oh, no, nothing so quick and neat." Maureen grimaced again. "I'll tell you what I'm about to do. I'm going to blow this place up with you both in it. It'll be like a cremation. The guns will be destroyed and so will the rest of the explosives, but that will prevent you from getting your hands on them."

"What about you?" I said, moving my leg a fraction closer to the torch. "You'll die as well."

She laughed in a grim way.

"They're going to get me anyway, one way or another," she said, almost to herself. "I betrayed them and myself when I told you where this place was. I suppose it's only right that my life should be forfeit. I'm a citizen of Ireland and a soldier in the fight for freedom. My life is theirs to do with as they will, but *you*," she said with a heaving breast, "*you* deserve to die. You destroyed the other dumps and you struck down two of our members."

I pointed to the Semtex drums.

"Maybe they are duds. You stopped to think of that? After all, they've been here twenty years or more."

"Well, let's find out shall we?" she said, raising the gun and aiming at the metal drums.

I leaped the rest of the distance between me and the torch and, scooping it in a sweeping gesture of my arm, succeeded in knocking it aside and down between a crack in the boxes. Immediately the chamber was plunged into darkness and I shifted my position several feet sideways just before Maureen shot at me. Momentarily, I felt the bullet fan the air past my cheek before I deliberately pushed Jeannie aside. I fell to my knees, pulling her with me as the gun blazed a further three times. I yanked my own gun from my shoulder holster and levelled it at the point where I thought Maureen was. I waited with the heavy pistol directed at her. Her gun crashed again and I homed in on the flash and squeezed the trigger.

A cry of pain rang out almost immediately, proving that my shot had struck home. I waited briefly for her reply, but the only sounds to be heard in the darkness were Maureen's sobs. After awhile I climbed to my knees and retrieved the torch. Revealed in the light, Maureen was lying in a heap on the floor oozing dark blood from a wound in her chest, which was visibly widening into a congealing pool beneath her prostrate body. She stared at the light with eyes closed to a slit and, after giving a sighing sob that wracked through her frame, coughed and lay still. I stood there over her dead body for awhile, shaking my head at the waste of life.

Other sounds entered the chamber and two heads popped into view at the entrance – the two railway men. They scoured the room with curious eyes and looked at me in puzzlement. The grey haired one who seemed to be in charge directed a question at me.

"I thought I heard the sound of a shot. Is everything all right?"

In the half-light they suddenly saw the body of the woman.

"Oh!" they said together.

"We had a little trouble," I explained. "As you probably know already, she is... *was* a member of an illegal organisation, the IRA. I'm relying on you to keep everything you see here under your hat," I said, nodding towards the body, "and that includes the woman. You also know that we work for the government in a secret capacity, but of that I will say no more. We'll seal this room and then it will come under the Official Secrets Act. Being officials, you will understand what we have to do. The location of it is and will remain a secret, is that clear?"

They turned and looked at each other and then at me, nodding in unison. To avoid any unwelcome speculation about Maureen's death, I left the body in the arms dump and resealed the chamber with the metal plate, plastering mud onto the steel to wipe out the marks and scratches I'd caused. After clearing away any signs that we'd been there we started the journey back to the underground station.

The station and surrounding tracks were closed to everyday rail traffic until the following day, so we had no need to hurry. The only incident worth recording is the fact that the torch gave up the ghost halfway to the platform and plunged us into a gloomy walk to the station. However, we managed, and after a little over an hour emerged into the light of Bank Station, covered in mud and brick dust, and smelling strangely of oil, but I put that down to the close contact we had with the railway lines.

I grinned with relief when we climbed out of the pit at the platform and ran smack into several men in plain suits, who turned out to be a mixture of railway authority, government officialdom and MI5. Out of sight were the shadowy forms of Scotland Yard and armed police, but as I knew, I skirted the jumble of gossiping men and, with Jeannie in tow, headed for the exit. We were questioned three times by uniformed men with machine guns and black and white check on their caps, before once again emerging into the daylight and a well-earned meal.

Later on, wolfing down a large hot breakfast in a café just around the corner from the station, Jeannie and I relaxed in the crowded tea room, looking exactly like a couple of down-and-outs. People sitting close by observed us with a mixture of curiosity and amusement, and one city gent with a bowler hat and striped trousers even offered to pay for our breakfasts, that's how bad we looked. I refused with a smile and the man went away, possibly congratulating himself on his show of charity.

"You do look a bit dirty," Jeannie said when I expressed surprise at the man's generosity. "Your clothes are covered with mud and grease from the walk along the track."

I shrugged in resignation and gulped down a large lump of toast and butter.

"I suffer from my devotion to duty," I explained, chewing a piece of fried egg. "If I get a little mucky in the process I put it all down to the dangers of my profession."

She giggled and the other diners stared at her. She reddened under their collective gaze and dropped her head.

Well into the afternoon, after cleaning ourselves up, we were walking in the park and enjoying the fresh air. Earlier on, an enthusiastic Lawrence had poured praises into my ear over the telephone and told me that, without a doubt, my future with the ministry was assured.

"You will like working for the ministry," he had enthused, "although those who work in the field are not necessarily the highly paid ones."

"I can vouch for that," I got in quickly.

As usual Lawrence was ignoring me by talking over me.

"They, the ones in the field," he was saying unabashed, "nevertheless, are those called upon to get the job done; you, for example. In this capacity your country is justly proud and forever indebted. You could be in line for an annual award in the honours list."

"What kind of reward?" I had asked dryly.

"*Award*," he had corrected. "BEM or OBE, or some such honour," he had replied.

"How much money is involved in these citations?" I had returned, visualising a welcome financial transfusion to my bank account.

"Not a lot. Anyway it's not the money that counts, it's the prestige and honour that goes with it."

As usual, the very mention of money had been sidetracked and moved to the back-burner by Lawrence, who had hurriedly changed the subject.

"I've got a couple of snippets of information for you, Cox. One is the boat from which you recently escaped has been seen up river at or near Lowestoft. It was boarded by some of our men, but when searched was found to be empty of any arms. It was hired from a local boatyard by a man who paid cash. It was returned to the owner on time by the same man who hired it. He's not been seen since."

At this point, Lawrence's smoker's cough had crashed into my eardrum and, as usual, I had waited for it to subside for him to continue.

"The other piece of information," he went on, "is that a big disruption is planned by the opposition. We don't know if it is a bomb or a demonstration. Sources say it might be one or both together. We only know it was planned by the army hierarchy after their setbacks with the arms dumps and bomb factory. You really are making an impression on them, Cox."

He had finished by promising me help in the fight as soon as the ministry was able to recruit the right sort of manpower within the resources of the department. The phone had clicked to end the discussion and I was on my own once more.

"Well, it's back to square one again," I said to Jeannie, leaning against the trunk of a tree.

Her face creased into a grin and she shook her head slowly.

"Not right back to the beginning," she disagreed. "More like square three with all the progress we have made."

I searched the sky for a cloud and only found an expanse of blue that stretched to the horizon. The leaves of the tree above me were stark green in colour and stood out against the azure blue.

"I like hopscotch, that game we played as kids," I said. "We threw a stone and hopped to a square then threw it out again and hopped to the next position on the square."

"Yes, but the object of the game, as you know, was to get home before the other kid and win," she said, sitting down on a park bench nearby. "I think you must be fast approaching the halfway mark. A few more giant hops and you will be home."

"I wouldn't have made it this far if you hadn't been there," I admitted, looking down at her.

"I did very little," she said modestly.

"Oh, yeah! Imagine me trying to work out one bottle of chemicals from another, waiting for the lot to explode. Why, the whole of London town and I owe you a great debt of gratitude."

Jeannie demurred at this and became rather self-conscious.

"It was nothing, Bill. My motives were entirely selfish 'cause I love you and didn't want to see you get hurt."

We fell silent at this admission, reliving the morning's happenings. A shout broke into my thoughts and I focused on the scene ahead of me. In the distance, across a wide expanse of well-razored grass was a stretch of rippling grey water. Several boats were being rowed across the lake by enthusiastic oarsmen who were shouting with excitement at the event. A small crowd of children had gathered at the edge of the lake, urging the boats on. Others were wading in the shallow water, pushing miniature versions of the boats with triangular sails puffed out by the warm breeze blowing across the lake. Other models danced on the water, powered by tiny engines, the whirring of these coming faintly to our ears, wafted to us on the wings of the same gentle wind that blew across the water and caused small wavelets to ripple.

In my mind's eye I saw the effect a bomb would have on the gentle scene and I felt a sense of anger at the men who would perpetrate such actions. I resolved to fight them with renewed energy.

"Quite a peaceful scene," Jeannie said, reading my thoughts. "Imagine what carnage it would cause if a bomb went off here."

I picked my lip and let my mind wander through other events. The situation read as the British Government three, IRA nil. We were ahead of them in the race and stretched out to score even more if the going continued in our favour. If the British Government was right in their count of the arms location, and other things came into play like the end of arms commissioning to all factions, more say in the running of their country in Northern Ireland and a fairer deal to all religious persuasions, no matter what their faith, then the dumping of arms on England's soil would come to an end. Nice work if you can get it, but it was now and we had to live in the present world, warts or not. The fight must go on.

'Humph, a fine and noble cause for which to aim, but not in the way of the IRA,' I said inwardly. 'They are determined to acquire total autonomy no matter who it hurts in the process.'

In my absence a telephone had been installed in my flat and when we got back it was ringing. I lifted the receiver and heard a gruff voice in my ear.

"Hello, Coxy, Brewer here. Just to let you know I'll be joining you tomorrow. The shoulder has healed quite nicely and I'm fit and well to continue."

"I could do with some help," I said, hearing the dog bark

in the background. "It sounds like the pooch is ready to go as well, George."

Brewer laughed.

"Yes, he is, but not this time though, I'm thinking. He still has to have an operation to remove a bullet fragment from his back, so it's out as far as he's concerned."

"What a shame, but his health comes first naturally."

"Quite so, but to get down to why I've rung up. How are you faring on the arms dump situation?"

For the next few minutes I told him all about the walk along the underground railway track and what happened when we found the third arms dump. I told him of the shootout and Maureen's death in the arms chamber.

"Whew!" He whistled in surprise. "Finally a prize and one worth finding. This will severely dent the ego of the army. Now they've got to treat us as number one priority to eliminate, so we can expect some backlash in the near future."

"That's what I'm thinking," I agreed. "We've got them on the run, and with your help we should keep 'em at it."

"To do so we've got to find out more about the rest of the dumps," Brewer said, obviously delighted by the news. "If we can continue the momentum we'll have them beaten before they know it."

"Maybe," I mused, thinking of the events in the tunnel, "but it will get harder now. Their backs are up against the wall and, like the rats they are, they will become more dangerous."

"Yes," Brewer agreed, "so our hits must be harder and more lasting. We must eliminate them before they have a chance to do it to us."

"Yeah, but there's the rub; we've run out of ideas. The trail has gone cold."

"That's because they are playing it close to their chest. In the past they've let slip valuable information that has led us to the dumps. They are keeping tight-lipped about it now, so from now on we can expect it to get tougher."

"We can try the other method," I ventured.

"What's that?"

"The one we tried on Mason."

"You mean by offering a reward? We can try it I suppose."

"It worked before and I've every reason to expect it will again. A million quid is a lot of money," I said, imagining stacks of the stuff before me. "It would tempt a saint."

"Especially on our small salary! It beats me how this country can ask us to do so much while receiving so little."

"It's called patriotism, George," I said dryly. "An indefinable something they bring out when they want something done. It's a well known con. They wave the flag and call you to arms. It's been worked in this country from time immemorial, so expect it at every opportunity."

"I will," Brewer said, with a laugh that was echoed by the dog barking at his reaction. "See you tomorrow, Coxy."

Brewer rang off, but he was destined never to keep the appointment. During the night, as he was preparing for bed, someone fired a .45 slug into his chest. He lived long enough to scrawl a name on the wall, written in his own blood: *Sweeney*.

CHAPTER TWENTY

I ground my teeth in rage when I first heard the news of Brewer's death. Sweeney, the one for whom I was searching to get a clue to the whereabouts of the next arms dump, was responsible for killing him. A seething pain of regret and sorrow entered my breast, mixed with a rapidly developing desire to put a bullet into the murderer's heart.

I racked my brain for a clue and found nothing. I argued with Lawrence interminably, but didn't gain a thing. I resigned myself to the fact that Brewer's killer would get away with murder, when a chance remark by Jeannie set the wheels in motion again.

"The map you've got, doesn't it give you any idea about it? You've been playing with it for an hour now," she said, toying with the glass from which she had been drinking.

I held out the scrap of map before me and searched the coloured surface of the paper for the umpteenth time.

"Just the name of the village and it's location on the map," I said, laying it down on the table and rubbing the traces of my growing beard with a cupped hand.

Jeannie upended her glass and drained the contents with one gulp. She yawned and looked at her watch.

"'Bout time for bed," she said, standing up. "You can worry about that in the morning. If I was you I'd go back to where it all started."

I snapped my fingers and looked at her standing before me, eyebrows raised in surprise.

"That's it! I'll go back to the village, Coney End. That's right it did all start there, so that is where I'm heading." I took out my pistol and opened the chamber then sighting through the empty holes, removed the spent cartridges. "Why didn't I think of that?" I asked myself softly as I reloaded the gun.

The memory of Brewer's recent death clouded the remainder of the night and it was well into the early hours before I could get to sleep. I dreamed Sweeney was chasing Jeannie down a dark country lane with me watching him getting closer to her with every step. He was grinning in an evil way, teeth exposed in a triumphant leer, his hands crooked before him ready to choke the life out of her. I struggled to keep up with them, but could feel myself losing ground. I screamed to Jeannie to run faster, but the yell died in my throat. I was panting for breath, shrieking for her to run faster, knowing he was gaining on her. I was desperate, and tried to make my legs go faster, but only succeeded in slowing down. 'Jeannie!' I yelled, 'Jeannie!'. That's when I awoke as she shook my arm.

"You've been dreaming," she explained. "You called my name and thrashed about, so much I woke you up."

I was covered in a thin film of warm sweat, and when I moved around my pyjamas quickly got cold as air entered the bed.

"Just a bad dream," I said, rapidly opening and closing my eyes to clear my head. "Must have been something I ate."

Talking about food stirred my appetite juices and my stomach began its usual rumble. We rustled up a double helping of scrambled eggs on toast washed down with mugs of steaming hot tea. I showered and scraped off my beard with a used blade, cutting my chin in the process. Jeannie covered the cut with a plaster and finished dressing by pulling a pair of sheer stockings onto a pair of exquisite legs, filling me with an urge to peel them off again.

"No, not now, darling," she said with a giggle as I made a grab for her.

I relented with a smile, and finished dressing. I led the way out to the front where I'd left the old wreck and stood with arms akimbo, studying it.

"I wonder if anyone has had a go at it while we were asleep," I said as Jeannie joined me.

I searched the underside and the engine compartment, and was relieved to find nothing. I looked for any disturbance of the rust coating the bottom of the car and saw none. At last I pronounced it clean, and drove away.

I filled the petrol tank at a garage close by and turned the car's nose in the direction of the village. The car's condition was that it was developing a few mysterious knocks and other strange noises as time progressed, and the raindrops were still dripping through the roof when it rained, but more so as the days went by. I glanced at Jeannie who was smiling to herself, and decided she was thinking along the same lines as myself, so gave her a sheepish grin.

"Looks like the jam jar is rapidly going home," I said.

Her reaction was to laugh out loud and pat my knee.

We entered the outskirts of the village sometime in the late morning, driving into the village proper within a few minutes. The place still had that deserted feeling and the quietness of the roads into it added to the eerie mysteriousness I had found before.

"It's quiet," Jeannie said, mirroring my thoughts, "just like it always is."

"So you've been here before?" I queried. "You never told me."

"Only to deliver messages and so forth. I've always known this place has got something to do with the army, but I've never been able to find out what."

"You must've had contacts to meet, what about them?"

"Same as you did, in the local where everybody meets. I had a pre-arranged meeting with someone who took the message and off I went, nothing more sinister than that."

I parked the car on the same spot in the car park of the pub and entered the building from the back, with Jeannie following. It being early and the locals busy in the fields, the place was almost empty and devoid of virtually any noise except tinny piano music coming from a radio resting on the bar. As we waited, from the pub's interior a voice began to argue, instantly followed by a female voice that sounded decidedly angry. They seemed to be arguing about something that we had difficulty in making out. After awhile I tapped on the counter. The arguing ceased immediately and quietness ensued, followed by the sudden appearance of the couple.

"Can I help?" the man enquired with raised eyebrows, shooting us both suspicious glances.

"Can we get a couple of drinks?" I asked above the music.

To me they seemed to relax at the apparent innocence of our visit to the pub and the request for drinks seemed to doubly convince them of it. They broke into simultaneous smiles and the tension visibly eased a couple of notches downwards. Even so, as I ordered the drinks I saw they were watching each other and mouthing things silently, occasionally nodding and shaking their heads in turn.

I eased into one of the chairs and waited as Jeannie sat in hers. I inclined my head at them and gently shook it to indicate we should be careful what we said. She nodded in return and leaned forwards ever so slightly to hear what I had to say.

"We can stay here or make a few enquiries outside," I said in an undertone, almost touching her forehead with mine. "They will arrive here eventually, so I'm thinking we'd do best by letting them come to us, agreed?"

She nodded in reply and put her hand on mine.

"Bill," she said, with concern written in her eyes, "you *will* be extra careful won't you? I'm sure we are getting closer to them than we think. I've got a nasty feeling they know we are here. Very soon they will make an appearance and this time they'll come out in force."

"I'm expecting it," I grated, sipping my drink, "but even they, with the way they've wrapped up this village, can't do anything in public and will wait for an opportunity to finish us off."

"Does nothing ever frighten you, Bill?"

"I look at it this way, love. We all have our destiny to fulfil and no matter what, the path is set out before us quite clearly to some people, hazy to others. I believe I have a duty to rid the earth of the scum who murder innocent people in the guise of patriotism." I sniffed. "Besides, I'm getting paid for it," I added.

It was well into the afternoon before they made their move. The door squeaked open and a skinny man sporting a thin moustache seemed to glide into the room. He sat at a table opposite ours and rested there, looking into space and smoking a cigarette. I gave him a casual glance and smiled when I got the message.

Jeannie surreptitiously nudged my knee with hers and nodded.

"He's one of them," she said beneath lowered lashes. "A small fry, but dangerous. He generally makes an entrance to see if the coast is clear."

I looked at her in a quizzical way.

"He's one of the expendable members, those used as cannon fodder. If it is, he makes it quite clear to the others who appear later."

I sniggered at this and Jeannie frowned in annoyance.

"You think it is all a game and they are acting like kids," she continued in a low voice, "and they are, but the game is deadly and the stakes are high."

The IRA man lit another cigarette with the one he was smoking and stubbed the end out. He blew a cloud of blue smoke from under the screwed up moustache, and studied the effects of the cloud slowly lifting above him. Slowly, deliberately, he turned his head in my direction and held the gaze. I turned to meet him and winked. A sneer crossed his face and he resorted to watching the smoke cloud again. That's round one to me, I thought, let's hope the next confrontation will be as simple. It wasn't.

Harvey was the next person to push into the pub. The two men greeted each other with false smiles and artificial handshakes that fooled nobody. Harvey ignored us and took a seat at the table with the thin man, engaging him in a low monologue that was barely above a whisper. The thin man listened intently, only interrupting to snigger at something he thought funny.

Another interval passed slowly then the two men were joined by another who copied the others and began to talk. He was a stranger to me as well as the first man, but Harvey was the dominant one. He made all the running in the talking stakes. He greeted the newcomer like a long-lost friend and, slapping his back in welcome, offered him a seat at the table. Although we appeared to ignore the play-acting being enacted across the room, we let little slip and listened to everything with great interest.

I studied the room as I listened, noting the avenues of escape. It had two entrances and in an emergency another quick exit could be seized by vaulting the bar counter. The window was of the double glazed type with thick glass and locked, so that way of getting away was obviously impossible. It occurred to me that if we wanted to get this thing over with it was best to approach it directly. I cleared my throat with a loud cough, which had the effect of silencing the three men who stopped talking and stared at each other. The music from the radio paled into insignificance and the clock on the wall above the bar seemed to hold its tick. For a few highly charged moments of expectant hush the silence held its breath, waiting for something to happen – nothing did. I relaxed inside with an evil smile dominating my face knowing full well they were just as vulnerable as myself, even though they had the advantage of numbers.

The music trilled out into the room and the clock pointed to the hour of 2 p.m. as the talk resumed. I fingered the butt of my pistol with sliding palms and felt the coldness of the metal against my skin. I congratulated myself on having the foresight to reload the weapon, and gently jingled together another half a dozen cartridges I had also slipped into my pocket. I had plenty of fire power, and with Jeannie's little automatic to back me up in an emergency it was more than adequate in the circumstances.

I was about to try coughing again to attract some deference when the door opened and another man entered. Instead of joining the three terrorists he paused, after holding the door open, and stood in the doorway looking straight at me. I gazed back in a mild way, curious that he hadn't seen fit to make his way to their table. He then made a move that surprised me; he dropped his eyes, shut the door and walked over to a vacant table. While his back was to me I studied his figure and the way he sat down on a chair facing the bar. I swallowed the cough and the chance of remonstrating with the others directly.

Two more surprising things happened within the next ten minutes. The three terrorists decided to leave. They looked at each other with significant glances they tried to conceal and, as one, stood up and trooped out, one following the other. I breathed a little easier then and eyed Jeannie with a weak smile. She copied me and showed her teeth through reddened lips. I was about to lift my drink to my mouth when the second surprise occurred. The stranger nodded to us and addressed me.

"I hope this will not come as too much of a shock, Mr Cox, me meeting you like this, but I'm here to take the place of our recently departed colleague, Brewer."

"Oh, you are," I said, sipping my drink, "and who might you be, sir, if it isn't too much of a secret?"

He arose and approached us with an extended hand.

"I'm Durrant from headquarters at the 'car park'. I know you are Bill Cox from your description; you are very well known by all at headquarters." He turned to Jeannie with a smile. "And you must be Jeannie. I've heard about you too," he said, taking her hand in his and bending with the effort.

"You've come in the thick of it, mate," I growled. "Those men you just saw are the opposition. The man who did all the talking is Harvey, a particularly vicious member. He is personally responsible for a number of deaths, mostly with bombs he has planted in this country, others in fighting against us."

Durrant dropped Jeannie's hand and gripped mine.

"I'll remember his face for future reference," he vowed. "Thanks for telling me."

"Better the enemy you know, etcetera," I said, pointing to a vacant chair. "Sit down won't you."

He dropped into the empty chair and offered to buy us a drink. Jeannie declined and I accepted, asking for a double whisky. Silence reigned during the time he ordered the drinks and brought them back. I took mine with a smile and waited as he settled into the seat.

"What did Lawrence have to say?" I asked to the side of his head.

He held me in a glance that jerked from his glass of beer to my face in quick motion.

"About what in particular?"

"Well, Brewer's death to name but one," I answered.

"He was upset, naturally, but Lawrence being Lawrence he did not dwell on it too long. He was more concerned with the present state of affairs than yesterday's news."

That sounds like Lawrence, I thought bitterly.

"*Yesterday's news?* Did he say that? What a truly wonderful way of putting it. One of his own men who gave his life in the cause for queen and country, and all he can do is refer to him as *yesterday's news*," I said, shaking my head in disbelief.

"Yes, he is a bit much sometimes," Durrant said sadly. "I'm thinking he has that underlying sadness that never manages to see the light of day. I suspect he suffers inwardly."

"Yeah, my heart bleeds for him," I said dryly, remembering his penny-pinching ways.

"He thinks a lot of you, Cox. He says he has one of his best men on the job chasing the terrorists."

I chose to ignore the laurels.

"You got any ideas on how to tackle these gentlemen?" I asked.

"Apart from the direct approach, no, I'm here to back you up, so anything you're happy with is all right by me."

I told him about the map and of the dot on the paper.

"I can't make out what it is meant to be. I saw the wood where the workmen were living and I also inspected the site where they built several houses – nothing."

"That's our best bet, I'm thinking," Durrant said, taking the piece of map that I had produced. "We'd better start there."

"What about those bastards?" I snarled, looking at the door. "They're waiting for us to make the first move."

Durrant looked up from studying the map.

"I think we have them at a disadvantage," he said, handing me the map. "They believe you to be two when in reality we are three. The odds are lessening all the time."

"Yeah, three against fifty - some odds."

Jeannie had been silent for awhile and now she suddenly piped up with a suggestion.

"How about throwing them off the scent by using the two cars?"

We looked at her with blank stares.

"I drive away Bill's car to lure them on a false trail while you two go in the other direction, simple."

"She's got something there," Durrant said enthusiastically. "She leads them away on a false trail while we inspect the wood – brilliant!"

"I dunno about it," I said slowly, watching her. "Suppose they catch up with you?"

"Look, they are obviously waiting for us to make the first move. We do so by going out of different doors at the same time," she persisted, pleading with me. "That way those watching the front door are fooled into thinking we are all leaving the same way. They call to the others, who leave the front door unguarded. That is when you make your move as I drive away."

I ran the plan through my mind furiously and could not think of an alternative one to match it. The only flaw was fooling them into believing we were all in my car. The quickness of our exit might take care of that problem. I realised we had no alternative and I reluctantly agreed with a nod of my head.

"Right!" Jeannie said, firming her perfect lips. "Just give me time to get to the back door and make a lot of noise then you go, and don't stop for anything."

She stood up, planted a kiss on my forehead, gave me a smile and made for the rear door. I gripped my gun between taut fingers and, as one, we got to our feet and waited for the signal. Suddenly the back door slammed three times, a wild shout echoed through the building and a dustbin rolled over with a crash on the car park tarmac. A shot rang through the air outside as Jeannie made it authentic by firing at them. My car's engine thundered into life and screamed away.

We immediately charged at the front door, hearing the publican's shouts as we went hell bent through the exit. The door crashed against its hinges on the way out leaving us to decide on the direction to take. Like lightning, I sped to a covered building only feet ahead of a pounding Durrant who was running behind me. We made the shelter of the outbuilding, listening to the beating of our hearts and the scream of protesting tyres burning a path away in the distance.

"Looks like they fell for it," Durrant said, panting into the back of my neck.

The publican came to the door and, after looking in each direction, closed it, complaining to the woman who was out of sight. The silence lengthened and we breathed a sigh of relief as we stepped out from the corner of the building and made for the car park and Durrant's car. After giving a cursory ear to any or sundry noises, I got into the car and together we sped off in the direction of the wood.

We arrived there without incident and stopped on the edge of a small clump of trees and stubby bushes, looking about us at the vegetation.

"Nothing out of the ordinary here," Durrant said, peering at the map intently. "The houses are here as you said and the wood is here as indicated on the map. What on earth was this bloke thinking when he pinpointed this place?" He rummaged under the dashboard for a couple of minutes and brought to light a large magnifying glass. "There's a big country house a mile or so away. Belongs to a sir or something I would imagine. It's called Longstone House. We going to pay it a visit?"

I nodded my head and he reversed away from the wood and headed for the house. We went through narrow roads little better than tracks, which got progressively smaller as the house got nearer. A pair of brick piers reared up before us with a double set of iron gates stretching between them, firmly fixed in the middle by a twice wrapped around iron chain held together by a huge padlock. It looked like we were going no farther by car, so Durrant edged it off the track and we both got out.

The track continued into woods and tall trees, and disappeared out of sight over a slight hill. We climbed over chain link fencing and followed the road up over the rise. I pointed out a small pool of black engine oil in the middle of the track.

"Now, that's recently made," I said, skirting the viscid mess.

Not long after, the house came into view. It was a massive black and white painted building with tall chimney pots rising to sixty feet or more above the ground. It had a wide central doorway with a flight of stone steps leading up to the entrance. Extensive well-kept gardens with hedges, fountains and razored grass lawns graced the front whilst a battery of newly built garages occupied the tarmacked side of the property.

A car sat on the gravel in front of the house and there were several figures standing in a group around it. As we watched, two more figures left the house and joined the group, gesturing wildly as an argument ensued. Durrant produced a pair of binoculars and swept the area in front of the house. As it was sited in a small valley it was easy to look down on the scene. From the shelter of a clump of beech trees we saw another car come into our vision and stop beside the first. Two men got out, bringing with them another person who struggled to break free.

"Jesus Christ!" Durrant exploded, gazing into the glasses. He tore off the binoculars and thrust them in my direction. "Here, take a look at this," he said.

I looked through the lens and slowly brought the face of the prisoner into focus and with a quick intake of breath was staring into the face of the captured Jeannie.

"Shit, they've got her!" I said, grinding my teeth in

shangrin. "So now we know this is the place for which we've been searching. This is headquarters to the IRA I'll be willing to bet."

Durrant slapped his hands together in glee and wound the strap around the glasses, smiling all the time.

"Well, we have them right where we want them. The SAS will make short work of them. This will end their campaign in England, or at least seriously dent it I'll be bound."

"Oh yes, but what about Jeannie in the meantime? They'll kill her for sure."

"They might not, Cox. If we get in there quickly we might save her yet."

"I can't risk it. I've got to get her out while they think we don't know they have her."

"The chances are you will also be captured then they will have two hostages. A good bargaining position for them, I'm sure, so I'm all for getting assistance in this situation," he said.

"Then you'll have to do it without me."

"If that is the case, I'll do so. Right now I'm off to contact Lawrence and arrange a clearing up operation."

"No you are not," I said firmly, drawing my gun.

CHAPTER TWENTY-ONE

In other circumstances the amazed look on Durrant's face could have been funny. His eyes were standing out from his head like organ stops and there was a half-smile frozen on his features. Gradually, in slow motion, the smile faded and was replaced by a look of disbelief. As he gazed at me he was stuffing the binoculars into his pocket. A frown of annoyance displaced the amazement and he shrugged his shoulders.

"You do realise what you are doing, Cox?" he said in a quiet voice. "You are duty bound to report this matter to the authorities." He eyed the gun. "It's an offence to threaten the life of a colleague in the execution of his duty."

"You're in no danger if you do as I tell you."

"And what are you telling me?"

"Delay the action until I have a go at rescuing Jeannie. If I'm successful I'll do my level best to let you know."

"Don't you understand?" Durrant protested. "Even if you did bring her out, the balloon will go up. The bastards will lose no time in dispersing to the four corners of the country. We will be right back to where we started only more so."

"I'm asking you for twenty-four hours."

I was pleading now. Durrant hesitated and that gave me the fillip I was asking for.

"Just twenty-four hours," I repeated, lowering the gun.

Durrant's eyes were on me and he was obviously running it through his mind. He was weighing the chances of nailing the birds now before they had a chance to fly, and risk losing Jeannie if he did. The very thought of rounding them all up in one go was attractive and irresistible to him and I knew it.

"OK," he said at last, "twenty-four hours and not a minute over. Regardless of what or where you are going in, no holds barred. Is that clear?"

I breathed a sigh of relief and nodded my head. I stuffed the gun back into my pocket and held out my hand.

"Thanks for the breathing space, Durrant," I said, gripping his hand.

I left him there watching me descend the hill, dodging behind tree trunks and bushes, and seeing the house and its occupants get ever nearer with each passing bush and tree. Now and again I paused, ears pricked to catch every sound coming from the house. There were little signs of everyday noises like a faraway car being revved up, distant dogs barking and, fainter still, an aeroplane droning in the sky. At the house very little was happening. The group had dispersed and taken Jeannie with them. The cars were empty and silent. I came to the last of the covering vegetation and hid behind the bush peering out into the garden.

The front of the house was the most open with tall wide windows looking out onto the lush garden. Voluminous silken curtains backed the wide glass panes, with carved oak shutters attached to each side of the white painted frames. I drew a quick breath and started for the garages, flattening myself along the high brick wall and inching my body forwards to the corner. I peered around the edge of the wall and pulled back when a man emerged from the entrance. I heard his footsteps on the stone steps and, out of the corner of my eye, followed his movements as he strode to the nearer car and got into the driving seat. It looked as though he was settled for awhile, so I slid my body along in the opposite direction and came to the other end of the garages.

I stopped to allow my heart to settle down and my pulse to stop racing. As if the movement was half-automatic, I found the gun in my hand, cocked ready to fire. I gripped it and pointed it forwards, ready to fire at anything in my way. I put my face around the corner of the building and gazed on a great expanse of lawn dotted with various fruit trees and flower patches that seemed to go on forever to the horizon.

A large conservatory was attached to the rear elevation of the house, with hundreds of exotic flowers behind the glass panes, in all sorts of stages of growth. Thanking my lucky stars I had more cover, I ran at a crouch to the side of the conservatory and waited there listening like mad. An engine roared into life and a lawnmower began to cut the grass. I blessed it for the noise and ran to the door of the conservatory, standing there with the gun raised high, looking around the edge of the wooden door.

I drew a hot, surprised intake of breath at seeing the figure of a man with his back turned towards me rear up before me. I froze into a statue with my jaw firmly clamped shut while, undisturbed, the man went on pruning a magnificent white orchid. With racing heart and sliding feet I backtracked and was about to retreat when he spun around and saw me. His eyes dropped to my gun and the way it was pointing at his stomach. His face blanched as his eyes stared at me. I almost felt sorry for him, for I guessed he was the gardener with no possible connection with terrorists, but my heart hardened and with a finger I ordered him to turn around. He did so tremulously, raising his hands. Reluctantly I hit him at the back of the right ear with the butt of the pistol, and caught his sagging body before it had a chance to slump to the floor. I rolled him into a thick cluster of leathery green leaves and re-arranged them about him. Once satisfied, with the foliage to hide me and cushion my footsteps, I walked away towards the back entrance.

The air in the conservatory was hot and soon brought me out in a sweat. I wiped a bead from the end of my nose with my sleeve and, gripping my gun with a sweaty palm, opened the outer door listening intently then went in. The room had the appearance of a vegetable store with rows of onions lined up on wooden shelves, and another raised shelf held a mound of muddy potatoes. The place had an earthy smell about it, so I had probably guessed correctly.

Beyond another small door the house proper began to emerge. Polished floors and woodwork began to appear, and ornate door frames with thick oak doors that hid silent rooms came into view. I was beginning to think the occupants were of noble rank and unaware of the things yet to be revealed, and was about right in my estimation. The silence prevailed right up to the last, huge, flat oak panel, when I detected the hum of conversation through the thick wood.

I kneeled down quickly and held my ear to the door. I could hear several voices through the wood, one of them the high falsetto of a female – Jeannie! I was about to smash the door open when reason struck me. I had no idea what was on the other side of the door, how many were in the room and whether the woman's voice was really Jeannie's. I was in two minds and the indecision was frustrating. I cast my mind about, looking for a solution then like a ray of brilliant light the answer came to me as my eyes fell on a gorgeous silk curtain masking one of the doors. I tiptoed over to it and felt the fabric with one hand while the other searched for a box of matches I had in my hip pocket.

I suddenly heard voices, far away above me in the galleries that ran around the inside of the massive room. Quickly now, I gripped the box and feverishly snatched one of the sticks. The voices were getting nearer with each passing second as I struck the match against the side of the box, beginning to sweat again as the match disintegrated in my hand. With quickening pulse, I tried again and the match flared into brilliant being. With flashing glances at the big ornate stairs I knew they were descending, I held the flame to the rich colour of the silk and watched it begin to smoke. I held the cloth up to encourage the flame and, as the orange blaze roared up to engulf the entire silk curtain, hurriedly dropped it and dodged behind a similar silk curtain masking the next room.

The smoke built up and rapidly filled the room. After a brief couple of seconds the fire alarm activated and water jets rained down from the ceiling. Shouts raced through the building, and the door at which I had been listening, was torn open, disgorging several men who stood in a group gaping at the flames. They were joined by two more men, the ones who had been coming down the stairs, and together they inspected the curtain, which was now a smouldering tangle of blackened cloth.

While their backs were turned towards me I slipped from the concealing folds of my hideout and began to edge towards the first room. My shoes were silent on the thick carpet, masking my movements as I slid one foot after the other. I hugged the wall and the rich embossed wallpaper, all the while casting fearful glances at the men's backs. I was almost there, preparing to throw myself at the door, when there was a movement behind me as one of the men chanced to turn around and see me. Quick as a flash I dashed into the room and heaved the door shut.

Three pairs of eyes stared at me, one pair belonging to Jeannie, with delight, the others with surprise and alarm. A tall individual with grey hair at the temple, wearing tweeds and holding a sheaf of papers, shot up from the desk at which he was seated, and stood there looking at me. I twisted the key I found in the lock and, with the gun directed at him and the other man, made my way to her side.

"You all right, Jeannie?" I said, encircling her waist with my free hand. "Now, who's this gentleman?" I asked, jerking the gun at the tall man.

"I strongly suspect he is the governor to whom they are always referring," she replied, standing beside me.

"What say you, sir?" I enquired, directing my question at him.

A furious knocking pounded on the surface of the door and the heavy brass handle turned incessantly. Calling voices filtered through the solid oak, asking if the man was all right. I pointed the gun at the centre of the richly carved door and pulled the trigger. The resulting crash and the bullet hole drilled in the centre of the carving brought instant silence and those outside scattered immediately.

"I was asking you a question," I said, once more covering him and the other man with the pistol.

"Obvious, isn't it?" he replied.

"So it is, so it is," I said with narrowed eyes, "so you'd best come along with me."

He laughed in a low voice and set the papers on the desk.

"And where might that be to?"

"Where? To the local nick where all the criminals end up," I said, with raised eyebrows. "From there we'll organise a suite in a high security prison where you can spend the rest of your days regretting what you have done."

"You make it sound quite attractive," he said, eyeing the gun, "but sorry to disappoint you, I intend to remain here."

I saw the shadow of a man's figure on the curtain edge and fired the pistol. A squeal of pain rang out and the shadow dropped down out of sight. One less to deal with, I said to myself, wearing a grim smile. The smoke from the explosion curled up from the gun and caused a momentary silence broken only by the faint ringing of the fire bell.

"You must be Cox," the grey haired man said in a matter-of-fact voice. "I half expected you to make a bid to rescue her." He inclined his head to include Jeannie in his gaze. "The amazing thing is you got here so quickly. It took us all by surprise."

"And whom might I be addressing if I may be so bold?"

"Me? Why, I'm known as Casper Branden, Sir Casper Branden if you will give me my full title."

"Well, Branden, in the name of the people of Great Britain, I'm taking you in to face your peers, so get ready I'm in a bit of a hurry."

Branden's lip curled into a sneer.

"You are the big optimist, Cox," he said, sitting at the desk. "You don't seem to understand I have a small army at my disposal. Why, outside at this very moment I have thirty men ringing this house, ready to knock you down at the first chance they see. Why don't you recognise this fact and give up your weapon now?"

I laughed at his proposal at the same time as the desk telephone jangled. Branden looked at me with raised eyebrows and then at the instrument.

"Are you going to let me answer it or not?" he asked, reaching out for it.

I nodded my assent and he lifted the receiver to his ear, listening to a deep voice that vibrated the plastic phone so that we could all hear it.

"You did," he said as the voice ended.

Branden was looking at me with a smug smile on his face. He replaced the instrument on its rest and the grin grew broader.

"My, my, things are certainly happening today," he murmured then he spoke to me. "You were saying, Cox?"

"I'll repeat what I said before," I said vehemently, fixing the criminals with a fierce gaze. "I'll risk going through the ring of gunmen if I have to, but you are going with me whether you like it or not. If you resist I'll simply put a bullet through you and save the state the trouble of trying you."

Branden lounged back in his chair, perfectly at ease with the situation and the gun directed at his heart. He placed a pair of steel rimmed glasses on the bridge of his nose and peered through them at me.

"You will begin to see that you are my prisoner the same as I am yours, Cox, only more so."

"Yes, I'd be a fool to deny you that, Branden, but all the time you are under my gun you'll do as I say."

"But you have no chance of escape, even if you were to shoot me. My men will massacre you and the woman, and the war will continue just the same."

"I'd die knowing I had rid the earth of arseholes like you."

"I could make you a rich man, Cox."

"What do you mean?"

"I'm offering you a million pounds to go away and forget us."

"And then what?"

"Nothing, just walk away, simply and finally."

"I can't do that."

"Why not, thinking of your country? Forget it. What's she ever done for you except keep her citizens in chains?"

"If you don't know I can hardly convince you, you being our enemy."

"That's just it!" he insisted with some force, eyes standing out through the lenses. "We are all united in the struggle against our oppressors. You are, in fact, one of us."

I shook my head in denial.

"No, I'm not," I roared, setting him back in surprise at the force of it. "I don't murder women and children and then claim it is love for my country that compels me to do it. You are politically motivated, possibly by money or position. You don't fool me or your own people."

Branden, breathing heavily with the power of his argument, regarded me through his glasses and spoke in a quiet voice.

"You don't expect to be rescued do you?"

I started, and the involuntary movement was not lost on Branden. He seized on it eagerly.

"I knew it! You are expecting some force to save you. Ah!" he cried in triumph as I visibly blanched in surprise. "Well you can forget it now, Cox. That phone call you just heard was to tell me they have caught your partner. Yes, we have Durrant in our hands."

CHAPTER TWENTY-TWO

My heart sank inside me and my spirit with it. All the time at the back of my mind was the expectation of help in the shape of a back-up force. Now that hope had been dashed with Durrant's capture and I felt luck had left us and joined the other side. Feeling thus, it was difficult to grin, but I did, even so it was an effort.

Branden's face was a picture to behold because he was expecting us to wilt at the news. He was chewing a brick when I deliberately broadened the grin, and it had the effect of knocking the gloating look from his face. He fixed me in a look of suppressed fury.

"That news doesn't alter my intention of shooting you," I grated, raising the pistol that had wavered at the revelation.

A look of naked fear crossed his features and he raised an arm as if to ward off the shot.

"Remember, Cox," he said, white faced, "if I get killed, so will the girl and Durrant. Think it over before you pull the trigger. My men will make it especially painful for the woman. She will take a long time in dying, I can promise you, Durrant will die immediately."

I felt the threat register in my consciousness and knew he would keep it, or the rest would ensure it was kept for him. Jeannie would die a horrible death, even if it was an act of revenge. I spun on my heels to meet Jeannie's gaze and smiled in defeat.

"Sorry, love, I'm afraid he has us over a barrel. He really would do what he said, so I'm not risking it by resisting any longer," I said, admitting defeat.

Reluctantly, I handed the gun to Branden and waited as he unlocked the door and let his henchmen in. We were trussed up and made to sit in chairs facing the desk. Durrant was brought in and left standing. He looked as if he had been in a road accident. One eye was closed and of a red and purple hue, blood dripped from his mouth and nose, and a string of congealed blood was caked in his hair. He stood there swaying, looking through half-closed eyes, wrists behind his back tied tightly together with thin cord. He coughed and fresh blood seeped out of his mouth.

One of the gang, a ferret-faced man who licked his lips as if to savour pleasure from each pain-ridden morsel, was describing Durrant's capture with more than a modicum of twisted pride.

"We caught 'im just as he was getting into his car. He tried to protest at first by saying he was lost, but we pulled 'im out of it. I hit 'im a coupla times with the butt of me gun and told 'im he was a bloody liar. We spread 'im on the deck and trampled on his stomach a few times to let 'im know we didn't believe 'im, then we brought 'im here after he told us about the others."

"Good work, Greb," Branden said to the man. "If every one of you was as diligent as Greb here, we wouldn't now be in this sorry state," he said to the assembled men. He frowned and pointed to us as an example. "With all the resources, with all the manpower at our disposal, with all the alarm systems installed, Cox still managed to get in, and when he did, through your laxness, he found me. If he lives, my cover will be blown, as will his friends', so it is vital we eliminate them without any more delay. They are sentenced to death by firing squad at the bomb factory. You are to see to it that the sentence is carried out immediately."

Up piped a red-faced man wearing a trilby on the back of his head.

"Can't do that, Sir Casper," he said. "You've got a meeting with the vicar in an hour and you must keep the appointment if you are to appear normal."

Branden frowned again and chewed his lip.

"The vicar... Yes, I was forgetting him. The silly old sod had to come today." He meditated for awhile as the assembly stared at him. "We'll have to put off the execution until tomorrow morning. In the meantime, we have to put them somewhere safe." He pointed to me. "Watch *him* especially well. I can't stress this enough as he has a habit of getting out of impossible situations."

We were dumped on the concrete floor of one of the garages. Jeannie and I were tied together tightly and then to one end of a heavy workbench. Durrant was trussed up and tied to the other end of the bench. We were then gagged with bits of cloth that tasted of oil. The garage was cleared of any tools that might help us to escape, and after the last man left he snapped off the light and plunged us into the dark.

Durrant was groaning through the gag and snuffling on his own blood. I tested the ropes by pushing them against my chest muscles and exerted pressure on the knots. I had no doubt that in time I'd get free, and as I started the process of stretching the fibres with constant weight I was studying the garage space. A crack of light filtered through into the garage and as my eyes became accustomed to the dark I saw it was a solidly built building of brick and tile. To help me, Jeannie began to see-saw the bonds in time with me and within an hour the ropes were beginning to loosen.

The fabric of the bonds was rough and caused a red welt to appear on Jeannie's arm. She must have gritted her teeth against the pain because she never stopped sawing for one minute. I sighed into my gag in sympathy and tried to lessen her agony by taking most of the friction rub, but it was still hurting no matter what.

The vicar must have been and gone long before I managed to loosen the rope holding us to the bench, and the daylight was fading into night before I tore the gag from my mouth and spat the taste of rank grease from my tongue.

"There's been no movement from Durrant for the past couple of hours," I whispered, helping Jeannie to strip the ropes from her body.

We went over to his prostrate form and felt his pulse. There was a faint heartbeat, but he appeared very weak. I knew my first priority was to get him to a doctor. We removed the rough ropes and tried to make him as comfortable as possible on the cold floor, but he never uttered a word.

I tiptoed to the door and listened, but if there was anybody outside he wasn't making any noise that I could hear, so I gave up after awhile. Next I strode around the walls, feeling the plaster for any cracks or indentations. I drew a blank and was about to sit on the floor beside Jeannie when I felt a little stirring of the air as a draught passed my face. That interested me at once and I circled the building carefully this time, searching for the draught stream. I felt the cold air on my forearm, entering a grill that I figured to be about six feet six from the floor. I circled my tongue around my mouth, wetting the dry flesh, thinking of what I could do next. I stood on the tips of my toes trying to see out through the grill and that's when I got the first whiff of petrol. Now, that's got a few possibilities, I said to myself. If only I was able to use it. I tested the strength of the metal grill and found it was embedded in cement – a formidable task to move it.

I circled the garage again and examined the entrance door before returning to the grill. I squatted on the floor to think it over and put my hand right on a six-inch nail. After peering in the dark at the faint glow of light coming through the grill I had made up my mind. With Jeannie's help I pushed and pulled the workbench along the rough concrete floor and set it in place below the grill. Next I climbed onto the oily surface of the wooden bench and, with my hand protected by my sleeve, began to work on it.

The first few strokes scored the cement skin and a small chunk of rendering broke off - a good start. I resumed my task with rising spirits, scraping and digging at the cement. Naturally I slipped occasionally and left a bloody mark on the grill. I gritted my teeth and fought the pain as well as the wall. After an hour I had dug a hole two inches in width and was able to get two fingers under the metal grill. Although the night air was cold and my face was constantly subjected to a draught stream, sweat slid down my face and slowly dried when I paused for a blow. I sucked my fingers without end and constantly tasted my own blood. Dust entered my mouth with every breath and the draught blew it into my eyes. I was spitting out the particles every time I tried to widen the hole.

The smell of petrol was stronger now, coming through the hole with increasing strength. Encouraged, I stepped up the attack on the wall, and just as the first streaks of dawn lit the sky I lifted the metal grill from its seating and handed it down to Jeannie. With aching hands and worn down fingernails I widened the hole and silently handed the pieces down to her to be stacked on the bench. With great effort I tore out loosened crumbling cement and the bits danced on the ground below with gathering force. I put my head into the jagged hole and found myself looking at the gaunt shape of a petrol pump outside, less than six feet away from me. The odour of petrol was overpowering now that I looked down. The pipe nozzle was dripping tiny drops of petroleum spirit into a bucket. Although it was evaporating almost as fast as it dripped down, there was still some in the bottom of the bucket. I wanted that bucket because I had an idea, but it was out of my reach by a long way.

"I can't reach it," I said to Jeannie, outlining my plan.

"Can't you hook it with something?" she suggested.

"What with?" I asked, moodily.

"With the nail," she replied, and I could have kissed her for thinking of that.

I rested the nail against the wall on the bench and gave it a mighty whack with the corner of the metal grill. It bent under the blow and folded in the middle. I hammered it into an L-shape with another couple of blows and looked at the result with glee. I had my hook and all that remained was to attach it to a rope. Jeannie supplied the tights and we were in business.

I cast the hook downwards and outwards, and missed. I rolled it up into coils and tried again. It wrapped itself around the bucket handle, and the black tights stiffened with the strain. I pulled, but the bucket resisted for awhile, stuck in the residue of grease on the ground. Suddenly it jumped up and clanged against the wall with a loud bang. I let it stay in that position, slowly revolving on the end of the taut cloth whilst I listened with sharpened ears. I let the seconds tick by, but no alarm sounded, so I reeled in my catch, pulled the bucket through the hole and stood it on the bench beside me. I had the petrol, but was not sure how to use it as we were still imprisoned in the garage.

I was scratching my head in confusion wondering what to do with it when the light began to filter through the door once more. Somewhere in the house came the sounds of someone moving around followed by the closing of a door and the crunch of soled feet on gravel stones. I guessed they were coming for us, so I quickly hid the bucket behind the door. The key soon rattled in the lock and the door swung open to reveal Ryan standing there looking very mean. He was backed up by another pair of villains holding sub-machine guns.

The moment Ryan saw me he made a grab for me and signed his own death warrant. With a sideways step into the shadows I dove for the bucket and with a mighty heave swung the contents at him and drenched him with petrol. He stepped backwards, staring through bulging eyes that watered as the fumes blinded him. I fumbled for the box of matches and, as the other two got ready to fire and in full view of them, held a match against the box.

"Drop the guns or he goes up in flames," I warned as threateningly as possible.

They smelled the spirit and knew how close to death Ryan was. They looked at each other and dithered, waiting for an order from Ryan, who was otherwise occupied. To further visual weight to my threat I scratched the match on the box and held it high, ready to throw. They still hesitated, mesmerised by the flame. Suddenly Ryan began to scream in pain and fright and they woke up. I threw the match at Ryan and as he burst into flames, launched myself at the nearest man. I wrestled with him, forcing the gun upwards, protecting myself with his body.

Behind me, the bonfire that was Ryan raged into a ball of orange and black smoke, emitting blood-curdling screams of pain and agony that rang out in the stillness of the soft morning air. The gun for which I was struggling clattered to the ground. I sprang for it just ahead of my opponent. I kicked the bucket at the other man who was ready to fire, and grabbed his gun. My finger touched the trigger and the gun recoiled, spitting slugs along the ground. One bullet struck the bucket with a loud, 'whee!', and the resulting ricochet flew off into space. I picked up the gun and, with my hip bone, bumped the first man into the fire. He screamed as the flames licked around him, unnerving the other man who had yet to fire a shot. A short burst took care of him, sending him to the ground clutching his belly from which a red stream of glistening blood was fast flowing.

Ryan was rapidly becoming a heap of ashes and, with a start, I remembered where he kept the directions to the next arms dump. I pushed the burning remains of the man to the floor and, after removing his scorched shoes and socks, began to examine his feet. I could see the blue marks of the tattoo and tried to make out what it said, but no matter what, I could not make head or tail of it. I fumed and guessed it was in Irish, his own language - of course. I snapped my fingers as a thought struck me – Jeannie, she would know, so I called her over.

Jeannie appeared, averting her eyes to avoid the burnt offering.

"Yes," she said, with disgust in her voice, "it is in Irish, but the fire has wiped out some of the figures. Part of the location is missing - somewhere in Kent, in a grave. The town is burnt away as is the church, if it is a church."

There were signs that the house had awakened as we heard shots, so the minutes before reinforcements arrived were ticking by. I only had a short time before that was due to happen, so I quickly made up my mind. The tools that had been removed from the garage were stacked up outside on the ground, and I noticed a saw amongst them.

Now the house came alive and lights jumped into view.

Soon the whole building was a blaze of light and figures came out of the entrance door running into the garden where they stood staring at me. I immediately opened up on the machine gun, sending them scattering for cover. Bullets hit the garages as they returned fire and I dodged into one of them. The gunman with whom I had fought was finishing beating out his flaming clothes, so he scrambled into the safety of the garage and retired to the rear with no more interest in the conflict. I emptied the gun and grabbed the other, ducking just as a screaming bullet buried itself into the place where my head had been. I was about to fire again when I saw an object on the ground, close to the body of the man I had shot. A hand grenade! I almost shouted with glee. It must have come from his pocket.

I flattened myself as low as I could and wormed my way to the hand grenade, stopping to cover my head as a bullet kicked up a gouging path in the gravel ahead. I fumbled in the dead man's pocket and found two more. That was more like it. As I clutched the bombs I breathed a sigh of relief now that the odds were more in my favour. The body protected me from the shower of bullets coming from the terrorists' side and I ducked down behind it, hearing the slugs thud into it and waiting for a chance to retaliate.

A lull in the firing gave me a chance and I rolled across the ground to the shelter of the garage. I pulled the pin from one of the grenades and, leaping out into the open, threw it with all my might. As it curled in flight towards my opponents I threw myself after it, making for the covering corner of the house. I reached it as a shower of bullets tore into the brickwork and I listened for the thump of the explosion. The bang came as the grenade disintegrated into a thousand missiles and, using the confusion it created, I leaped from my cover across the lawn and behind the protective figure of a Greek statue.

I peered around the stone belly of the effigy and caught sight of a car parked in front of the house. The very thing, I mused, if only the key is there. I threw myself across the open space and into the driving seat. Christ – no key! Thinking furiously, I ripped the wires from the steering wheel column and, with nerves jangling at breaking point, feverishly joined them together. The car roared into life and I trod viciously on the gas pedal, fighting the wheel as I reversed. With tyres screaming on flying gravel the car shot away, heading for the garage. I yanked the wheel in a spiteful turn and the car thundered into the garage, emitting a blast of engine and smoke as it squealed to a stop.

"Keep 'em busy," I yelled to Jeannie, tossing her the machine gun.

I grabbed the saw and went to work on Ryan's corpse. I heard Jeannie open up with the gun at the same time as the saw crunched through the ankle bone. I wrapped the dripping limb in the remains of my coat and stuffed it into the car boot. With careful hands I lifted Durrant into the passenger seat and leaped in beside him. The car's engine screamed louder as I pressed the accelerator, vibrating with power as it waited to speed off. I roared at the bending down figure of the woman firing the machine gun and she hurled herself across the space dividing us and into the car. Jeannie slammed the car door with a crash just as I gunned the engine into shuddering power. The ear-deafening roar echoed through the garage as I trod the pedal to the floor, and the car shot forwards through the entrance, hitting the open air with a shattering blast of power.

I wrestled with the spinning steering wheel and yanked it around hard. The car answered, and with screaming tyres lashing the gravel against the underside, lurched to the right and roared up the road. As I approached them I saw the startled faces of the gunmen turn to me and watch my progress. Branden was waving them into action as we got nearer. His features were a picture of surprise and fury when he shouted something at me.

Inside the speeding vehicle I readied the remaining hand grenades by spreading them on my lap, keeping one eye on the road ahead. When we were amongst them, scattering them aside, I picked up the first bomb and, pulling the pin out with my teeth, lobbed it out of the window into the knot of fleeing men. The second and third followed as I yelled defiantly:

"Share that lot amongst you, you stinking bastards!"

In addition, Jeannie emptied her gun at them through the open window, twisting around in her seat to see one terrorist crumble to the ground. Within seconds, the bombs erupted behind us. The car responded with a roar as it hurtled up the road, and inside we laughed long and loud with success and utter relief.

CHAPTER TWENTY-THREE

Our elation was short-lived, however, because we had travelled only a couple of miles when I spotted a car in the rear-view mirror. I put more pressure on our car by treading the pedal down harder, and it responded with more speed. The engine scream increased in volume and the vehicle tore at the road. Studying the mirror, I saw that we were holding them.

Three cars seemed to be following us, gaining a little at the outset, but now maintaining the distance between us. I breathed more easily and began to whistle tunelessly, affecting Jeannie, who laughed at my efforts to form a tune. I continued until a dark shape swept over the car, causing me to look up suddenly.

"Bloody hell, a bleeding helicopter!" I yelled, seeing the squat shape dive down in front of me.

It was one of those little jobs with open cockpits.

"We must be important for him to use all his resources in one go. Let's hope he isn't armed," I said, as the helicopter executed a turn away rise into the sky and flew out of sight.

The road ahead dipped into a valley, and a small forest area came into view. Tall oaks with big canopies rose up before us, and I drove the car into the shelter of the trees. The road ahead forked, the main one snaking to the valley bottom and a minor one shooting off to the left. I yanked the wheel over to the small road, shot around a wooded corner and stopped in a cluster of tree saplings. The car shuddered to a halt surrounded by half-grown trees, hidden from view by anything passing by.

The helicopter blades swished over us and swept away down the valley and the cars roared past down the incline on the other road. I breathed a great sigh and congratulated myself on our lucky escape. I gripped the wheel thinking, but for how long, how long before they smell a rat and realise they have been tricked? Better to get out of here and follow the minor road. I reversed out into the road and revved the engine. The helicopter circled the sky above the trees several times, each time without spotting us. The trees were beginning to thin out and the perimeter of the forest was fast approaching, but when the last leaf overhead flew by to the rear, the helicopter was out of sight behind a range of distant hills, finishing its turn before returning.

We crested the rise and settled into flat grassland that promised very little in the way of concealment, so my glances and thoughts were about the amount of time we had before being seen. With my head twisting every so often to spot the helicopter, I sensed rather than saw the dot swing around the hills and swoop down towards us. Raging engines filled the air with sound and the aircraft, rotors spinning furiously, swept down in a dive towards us.

"You can bet he's pinpointing us and radioing Branden

at this moment," Jeannie shouted, following the flight of the helicopter as it streaked over the roof of the car. "Then they will arrange a hot reception for us farther along this road."

That was also my reasoning as I watched it climb into the sky.

"I don't think it's armed or we would've known by now," I yelled above the hubbub of the two engines. "Best I can do is cut out across open country the first chance I get."

The chance came sooner than expected for, as the aircraft grew smaller and finally disappeared, the fence lining the road came to an end and a farmyard came into sight. A dirt track ran by the building and vanished over a small rise in the grassland. I shot through a metal gate and, in a cloud of dust and straw stalks, drove up the narrow track and sped over the hill. The road, running between waist high wheat, stretched for half a mile, twisting and turning until it ended at a derelict barn resting between two hills. I came to a stop outside the barn and hung my head wearily.

"This is as far as we go," I said, resting my head on the steering wheel.

Night was fast approaching and I felt dead tired. Nothing disturbed us as the hours went by. I slept where I sat and only woke up a couple of times, once when Durrant groaned and then when I thought I heard the faint sound of passing cars, but after that I passed out and was soon dead to the world again.

The racket made by a nearby tractor awakened me. I had shifted during the night and Jeannie's head was resting in my lap. I rubbed my eyes and glanced at my watch – 5.45 a.m. We had more than slept the clock around. I stretched and yawned just as the tractor crested the rise in the surface of the track. Beside me in the middle seat, Jeannie was sleeping peacefully, as was Durrant, who had his head on the headrest.

I fingered my sprouting beard bristles, watching the tractor turn away off the track and into the growing wheat. I bent down and whispered in Jeannie's ear, and she stirred and awoke, blinking at the light.

We slowly drove away from the barn down the track and, after waving at a surprised farmer who gaped at our sudden appearance, entered the road once more and sped away. The late August sunrise painted the clouds a vivid red and I mentally recalled that a red sky in the morning was supposed to forecast rain.

We had only gone a matter of five miles when our luck ran out. The nearside front tyre picked up a nail lying in the road and before we knew it, it was as flat as a pancake. Cursing the tyre and the roughness of the road, I got out the tools and went to work. The wheel nuts were rusted in and made me sweat, but I persisted and removed them using a hammer. When I was putting on the spare wheel, a lorry with a load of hay passed by with the driver ogling us, but he didn't stop, just shot by in a cloud of dust and flying straw stalks.

We arrived home at eleven and, after depositing Durrant in the local emergency hospital and dropping Jeannie off near her place, I called Lawrence and told him what had happened.

"Ahem," he said," Durrant is a good man. Shame it happened to him so quickly before he had a chance to make his mark against them. This man, Branden, is a big noise in political circles, so we must be sure we have the goods on him before we make a move. Incidentally, he was one of the names in the diary you found in the house near Waterloo Station."

"What about Ryan's foot? How can I find out where the arms dump is?"

"Go to the 'car park' and take the object with you. They are equipped to investigate it. The lab technician will find out what the tattoos mean then you can go on from there, Cox."

We waited for the results of a test on Ryan's foot, watching the white coated figure of the lab technician examine the flesh of the sole through the powerful lens of an electric microscope.

"It's pretty burnt up," he said, "but from what I can make out it is some sort of roundabout or circular thing, with a few words written in a foreign language tattooed underneath the designs." He copied the words down on a sheet of plain notepaper and handed it to me. "It's not a lot to go on, but it is all I can see without running a bigger test on the skin, which will take a week or more."

I handed the slip of paper to Jeannie, who was studying the words over my shoulder.

"It's not a grave as you thought," I said, "but a round object, more like a roundabout."

She read the scribble and bit her lip thoughtfully.

"It's a bandstand," she said at last, frowning.

"In a park in a village in Kent. Jesus Christ, how ordinary

can you get?" I said with raised eyebrows. "What village might that be?"

Jeannie was trying to make out the words that were affected the most.

"Looks like Midhurst or Mendith or some such place. We can check it on the map."

"A bandstand you say?" I questioned, over her shoulder. "Now all we have to do is find out how many open spaces with bandstands there are in Kent."

"Quite a few, I'm thinking," she said, handing me the paper. "We can rule some out by knowing how to spell the name of the village."

"A big task, but not too big," I said, with little more than a spark of optimism in my voice.

Later, pouring over a map of the county, I pointed out a number of like sounding villages and tapped the page with the tips of my fingers.

"There we have it. Now all we have to do is pay each one a visit until we find the right village with a bandstand in the local park – simple!"

"Where do we start?" Jeannie wanted to know, pinpointing one of the black dots that indicated a village. "Now, here's one in the north of Kent starting with the letter 'm', Milworth, can we begin there?"

We began in Milworth, but after making a few enquiries we drew a blank. All afternoon we went from hamlet to village, small town back to hamlet again, all beginning with the letter 'm' displayed quite clearly, but we still came up with nothing.

We were sitting in the window seat of a local tea shop sampling a newly baked scone and butter. The tea was served in dainty china with pictures of birds in flight on each item. I sipped the tea and spooned strawberry jam onto the scones.

"Perhaps we will be lucky tomorrow," Jeannie was saying as the waitress was passing our table. "The damned bandstand must be around here somewhere. All we have to do is find someone who plays in a band. They'll surely know if there is one in the vicinity."

The waitress spun around until she faced Jeannie.

"Pardon me," she said, with a polite smile, "but I couldn't help overhearing what you said. I am a member of a brass band and we play on Sundays over at Meekly. There is a bandstand there."

I sat bolt upright when I heard the words, and nudged Jeannie's knee with mine.

"Meekly," I said, pushing the cup away, "is it far from here?"

"A couple of miles across country if you know the way, but five miles or more if you go by the main road," she answered.

I left her a large tip and we headed for Meekly.

I pulled up outside the black iron gates of a municipal park, and peered through the railings. From the pavement we could just see the top of the bandstand and the iron pillars supporting the roof. I looked with annoyance at a wrapped around chain and padlock holding the entrance gates firmly together.

"Looks like we've some climbing to do," I muttered,

holding one of the railings that stretched from either side of the gates.

I heaved myself upwards and swung a leg over the fence. The other leg followed and I waited on the low supporting wall until Jeannie joined me. I hopped down and she landed by my side me with a little jump. We found the pathway through the bushes and headed for the bandstand. We came to a clearing and beheld it standing in a stretch of grassland, and received quite a shock for the bandstand was there, but different, to say the least.

"Bloody hell, the thing is square shaped!" I said, and it was.

If in the past the bandstand had followed traditional lines and presented a circular front to the audience, it had certainly changed over the years. The base was square, the balustrade square and also the roof. What was more significant was the pathway around the base. It was composed of gravel and ran completely around the bandstand.

I shook my head in bewilderment and looked at Jeannie sadly.

"Looks like we've slipped up somewhere," she said, with a look of sympathy. "Everything pointed to it; the name, location and even the amount of time it has been here…"

Her voice trailed off into nothing and a blank stare ran over her face. We retraced our steps and climbed back over the railings, engrossed in silence all the way back to where we had parked the car.

"Pity about that," I said, turning on the engine and drawing away from the kerb. "It looked so right I thought we were on to a winner. Let's have another cup of tea, I'm parched."

We were in strange territory, so I made for the same tea room we had visited before, and we were soon sipping piping hot tea, sitting in the rays of the dying sun as it descended towards a line of tall oak trees.

"Did you find what you were looking for?" asked a voice, and we looked up to see the same waitress standing by our table.

"Not really, for we are looking for a round bandstand and not the square one in Meekly," I answered.

"Oh, what a shame," she said, shaking her head, "but you are a little late for the round one. Meekly town council had another one built ten years ago. The old one was round and sited about fifty yards away."

I nearly choked on my tea when she said those few words. The waitress looked astonished as Jeannie pounded on my back to relieve the fit of coughing I was having. The sudden knowledge was too much for me.

"Go down the wrong way, love?" she enquired sympathetically as my eyes watered.

I nodded through the tears and pain, trying to regain my breath.

Jeannie laughed later as we were making for home.

"I thought you would suffocate. For awhile there it was touch and go."

"It caught me just as I was taking a long drink," I said, joining in with her merriment.

CHAPTER TWENTY-FOUR

Jeannie and I were back at the park the next day. Surprisingly the gates were open and the long chain dangled from the black ironwork. We entered and made for the square bandstand, standing before it, trying to figure out the location of the original one. I pointed to a clump of brushwood fifty yards away.

"You go that way and I'll go in the opposite direction. Go in a circle and meet up on the other side," I said, waving my hand. "I don't know what it will look like, so search the ground carefully."

Jeannie nodded and stepped away through the wet grass. I stood for a moment picking my lip, giving the area about me a once over. I was about to head in the other direction when Jeannie's shout brought me to a halt. I saw her standing at the edge of the cluster of trees, waving at me. At a trot, I sped over to her and she spoke with a voice full of excitement.

"There's something over here. I ran right into it."

There certainly was something amid the undergrowth because when I parted a tangle of bush branches I got my first glimpse of a circular hump covered in weeds and creeper tendrils. I pushed in farther and kicked up against concrete, realising, with a jump of my spirit, that we had found the old bandstand.

"Looks like it," I said over my shoulder. "We struck it lucky first time around." I strode around the mound, tearing at the weeds murmuring, "I wonder where the entrance is?"

Using my shoes, I kicked at the mass of clinging bindweed and ripped the roots away from the soft earth with my bare hands. Several layers of weeds hid the concrete lump and fought back with tenacious stubbornness as I tore at them. The creeper fronds and stems resisted my efforts for awhile and meshed together, clinging onto the concrete surface like mad. Suddenly it all came away; stickers and suckers in one large blanket. I paused for breath and looked at Jeannie, who had straightened up as well.

She was looking over my shoulder at something holding her complete attention. I followed her gaze and saw the figure of a man standing behind me. He was dressed in the uniform of a park attendant and he was frowning at me.

"What do you think you are doing?" he asked, striding forwards until he stood by me and looked at the pile of mixed vegetation at my feet.

"It's a government secret," I said as he gazed into my eyes.

I gave him a slow wink and a smile, all of which he ignored with a stern look.

"You realise you are destroying council property?" he said, including Jeannie in the charge by transferring his gaze to her. "If you persist, I'll have to call my governor, who will call the police."

"Call who you like, mate," I said, a little peeved by his attitude. "I'm on government business and it is vital I carry on, so stand aside and let me continue."

He gave me an odd look and slowly backed away, turning his head to his rear to view his retreat then, turning his back on me, he dashed into the bushes and vanished from sight. We cleared the concrete slab of all vegetation and I gauged it to be about twenty feet in diameter. I strode the circle, stamping on the flagstone surrounds until I thought one sounded hollow.

"We'll try here for a start," I said to Jeannie, and went back to the car to fetch the spade I had left in the boot.

With Jeannie watching me, I attacked the paving stone by ramming the blade in between the cracks and levering upwards. Within ten minutes it lay to one side and I was busy digging up the ground beneath. It was then that authority decided to come on the scene in the shape of a fat man flanked by two other men, one of whom being the man who had run away.

"What's all this about?" the fat man demanded. "This is county property and you are creating a misdemeanour by your actions."

He adopted an important stance before his underlings and edging forwards, but not too far, stood before me full of piss and eminence. He wore a black cap with a 'Head Park-Keeper' badge pinned to the centre of the fabric, with a shiny peak resting tightly above a pair of thick rimmed glasses. He had a podgy face from which two full lips were protruding, they being made wet by a pink tongue sliding from side to side.

He was panting a bit with exertion, all the while treating me to a look of extreme annoyance.

"You can't come into our park and dig it up willy-nilly when you like, sir," he said, glancing at the other two who were nodding in unison.

"I told your mate I was on secret business and that is what I am, so I'll thank you not to interfere," I grated, lifting the spade in one hand.

He must have thought I was about to use it on him because he stepped back a bit, his face whitening with fear. The three men went into a huddle, talking in a whisper, with glances occasionally aimed in my direction. I ignored them and went on digging. I was about three feet down when I decided to give up and try somewhere else. They took it as meaning I was giving up completely, and stared at me. I continued digging, but in a different place, so they went back to their discussion.

Within the space of about an hour, the head keeper called someone on the phone he had produced, and another two men had made an appearance just as I hit the beginnings of a flight of concrete steps. With rising excitement, I cleared the steps of clinging clay and exposed a square flagstone at the bottom. Jeannie, looking at me in a meaningful way, grabbed the spade and, with several quick strokes, scraped the black earth backwards and then stood over me.

"The door is under a layer of the clay in front of you. You'll need a hammer and a screwdriver," she said as I nodded in agreement.

She was just handing them down to me when the police arrived. I gave them a phone number to call and they complied with their hand sets. Within a quarter of an hour the place was cleared. I exposed the metal door and Jeannie was ready to make her contribution. With shoes slipping and sliding in the mud, I twisted the first of the screws in an anticlockwise direction and started the familiar pattern of removing the sheet of corroded iron plate. They were rusted in as usual and resisted all and every effort on my part right until the last minute then they just fell out.

To make matters worse, a light rain began to fall and was gradually filling the pit. As I progressed, the water level rose and I was soon sloshing around in three inches of rainwater, which soaked my feet to a pair of freezing cold lumps. I gritted my teeth and turned the screws, water cascading down my face as the raindrops increased. I cursed when the tool slipped and drew blood. I sucked the wound with a warm tongue and tasted the acid of rust oxidation, spitting and wiping the red from my lips with a wet wrist. My hair was a saturated mat with streams running down my forehead and nose to a jacket black with rainwater.

With heartfelt thanks, the last screw eventually fell into the pool and I began the task of separating the plate from its bed. I hammered the screwdriver in beneath the plate and felt the metal part from the frame. I lifted it off the protruding bolts and gently lowered it to the ground. I wiped the rainwater from my face with a soaked sleeve and turned to Jeannie who was beside me in the hole. She gave me a knowing look and ducked into the well. I stood in the teeming rain behind her, with the full knowledge of what she was doing, willing her to succeed.

The second door came open and I waited, imagining the

frightful prospect if Jeannie made one little mistake, then she pulled out of the hole with a worried look on her face. I swallowed with a little difficulty and looked at her. Her hair was running with water and flowing from the ends in streams. She pushed it back behind her ears.

"There's something in the way," she muttered, swallowing water. "I can't get my hand in behind the bottle. Something is stopping me."

With rising apprehension I ducked into the hole and felt for the bottle. She was right; something had fallen down and blocked the entry for my hand. It felt like a piece of masonry by the shape of it, well and truly wedged in between the wall and the bottle. I was fuming and looked at my watch then at Jeannie.

"I make it we have only forty-five seconds to clear out before it is due to go off."

I gave her a sidelong glance and slowly mounted the steps. She shook a fringe of raindrops from her hair and followed me. We made no pretence of hurrying, but just sauntered over the ground to the protection of a pair of sturdy oaks and waited behind the grey trunks. The seconds reached the full minute and stretched beyond it, but no explosion occurred. I peeped around the gnarled tree trunk and through the rain, staring at the concrete block, but it remained the same.

"Perhaps it's a dud," I said, smiling through the drips dropping down on us from the tree.

"I think it is something to do with the obstruction. It's preventing the two chemicals from reaching each other and starting the explosion."

"Do you think we can get in there without triggering it to go off?"

"What's the point? We've found the dump, let others do the rest of it. Why risk our lives to see if it is still active?"

"A lot of things can still go wrong."

"Such as what?"

Branden knows we have the location. He might step in and move the munitions before the authorities have the chance. There is still the chance that it might explode, and there is also the likelihood that a general panic would begin, what with all the houses so close by. That's not taking into account the area will have to be evacuated."

Jeannie firmed her lips and shuddered.

"Then we will have to go back in to make sure the place is safe."

"Most certainly we will. It's like waiting for a bomb to drop; you've either got to diffuse it or clear the general public from a wide area while it is being dealt with safely. Just imagine the widespread terror this action will cause, not to mention the cost," I said, glancing at my watch again. "Do you think you can do it?" I asked softly, wiping the rain from my face.

Jeannie drew up to her full height and pulled in a deep breath.

"If that be the case I suppose I *must* do it," she said.

We looked at each other and exchanged shallow smiles just as the rain stopped and a watery sun appeared. We walked back to the hole in the ground and sloshed down to the bottom.

"I can feel the obstruction with the tips of my fingers," she announced, with excitement in her voice. "It is wedged behind the top bottle and stopping it from shattering."

"Can you shift it a little by sliding it sideways?" I asked, talking into the hole over her shoulder.

"I need something thin to push it away," she said, her muffled voice filtering through to me.

I stooped and grabbed the screwdriver, handing it to her. She worked away inside the hole. I could hear her scraping with the tool and the dulled oaths when she slipped with it.

"I'm moving the lump now," she shouted, "but when I do, the bottle will be free to shatter when I open the inner door, so be ready to do another bunk if I fail."

I heard a dull thud as the offending lump of concrete fell away, and the squeal of the inner door as it opened. I began to count methodically, willing her fingers to stop two chemicals from coming together, looking about me just in case we had to run for it. I remembered the others we had succeeded in disarming and the ones we had run away from, and my heart began to pump faster. Jeannie suddenly uttered a cry of triumph and backed out of the hole, tears of relief in her eyes and holding the bottle towards me at arm's length.

"It was touch and go for awhile, but I was praying like I never prayed before," she said breathlessly, her chest rising and falling with emotion.

I took the glass tube and set it aside on the mound of discarded clay and then gathered her into my arms. Her body was trembling and the tears began to flow faster. I whispered into her ear and kissed her cheek with tender kisses, holding her until the shaking subsided and stopped.

"I was really frightened," she whispered, and shuddered.

I planted a gentle kiss on the curvature of her lips and held it. Her frame bent to my angled body and clung with a fierce and passionate embrace that surprised me for a moment. She drew back with a self-conscious smile and reddened slightly.

"Phew! You had me going for a minute," she said. She held my hand and gently dragged me to the chamber. "Let's not forget why we are here, darling, more of the other later."

The room under the bandstand was smaller than the other dumps. It was a square chamber, about twelve by twelve, but packed to the roof with boxes, so that we hardly had any room to inspect the contents. Even so, we estimated it contained something in the order of five hundred pieces; a staggering amount of arms in so little a space.

"It's surprising the amount of arms the IRA has," I said, levering a heavy box aside.

I was using the screwdriver and managed to prise open and lift the corner of a lid. A suppressed light was coming through the doorway, enabling me to see the plastic wrapping around the contents. The thick plastic cover was heavy with caked grease, and the wink of bright metal was only just visible, however, I was satisfied and dropped the lid back to its original position with a bang.

"So, number four," I said joyfully. "We've got three more holes to discover."

I began to wonder where the other three were located. The thought occupied my mind until the faint sound of a man's voice filtered to my ears. Almost at once a head wearing a bowler hat popped into view framed by the square doorway, and an upper crust voice, dripping with conceit, entered the chamber.

"Hello there, I'm Soames from head office!" the apparition said. "You won't know me, but I work in another division.

Lawrence sent me to support you in your hour of need, as it were." He laughed in a hoarse voice almost like a donkey's bray. "I see you've found the dump, so congrats on that, old chap."

Jeannie and I climbed out of the hole, blinking at the light and giving him the once-over. I decided he was a typical public school product with all the consequences of the privileges it projected. He had the manufactured voice taught by the school and used it constantly.

"I've never heard of you," I said with narrowed eyes. "If your division, as you call it, sent you here where are your papers?"

"All in a moment," Soames said hastily. "Right now we have to ensure the location of this place is kept secret."

I laughed out loud.

"What about the police, and how do you silence the council employees?" I pointed out, still gurgling with mirth. "In a couple of hours the whole world will know."

Soames narrowed his eyes and thinned his lips.

"So you've not made any other arrangements apart from them, is that what you are saying?"

"You've got it in one, brother, you certainly catch on quick."

Suddenly Soames stepped over to Jeannie's side and, pulling out a Luger pistol, grabbed her, stepped behind her and held the gun to her head.

"Now, Mr Cox," he said, with menace dripping from his tone, "you'll do as you are told or the girl will die fast." He appeared to relax and continued. "Now, that's better. Pull your gun from your pocket very slowly, and I mean *slowly*."

Soames tightened his grip on Jeannie, pointing the pistol at her right temple with an arm circling her throat.

"I had a feeling about you, mate, right from my first sighting of you," I growled, letting my gun fall from my hand. He put his hand to his mouth and blew a soft whistle. The bushes parted and three figures emerged, Branden leading.

"Cox, you certainly are a pest, your persistence would be admirably used in another direction. As it is we are getting heartily sick of your constant interfering in our affairs," Branden said, walking across the open space towards me. He was holding a small hand gun and it was trained on my chest. "Now we are going to finish you once and for all."

"I'll haunt you until you are safely behind bars," I said threateningly, "with all the rest of your cut-throats alongside you. When Lawrence hears of this he'll-"

The rest was cut off when someone caused the world to collapse on top of me.

CHAPTER TWENTY-FIVE

I came to, feeling a lump the size of a table tennis ball growing out of the side of my head, and realised I had been knocked out. I raised my head in pain as the bump stabbed at me and I twisted sideways to see the concerned face of Jeannie looking down at me. She peered at me after assuring herself I was back in the land of the living.

"Hello, someone hit you with the butt of a gun, darling, and knocked you unconscious," she said.

"That situation's normal with me lately," I said, swivelling my head around to make sure it was still there, "and I'll make an informed guess that my assailant had an Oxford accent as well as being the traitor everybody at the office is seeking – the man called Soames."

She nodded in agreement, her face serious.

"Well, he's rooted out once and for all. He can't do any more harm now we know who he is. Lawrence should be pleased he's been rumbled."

"It surprises me Lawrence will be pleased about anything."

I sniffed, wincing with raw pain as I got to my feet. "Where are we now?"

"Back at Branden's house," Jeannie replied, helping me up, "in a small room that smells of damp and rotten vegetables, so I guess it must be some sort of storeroom."

I had recognised the room. It was the same one I had used to enter the house before, so I knew where we were. It was a great help knowing where to run in an emergency, the only trouble being how to get out as there was a huge lock on the sheet iron door. I sat on a sack of potatoes and rubbed my sore spot again.

The middle door opened and a head popped into the room. Branden stood there sneering at me. He was accompanied by four of his cronies who spread out around him, ready to defend him if I was to attack. I would have done, but I didn't fancy tackling all five, so I let it pass.

"Bring them along, Phelps," Branden growled to the nearest man.

We were bundled through the doorway, held by our wrists and elbows. We passed under the smoke-blackened ceilings and scorched curtains of my first foray into the country house, were ushered into the same big room and stood behind the same desk where I had first met Branden. We were manhandled into an upright stance and tied wrist to wrist with rough cord. The men stood aside respectfully as Branden sat at the desk as though he was a presiding judge.

"Cox, as I have said before, we need dedicated men like yourself to join our organisation," Branden began. "I offered you a million to come in with us and now I'm increasing it to two million, are you interested?"

I shook my head and glared at him.

"No deal," I growled.

His eyebrows shot up in astonishment and he sat back.

"We know how much you earn at the ministry and it is peanuts compared with this offer, so why the misplaced loyalty?"

"You wouldn't understand even if I was to spell it out to you in words of one syllable."

"You understand money though?" Branden persisted. "Your country is noted for the way it pays poor wages. Where's the harm in making a quick buck like the rest of them?"

"No harm provided it doesn't harm anybody in the process."

"We don't deliberately set out to harm anyone. If someone is killed in our offensive we treat it merely as an accident."

"You would," I said with rising anger, "and what about us? We gonna be another accident?"

"We'll deal with you, you can be sure of that."

"No doubt, and what about the arms dumps you've secreted around the country?"

"You have destroyed four so far, but you won't do it any more."

"You'll have to kill me first."

"My sentiments entirely, Cox, because that is exactly what we are about to do – both of you." His eyes travelled to Jeannie as he said this and briefly rested on her before coming back to me. "You have been sentenced to death before, so it won't come as a surprise to learn it will be carried out at once. You have slipped through my fingers before, but you won't do it again."

Branden glanced at the men behind me and at once we were gripped by several hands and forced to march from the room around to the back of the house where there was an open space. I was waiting for them to tie me to an upright iron stanchion, when another of the gang made an appearance. When I saw who it was I could hardly contain my rage.

"We meet again, Cox," Sweeney said, grinning in his evil way, "but not for long though 'cause the boss has given me the job of finishing you off. May I add that nothing will give me more pleasure than putting a bullet into your brain – nothing at all."

"We've a score to settle, Sweeney," I growled, "but it seems you've got the whip hand this time. If I get the opportunity to reverse it I'll make sure-"

"Stop right there, because there ain't going to be any opportunity," Sweeney interrupted, pushing me aside to get to Jeannie. "You and the woman go together and that's a promise."

He fixed the cords to the post and waved the others away, drawing an evil looking pistol from his armpit. I stood upright, watching him take off the safety catch and check the magazine. Amid a whirring and a loud ring of aircraft engines, a helicopter appeared over the line of trees on the horizon and swooped down on the gang of waiting men. I cheered in a loud voice as they instantly scattered to the safety of the house, then began work on freeing myself and Jeannie. She held out her arms as I dropped my own bonds to the ground. I was on the last turn of the cords holding her when I noticed a look of horror come over her face as her mouth set in a warning scream. Instinctively I whirled on one foot and in the same movement cast my bulk at the figure of Sweeney, who was about to fire the gun.

The bullet clipped a sliver of skin from my left cheek and whizzed off through a large pane of glass. The shattering glass seemed to unnerve him or at least put him off because he hesitated for a fraction of a second, which gave me time to launch myself at him. The second shot exploded harmlessly over my right shoulder and sped away with a zing, but I had him now, although he tried to raise the gun for a third shot. We were too close for him to succeed, and my hand closed around his wrist in a vice-like grip. We wrestled for possession of the gun, treading great holes in the surface of the lawn with our scuffling feet. He was a big tough man and fought like mad to retain the pistol. For about a minute we gyrated around, trying to gain the initiative, and again it was a noise outside that transferred the advantage to me.

The helicopter blades suddenly whirled around in a burst of renewed power as the machine settled down on the big stretch of manicured grass, causing Sweeney to glance sideways towards the source of the sound. I followed up with a tremendous left hook to his exposed jaw and slammed my knuckles on his front teeth. He staggered back with surprise and anger, blood dripping from bruised lips and panting heavily. His eyes darted to the fallen gun that lay halfway between us and he made a sudden dive for it just as half a dozen soldiers piled out of the side of the helicopter.

As Sweeney straightened up with the gun almost turned on me, I aimed a kick at his groin and connected with the toe of my shoe, which bounced off the top of his thigh. He retaliated by heaving his bulk at me and we crashed to the ground together trying to score with short jabs. I wound my legs about his waist and managed to get a hold on his throat with one hand whilst holding him off with the other. He wriggled about then, with a mighty heave, he broke the stranglehold and clipped me in the face. He rolled clear and scrambled to his knees hurriedly searching for the gun, then straightened up with narrowed eyes staring at it clutched in Jeannie's hand and pointing straight at his heart.

The soldiers circled us and put handcuffs on Sweeney, who gave me an evil look and dropped to his haunches gazing at the ground sullenly. I took the gun from Jeannie and patted her hand in thanks. A sergeant holding a machine gun directed the men to surround the house and pointed to the sullen Sweeney.

"Who is he and how many more of them are in the house?"

I indicated Sweeney with a nod of my head.

"This one here, the one I've been trying to put under restraint, is a well known hit man for the IRA. He is personally responsible for a number of deaths, one in particular being a government agent he shot quite recently. You saw the rest disperse for cover when you dropped in. There are roughly thirty or forty men in the house and God knows how many scattered around. They are controlled by a man called Branden. He is in the house with them and cooking something up right at this moment I think."

The sergeant eyed me and shouldered his gun.

"You are Cox, I know by the description I was given," he said. "You know the situation, so where do you go from here?"

"I'm engaged in finding out where the IRA has buried a number of arms dumps in this country. The boss, Branden, controls all terrorist activities here and must know where they are located. We've found four so far and we need the other three, making a total of seven suspected sites."

"And how do you propose to make him cough up with the info?"

My answer was interrupted by gunfire as the man in the house opened up with machine guns and other weapons. The sergeant sped away to direct his men, leaving me to guard Sweeney who was cocking his head, listening to the barrage.

"I heard what you said," he snarled, fixing me with a vicious stare of pure hate. "You'll get nothing out of the boss. He's got a few nasty surprises up his sleeve for you, I can tell you for nothing."

I gave him a dirty look and ignored his outburst as the khaki clad soldiers began firing around the front of the house. The resulting fusillade of exchange fire echoed across the open countryside. I heard the sound of shattering glass as the windows collapsed, and the ping and whine of flying slugs gouging out lumps of masonry as they connected and then flew off into space.

I pulled Sweeney to his feet and, with the gun pressing into the small of his back, propelled him forwards around the conservatory up to the corner of the house where I peeped around the stonework. I spotted the sergeant taking shelter behind a small garden shed and called to him.

"I'm going to make a try for the house using *this* for a shield." I prodded Sweeney with the gun as I spoke. "You give me covering fire to keep their heads down, while I try for one of the windows."

The sergeant nodded and yelled to his men to concentrate their fire in one swift blast at all the windows except the nearest one. A whistle shrilled from the sergeant's position and the terrific explosion of concentrated weaponry began. The rain of bullets of small and large calibre doused the building in dust and flying chunks. The massive front door was reduced to pepper pot remnants and teetered crazily on its hinges before sagging down. In addition to this, flower pots and wrought iron containers with magnificent plants in the process of growth and splendour, exploded into bits and showered their contents onto the ground.

I waited until I judged the time to be right, listening to the tremendous battering of the house, then snarled for Sweeney to move out, spitting out a warning of dire consequences if he didn't do as I said. I pushed him forwards as the firing slackened, and came up to the nearest window, peering through the glassless gap ready for anything. The room was empty, however, due to the amount of damage inflicted by the incoming projectiles. I swung a leg over the sill and jerked my head at the terrorist to follow my example. He did this grudgingly, and we stood in the room panting slightly, listening to the soldiers' firepower tailing off.

I pulled a fierce face at him and indicated that he should go forwards. I followed behind closely, nudging him with the snout of the gun, which was poking in his back.

"One wrong move, mate, just one little one and I'll kill you!" I threatened, through gritted teeth.

We stepped over ripped and torn furniture, past splintered

plaster and hanging wallpaper to a brown carved door that was standing halfway open. I looked through the crack between the door and the frame and, partially satisfied, pulled it open wide and pushed the gunman through the gap. Ahead, a scurrying figure stopped in mid-stride and goggled at the stiff image of Sweeney appearing before him. His cries soon brought others to the scene and, after seeing me in the house, they levelled an assortment of weapons in my direction. I edged farther behind Sweeney's protective back and called to the nearest man.

"I want to see Branden," I demanded, breathing down the neck of my human shield. "I want to make a deal with him."

After a moment, Branden came into view, showing incredulity. He cuffed the nearest gang member on the face and yelled at him.

"I thought I told you to guard every window, you fool!" He turned to me. "Once more you've escaped my punishment, Cox. You bear a charmed life, but this time the jig is up. You've walked into my house once too often, so I'll-"

"I've come to offer you a deal," I interrupted, looking over Sweeney's shoulder. "One you'd be wise to accept."

"What kind of deal?" Branden questioned, shushing those around him, who were shouting for him to ignore me.

"Your life for the whereabouts of the other three dumps," I answered, inching Sweeney forwards.

Branden laughed out loud and was joined in the merriment by several of his henchmen.

"You fool," he shouted above the hubbub, "do you think I'm unaware of the dangers in the life I lead? That is why I've made arrangements for any contingency like this that might arise."

"Arrangements? What arrangements?"

Branden's laughter erupted again and he turned to the others.

"Shall I tell him, boys?" he asked.

"Yesss," they all chorused.

"There you are, general agreement," Branden said, beaming. "Listen. Under this building we have dug a long tunnel. It runs for five hundred feet and ends in a copse west of here. Several of my men are currently escaping via this tunnel and soon we will all disappear through it, leaving you and the soldiers attacking an empty house."

"Very good, Branden," I said, "you've thought of every eventuality except one. Your men can use it, but you can't."

His face was a picture as he puzzled over my statement.

"What do you mean?" he queried with a half-laugh.

"You're too well known," I insisted. "You'll be picked up before you go fifty miles."

I felt Sweeney move and jabbed him in the back. Outside the bullet storm was lessening and now only an occasional stray slug sang a lone song against the splintered masonry.

"I could decide to risk it anyway," Branden retorted. "I could blow up the house and while they were busy searching for my remains I would vanish into one of the safe houses we have in this country."

"Maybe so, but my way you wouldn't have to do all that," I argued. "I will guarantee you a safe passage out of the country to Southern Ireland and no questions asked. Your associates would have to stand trial for their various crimes, but under the agreement you would be free to go. All you have to do is tell me where the arms are stored."

I knew the last part of the deal wouldn't sit too well with the rank and file of the gang and I waited for their reaction with baited breath. It wasn't long in coming, and trouble came in the shape of Soames, the public school gent, who pushed his way through the rest, piping up as he came.

"Can't you see what he is doing? He's trying to drive a wedge between us by offering us different deals. I say we should all make a break for it right now. We have the tunnel, so there will be no problem. I say rush him and get it over with."

"How long have you been head of operations, Soames?" Branden fumed, fixing him with a withering look. "*I'll* make the decision whether we go or not, is that clear?"

"Yes it is," Soames mumbled, half under his breath.

"All of you," Branden said to the gathering, "listen to me. If you want to go you can use the tunnel. I'm going to stay and set the charges to blow up the house then I'll join you, but first I must make sure we will not be prevented." He reached under his coat, produced a hand gun and levelled it at me. "Perhaps this will answer your question, Cox," he said and, pressing the trigger, shot Sweeney in the chest twice.

CHAPTER TWENTY-SIX

I felt two bullets thump into Sweeney's body and he started to collapse. To say I was surprised by the move was to prove an understatement. I was totally shocked and, for the moment, dumbfounded as well. The echoes of the gunshots died away among the varnished timber rafters overhead and I jerked out of my trance to hear Branden's triumphant laugh.

"Now that has got rid of your shield," he said, as I grabbed the falling villain around the waist. "Now it's your turn, Cox."

Branden's face turned nasty and he loosed two more shots, obviously meant for me. I hiked the body up and ducked my head behind it. The strike of the lead slugs caused it to quiver, but the dead man took the full force of them in the chest. I had to act now, and act fast. The dead weight of the body was resting on one arm and was slipping fast. I made a decision and, letting it slide away, dived to one side to the safety of an exquisitely carved sideboard. From behind the solid wooden boards of the polished piece of priceless furniture, I opened up with the pistol, scattering the gang. As they dived for cover one of them let rip with his weapon and the bullet gouged a long splinter of polished wood from the carved surface and rebounded into the wall.

Out in the open, the helicopter engine roared with deafening force as the aircraft took to the air. The noise began to recede as it gained height and headed out for the horizon.

Inside the house I was exchanging shots with those who were brave enough to poke their heads from safety and risk a snap shot at me. I replied in kind until I saw the chamber only had one round left, so I was more or less forced into my next move. The next head to pop out from cover got the last bullet from my gun and, when it pulled back, I immediately jumped up and threw myself behind the wall protecting one of the terrorists. The next time his pistol came around the door jamb he had the shock of his life when I wrested it from his grip. He did a foolish thing then. He looked around the corner to see where his gun had gone, I righted the gun and shot him full square between the eyes. He fell back and hit the floor with a crash.

I waited for another head to break cover, lying on the thick carpet for awhile and sighting the gun forwards ready to fire. A brave man leaped into view hoping to catch me unawares. He was facing in the wrong direction and, before he had time to adjust to my position, fell prey to my next bullet. He was carrying a machine gun, however, and the heavy weapon clattered to the floor moments before I flung myself forwards and scooped it up in my arms. Branden made an unexpected move by yelling to his troops to rush at me and overwhelm me with numbers, but no one was feeling compelled to obey his commands. They contented themselves with a little display of courage by taking hasty shots at me and quickly withdrawing to safety.

It was then I caught sight of a figure darting across the room and vanishing out of sight behind a wide screen. My senses were alerted immediately and flared into interest then another man flung himself across the room and behind the screen. So, I thought, the rats are leaving the sinking ship and are making a bid to escape the net. That is why Branden is trying to pin me down here before trying to break out with them. I resolved to scotch his plans if I was able, and made it plain.

"Branden," I shouted, "I'm on to your game; keep me busy here while you creep away one by one. You won't succeed, you know. I'm gonna do all I can to stop you, so you might as well do the right thing and give up now. The deal is still on."

"Fuck you, Cox, for your damned meddling," Branden roared from his cover. "Now I'm going to kill you piece by piece, nice and slow, so I can savour every part of your screams for mercy. You'll rue the day you ever tried to better me when you feel the full force of my anger."

I laughed at the threats and watched another pair of ruffians scoot across the end of the room. I loosed off a burst in their direction and saw them leap behind the screen quickly, emitting loud howls of pain.

"That will convince you I'm serious, Branden. Your escape route is open, but you have to make it before you can use it. I'm thinking those others don't seem like they did."

I grinned with an upwards twitch of my lips and, with my arms and elbows, inched my body forwards again, cuddling the cold barrel of the machine gun close to the roundness of my right cheek. Outside I could hear the close proximity of the soldiers as they began to close in. The firing trailed off to be replaced by shouting mixed with scuffling hobnail boots on the gravel pathway.

"You hear that, Branden?" I shouted. "They're coming for you. You only have minutes to make up your mind. In a little while there will be no more soldiers then you will be able to handle everything."

Nothing from Branden then suddenly there was, for he did make up his mind and launched himself into view, haring for the screen and a fond hope of escape. The movement was both abrupt and swift, catching me completely off guard. Even so, I managed to loose off a brief burst before the gun chose to jam. The slugs bit off a shower of woodwork that sprayed the shoulders of the running man an instant before he vanished behind the screen. I was swearing and shaking the gun, but to no avail, so casting it aside I started forwards, dragging my hand gun from my waistband. The head of another member of the gang popped out and, as I hurled myself towards the screen, I snapped a shot in his direction watching the head withdraw hurriedly.

Reaching the screen I heaved it aside to reveal a large cupboard with double doors that were thrown open wide. At the rear of the cupboard yawned the entrance to a roughly hewn tunnel measuring some six feet by three and sloping downwards. As I stepped into the hole I could hear the faint sound of running footsteps, which seemed to echo through the walls of the building. The leather of my shoe touched packed earth and gently slithered on protruding pieces of granite rock. The way ahead was lit by low voltage bulbs hanging from wooden pegs driven deep into the earthen walls, each fixed to a long cable looping its way down the tunnel.

The path ended and became a flight of stone stairs. Cracks with lichen thrusting through edged the stones aside so that each stone surface was rough and uneven. I descended with care and several times grabbed for the rope handrail that had been put there for the purpose. As each bulb periodically passed by my eye it cast me into partial shadow before the next one. I was listening for any sound and was tuned to a fine degree to expect a sudden assault. I pointed the barrel of my gun in a downwards direction, finger curled on the trigger. My feet touched packed earth again and the tunnel levelled out into a wide area dug out of solid rock.

The massive subterranean room was well lit by naked bulbs hanging down from the roof of the cavern. The shadows of the roughly hewn rocks danced to the insistence of a current of cold air coming from the continuation of the tunnel in the far end of the cavern wall. I watched the bulbs drift slowly on the end of the wires and lowered my gaze to take in a huge iron door set in the rock face some seven feet in width and of equal height. The door was supported by two massive iron hinges welded to the surface of the iron plate and fixed to a pair of iron girders, both set into the rock. I marvelled at the size of the construction, but what held my attention the most was the fact that the door was open about a foot and light was shining through the crack. I crept across the rough floor and edged my body into the chink of light, stooping as a shadow stepped in front of it.

"Come in, Cox, I was expecting you," Branden said,

silhouetted by the brilliant light. "If you look around you will see where another arms dump is situated; the biggest one I will inform you."

"Never mind that now," I grated, pointing the gun at him. "I'm taking you in like I said I would."

"You fool," Branden snarled through bared teeth. "I credited you with a little more savvy than most. You must know I've made arrangements for any situation like this to arise."

"You mean your threat to blow up the house? Well, you can forget that now, you've made your point so give up."

Branden held up a metal box so that it was framed by the ray of bright light. Two wires were visible, fixed to the underside of the box and running away out of sight into the darkness beyond the light.

"See this?" He shook the box to emphasise the point. "When I press a button on it, a sequence of events will be set in motion leading to the destruction of this arms depository and the house above. You have only ten minutes to clear the area if you want to live, Cox, so I suggest you start running now."

"And suppose I don't?" I said, blinking in the strength of the light. "Suppose I was to shoot you and stop you from pressing that button?"

"Then you would be a fool," Branden said, with a hoarse laugh slipping from between tense lips. "This box is constructed so that if the wrong button is pushed the result will be instant detonation. We would all be killed as would everybody within a certain radius of the explosion, and that includes the British soldiers currently searching the house upstairs."

"What about your own men? They'll be killed as well."

"I wouldn't worry about them now."

"Why not?"

"Because, my interfering friend, at this moment they are right behind you ready to shoot on my command, so I suggest you stay perfectly still and lower your weapon."

"You're bluffing, Branden-" I began then stiffened as the sound of a scraping shoe caught my attention.

I reluctantly let my arm fall and was immediately held by the arms as they moved in. They bound my wrists behind my back as I cursed myself for getting caught so easily and bit my lip in annoyance.

"Well, Cox, you have come to the end of your luck I'm thinking," Branden said, smirking and moving closer. "I had dreams of cutting you into little pieces and roasting the bits over an open fire, but this end will do as well as any. The fragments of you will be spread over a large part of the landscape after the blast and any left will be eaten by wild animals, so it more or less winds up the same way."

"If I get out of this, Branden, I'll-"

My threat was cut off as they smothered the flow of hot words with a rough cloth that was tightened around my mouth.

"You'll do what?" Branden questioned, pushing his face into mine, so I had a close view of a pair of bloodshot eyes staring into mine. "Stop me from blowing the place up? Well, I'm about to do just that to prevent the contents from falling into the clutches of your government."

He laughed as I glowered at him and mumbled into the gag.

"What did you say? You don't believe I'll do it? You are so wrong. If it suits my ends I'll blow up the whole country." He straightened up to throw out a hand that swept the four corners of the room with one movement. "You want to see what you have missed? I assure you it will take your breath away."

Branden strode to a dark corner and, with a downwards stroke, bathed the room in brilliant light. He was right. The sight of row upon row of wooden boxes stacked together tightly and rising to a height of twenty feet or more made it hard to breathe as the excitement of discovering the whereabouts of the major arms dump welled up inside me. I craned my neck to see more, and in wonderment saw sacks of the plastic explosive, Semtex, occupying shelf after shelf, with detonators and fuses neatly placed to one side. Box after box of what I reckoned was ammunition rose into the air and close by, smothered in thick yellow grease, a dozen mortars reared their ugly barrels. I twisted my head in the other direction and noted more boxes, knowing full well they contained automatic guns sunk deep in protective lubricant. Also in full view, suspended from iron pegs and glistening in the harsh light with a skin of the same coloured oil, were two bazooka anti-tank weapons.

I drew in a sudden breath of surprise while my eyes widened in sympathy, which I quickly hid by dropping my gaze to the floor when I saw Branden eagerly drinking in my astonishment. A look of triumph leapt into his gaze and his laugh rang out through the confines of the cavern. The shadows returned when he switched off the power and plunged us into gloom once more.

"I bet that was an eye-opener," he said, coming over to me

and standing by my side. "Those boxes hold over two thousand sub-machine guns and the square ones contain a quarter of a million live cartridges."

I shrugged my shoulders to denote my disinterest and wondered what sort of damage a box of matches would do. I was aching to tell him, but breathed hot air into the gag instead.

"So you pretend to show no feelings at the sight of all these weapons, although I know you would dearly love to report it to your superiors," Branden said, straightening up. "You have no chance though, as you will see. I know in the past you have had phenomenal luck in your campaign against the army, but now the luck has started to run out."

With a wave of his hand, he signalled for the others to leave, and waited until the last man had exited via the iron door.

"Cox," he said, picking up the detonation box, "you see before you a dedicated man. I will relinquish quite a lot now that you have exposed me to my enemies. The position that I have maintained is now untenable and I must quit this country." He stroked the box with the tips of his fingers and stared into space. "The job I held the enormous salary I enjoyed – all gone. My title, given to me by a grateful country in recognition of my services to a well known charity is also gone, and all due to a hairy arsed upstart with as little breeding as the animals in the field. No wonder I demand retribution for the huge losses you have cost me and now," he tapped the box, "I have the power to do just that."

He twisted me around and pushed me over to a metal drum, forcing me to sit on the floor with my back to it. He tied my ankles together with a length of rope and fixed the long end to one of the mortars. He then placed the box on top of the drum and fiddled with the controls for a few seconds before looking down at me.

"There you are, Cox, it is set to go off in ten minutes, so I'll bid you adieu. Give my regards to the Devil when you meet him," he said over his shoulder and vanished through the doorway.

CHAPTER TWENTY-SEVEN

Ten minutes! I raged inwardly. Jesus Christ! Ten minutes to live and even less now that the countdown had begun.

I had to warn the soldiers, but I knew I didn't have an earthly chance of retracing my footsteps up the tunnel in time to alert them to the danger. There had to be a way to prevent the bomb going off. All I had to do was find it and... I stopped thinking and fought the bonds holding me. I kicked at the rope tying me to the mortar and felt the weapon slide inside. I slashed at it with the side of my shoe, but it held. Sweat was beginning to pimple my brow and run into the gag, making me taste salt.

I looked up and saw the metal edge of the detonator protruding over the edge of the drum and began to wriggle my body upwards, but the rope on my ankles stopped me from kneeling upright. I was counting the seconds now and the first minute slipped by. I began a rocking motion, hoping to tilt the detonator and get to the controls. The drum teetered on an uneven bit of floor and spun away, dislodging the metal box, which crashed to the ground and sprang open revealing the works. I shut my eyes waiting for the bang and opened them again just as rapidly when nothing happened.

I judged that five minutes had passed and the margin to the explosion had narrowed, then I saw wires leading from the detonator and running out of sight to a bulky object just discernible in the corner. I decided it was the charge, so wrestled with the ropes again and got precisely nowhere. The ticking of my mental clock pounded out the seconds and the last minute was fast approaching, beating in time with the hammer blows of my heart. I then made a final desperate attempt to forestall the explosion. I gathered the detonator behind my back in the claws of my aching fingers and began to pull on the wires. My efforts were resisted for a time then the plastic coating began to stretch with the strain and I didn't think I had the strength to break them. Suddenly all three wires parted from their hold on the bomb and whipped away from it just as the box gave a little click.

I sat hunched into a half-ball waiting for the explosion and oblivion, but the seconds ticked by and my hopes soared in reply. I raised my head in the half-light and realised I wasn't going to die there after all, well, not in the immediate future anyway. I struggled to free myself and paused for breath when I saw I wasn't getting anywhere. I heard the sound of a man's voice and the scuffling of boots on the hard rock floor. As the gang had departed I could only conclude it was the army, so I shouted through the gag, although my efforts came out as a muffled cry.

The door was pushed open a bit more and the sergeant stepped into the room. He showed surprise when he saw me trussed hand and foot, and quickly strode to my side. He wrenched off the gag and waited as I drew a welcome breath into my lungs.

"Be careful, I've just disarmed a bomb," I warned, handing him the remains of the detonator and pointing to the shape in the corner. "It might go off yet, so I'd get someone to look at it."

We were joined by others in camouflage clothing, and the sergeant spoke to a corporal who examined the bomb. I undid the ropes tied to my ankles and stood up, stamping my feet to increase the blood supply to my toes. When I turned on the main lights the sergeant whistled with surprise at the sight of the weapons looming up before his startled gaze.

"The bastards have been busy stockpiling this little lot. I'm thinking there's enough here to start a small war."

"And the instigator of it all has escaped through the other part of the tunnel," I said, with some changrin in my voice.

In walked over to Jeannie and my smile returned. She put her arms about me for a minute and then drew back, looking into my eyes.

"I was worried about you, Bill, so I followed the soldiers down the tunnel," she explained.

She shivered in the dampness of the place and took my arm as I went to the door.

"Branden got away," I said, leading her through the doorway.

We walked past a couple of soldiers who were guarding the dump and headed for the far corner and the remainder of the tunnel. Rising in a gentle slope it continued for about a hundred yards before getting decidedly steeper. It was almost a climb on hands and knees before daylight flooded in and we stepped through the exit into fresh air.

We found ourselves outside surrounded by the meshing arms of a thickly grown clump of gorse bushes, then pushed our way through the prickles to see the house resting in a hollow some two hundred yards away. I ground my teeth together in silent rage, knowing full well Branden was miles away and hoping I was reduced to a cinder in a pile of powdered rubble. Sorry to disappoint you, Branden, I thought. Jeannie and I walked down the slope to the house below.

A clean-shaven officer with three pips on his shoulder was directing orders to a group of camouflaged soldiers, who circled him and ignored us for awhile. After the last trooper had departed to carry out the orders, he turned to me and, to my surprise, saluted. I returned the gesture with a 'one up' of my own.

"Glad to see you, Captain. I've just come through the bolt hole, but the birds have flown." I said.

He hitched a heavy looking sub-machine gun to a higher position on his shoulder and cast a curious look at Jeannie.

"I hope the lady is OK. We saw her sheltering from the gunfire in one of the garages and she told us of your foray into the house. After we made sure the house was secure we allowed her in to find you. You know the rest."

The sergeant appeared at the entrance to the house and waved to me.

"Someone wants to speak to you on the phone," he shouted, "a Mr Lawrence."

I groaned and walked over to the huge oak door where the NCO pointed to a dust-covered phone set then left me to it.

"Cox here," I said, blowing white powder from the instrument.

"I hear you have unearthed the main arms dump, Cox," Lawrence rasped, chest wheezing. "Too bad you didn't catch Branden at the same time. He's still a big noise in the army even though he's had a few setbacks recently. I must impress on you that there are still two more undiscovered dumps and while they remain so the IRA is still the biggest terrorist organisation in the country."

"You make it seem like it is a treasure hunt instead of a fight to the death every time we meet," I said, inwardly fuming at his apparent lack of gratitude. "I'd like to inform you that we are presently standing on an unexploded bomb that Branden set before he flew the coop. The thing might go off at any moment, so you can at least sense my nervousness."

"I can appreciate that," Lawrence said with the ghost of a feeling. "We're not completely without sensitivity you know, Cox, however, if we are to better the enemy we must forget our finer feelings and go forwards together."

I just caved in and closed my eyes in surrender. What can you do with him? I thought, saying nothing but an occasional 'yes' as he droned on. He was having his say. He always did and, as usual, I closed my eyes and ears until he had finished.

Outside, the sergeant came up to me and pointed out something I had missed.

"On the floor of the tunnel to the outside I saw congealing blood spots in the dirt. You could hardly see them in the dark. Someone must be hurt and leaking blood. Looks like you scored a hit, Cox."

"Yeah," I said, thinking fast. "I wonder if there are any

more spots on the outside of the tunnel. I might find some sort of trail if he keeps on bleeding."

I climbed back up to the tunnel exit, leaving Jeannie on the phone to one of her friends, and weaved in and out of the bushes, searching for any telltale stains. Immediately I saw a red smudge on a leaf several feet from the tunnel and looked around for another to draw a line in the direction in which he was heading. I found more, with a pool of congealed blood where he had stopped for a rest. Farther on I found a blood-soaked shirt sleeve and more blood stains on the ground, and I knew I was gaining on the wounded man.

Within half an hour I found him sitting down propped up by the tree trunk of a tall ash. Although my footfalls were light on the lush grass growing around, he heard me and raised a sunken face, it changing to a fierce grimace as his hand shot to his pocket and plunged inside. Seeing his intention I leaped across the distance between us and grabbed his wrist as the gun emerged clutched in his hand. He yelled loudly and aimed a bunched fist at my face as I twisted his arm, but he missed by a mile and took a punch in return, which caught him flush on the nose. I wrenched the pistol from his grip and stepped back with the gun on him, watching as he tried to sniff back the gushing blood coming from his nose.

"You scumbag, I want to know where Branden is making for," I demanded. "You tell me the truth and I'll get you a doctor."

He squinted at me through a waterfall of tears, trying to stem the dribbles of blood coming through the cracks between his fingers as well as dash the tears away.

"You can go to hell!" he shouted, gritting his teeth against the pain. "You'll get nothing outta me."

His right trouser leg was saturated with congealed blood, so I guessed the bullet had hit him high in the thigh. I concentrated on that area by putting my foot on the wound and twisting in a clockwise motion. He immediately screamed in a high-pitched voice and tried to dislodge my foot by pulling at my trousers. I twisted again and the blood shot out from beneath my shoe accompanied by a blood curdling scream that rang through the trees and frightened a flock of wood pigeons nesting above.

"You tell me, you stinking bastard! Tell me or I'll kill you where you sit, you whore's bastard."

To add weight to my threat I cocked the pistol and levelled it at him six inches away from his left eye. His eyes opened wide, despite the tears, and he stared up the open end of the barrel. He swallowed a gob of restricting spit and cried in a piteous way.

"I daren't tell you. Branden will kill me," he whined.

"He'll be in prison for the next thirty years, so how can he harm you?" I argued. "Now talk or I'm going to pull the trigger... Talk, you bastard, talk or I'll..."

I pushed the gun against his forehead and pretended to press the trigger. He closed his eyes in fright and sound gushed from his mouth.

"OK, OK, I'll tell you what you want to know only don't kill me."

A stream of watery blood slowly drooled from the corner of his mouth, joining the thicker variety that was seeping from the wreckage of a badly flattened nose, running in two lines down his chin and dripping onto a sodden jacket. As I watched, a hideous blood bubble formed and foamed at his lips, growing in size until it suddenly popped leaving a blood red stain on his two liver coloured lips.

"He's on his way to a house in the Thames estuary from where a friend will take him to Ireland in a small boat." He coughed and clutched at his thigh, twisting his features into a look of pain. "It-it's been arranged like this for a long time," he stammered, holding his leg.

"And where is this house situated?" I demanded, pushing the gun harder against his skin. "Give me the area."

The man grimaced as another spasm of pain knifed into the wound.

"Gimme a break, will ya," he moaned, coughing up bright red blood.

I was beyond giving compassion to a terrorist and swiped the barrel of the gun in a scything motion down the angle of his chin.

"Now," I spat, watching the new wound spout fresh blood, "are you going to give me the whereabouts or am I going to beat you to a pulp with this gun?"

The IRA man screamed with pain and terror, raising his hands above his head to ward off expected blows. Tears coursed down his ruddy cheeks, mixing with the bloody flow coming from his mangled face.

"Don't hit me any more," he pleaded, as I raised the gun. "The place is on the edge of a small village called Wycliffe, a few miles from Whitstable."

"How do I know you are telling the truth?" I demanded, listening to him snuffling on his own blood.

"It's the truth I tell ya, anyway, Branden's gone and left me in the shit, so why should I protect him? Now, get a doctor will ya, I'm bleeding to death here and the pain's killing me."

I straightened up pocketing the gun then reached down and pushed him against the tree.

"You stay there and don't move. I'll get a doctor to see you before long," I said.

I left him there and listened to his moans, which gradually became weaker as I put distance between us.

The captain heard what I had to say and dispatched a first aid man to help the wounded gunman.

"Did you get anything out of him?" he asked, watching the soldier run off up the incline.

I ran a hand over the rasp of my beard and thought of Jeannie. She was nowhere in sight and the captain's enquiry remained unanswered as I looked in every direction for her.

"If you are looking for the lady, she got a lift in our helicopter," the captain said, with a smile. "She said she's got some urgent business with a lady in prison. That right?"

"Suppose it is," I said, picking my lip thoughtfully then realising what I had to do. "Captain, I think I know where Branden has run to," I said. "I need someone whom I can rely on in an emergency, in case anything goes wrong," I continued, having noticed his look of interest.

"If I can help in any way, you only have to ask," he said, watching me.

"I'm about to depart to pick up Branden's trail. He's hiding in a village in Kent and before long will escape to the Irish free state and disappear I reckon."

"That he will if given half the chance."

"Well, I'm not giving him the chance. I'm out to scotch his plans before he has the opportunity to escape. I want you to organise a force to back me up if the going gets rough."

"Count on me."

"Good, I knew I could."

Later on I found my car where I'd left it and turned the nose in the general direction of Whitstable. The car hummed in reply to my insistence on the accelerator and, with little effort, sped along the short distance to the seaside town.

In the gathering gloom I made out the way to the village of Wycliffe with the aid of a tilting signpost, and squealed to a halt in the middle of a small tree lined square. The odour of fish hung in the air and the hiss of the estuary tides came from behind a row of granite and red brick terraced houses. I stepped from my car and headed for a lit building on the other side of the square and, pushing open the glass door, entered the stuffy atmosphere of a fish and chip shop. I nodded in reply to the woman's greeting and spoke jovially.

"How are you, darling?"

She smiled, flashing a surprising set of perfectly formed teeth.

"Not so bad," she replied, wrapping a large parcel of cod and chips in a tight bundle and putting it down on the greasy counter. "What can I do for you, sunshine?" she asked with a smile.

I was feeling famished. The sight and smell of so much food within reach and emitting such delicious odours caused my stomach to groan, and it replied with a loud belch that caused her to snigger.

"Sounds like you can do with it, love," she laughed.

I ordered a large portion of cod and chips while trying to ignore the saliva that came to my tongue and lips as the delicious flavour of the cooked food invaded my nostrils with its fragrant aroma. It was then I felt in my pockets and realised to my embarrassment that I was flat broke. I gave her a rueful smile and inwardly kicked myself.

"I can't pay you, I'm afraid, I haven't any money," I confessed.

She stood there searching my face, trying to see if I was genuine. She must have seen something because after the scrutiny she broke into a smile.

"That's OK, honey, I've got plenty of people who owe me money, so another one to add to the slate won't make all that amount of difference. You pop it in later when you're flush," she said.

The hot food was burning a hole in my hands as I carried it over to my car. The salt covering the fish and chips stung the open cuts on my mouth and lips, and nursed them until the food slowly cooled. As I munched away, my mind was racing, trying to recall the words of the IRA man who had given me the information. A house, he had said, a house a few miles from the seaside town of Whitstable. As I mused I realised I was at a dead end. I sighed at the thought. A dead end! I was in Wycliffe, but the trail was growing colder by the minute. I sat there undecided, looking in the rear-view mirror, eyeing the way I had entered the village and viewing the prospect of tracking back to Branden's bolt hole in the country.

A movement caught my eye. Into the reflection floated the square shape of a big black saloon car. It was slowing to a halt outside the illuminated fish and chip shop window. It stood there for a moment silently then two muffled figures got out and entered the shop, their black shadows striping the gleam of the lit glass. My heart leapt as I recognised the vehicle as one I had seen at the country mansion. So, I thought, the rats are turning up to join the rest of the pack. They are swarming to their leader, Branden, king rat himself. I could barely smother a laugh as I pictured their misbegotten loyalty.

"Now, if I'm not too wrong, with a little bit of luck they will lead me to Mr Branden," I whispered to myself.

My car was in the shadows cast by a tall office building and with the gloom offered by an unlit lamp post it was almost invisible to the eye. I waited with nerves almost stretched to breaking point before the two figures made an appearance, clutching paper parcels. Within seconds the car pulled away from the shop, silently gathering speed as it passed me, the black gleam of the paintwork flashing in the lamplight as it glided by. It headed out of the square, its faint tail lights growing dim as the saloon increased speed with hardly a murmur from the engine.

Gritting my teeth, I waited as the car disappeared from view then, ever so slowly, let in the clutch and watched the shadows pass by on either side. I squeezed the accelerator with the ball of my foot and felt the car answer my call as the revs increased. I couldn't use the headlights, but the moon was full and bright, so the road was a dull grey ribbon that wound away along the estuary riverside. For several miles I watched the red lights ahead. The road was empty of traffic and rapidly becoming smaller as it narrowed.

I cursed as I nearly ended up in a ditch that suddenly came out of nowhere. With a grinding of gears and swishing of pebbles hitting the bodywork I righted the car with a sideways wrench of the steering wheel and brought the swaying vehicle under control. During my tussle with the car I hit my head on the dashboard and, feeling rather dazed, pulled the car up, engine racing and roaring, swearing and cursing my luck. I got out of the car and swore a bit more when I saw the flat tyre that was the result of my encounter with the ditch.

The red light had long gone and I visualised the harrowing thought that I would have to spend the night at the side of the road. I settled down on the hard rear seat and was just about to close my eyes when dancing shadows on the rear window instantly brought me back to reality. A mousy-haired woman in a mini drove into view. She eyed me with some trepidation when she saw my scarred face, but when she saw the bleeding cut on my forehead she offered to take me to Whitstable, her destination.

I managed to persuade her to lend me twenty pounds and after I found a room for the night in a guest house and doctored my cuts in the bathroom mirror, I fell onto the double bed and was soon fast asleep.

I had a dreamless night. A distant church bell chimed the hour of nine o'clock and I cursed my laxity by not having breakfast. I found a telephone box and called Lawrence. The rasping voice grated in my ear once again.

"I need a car," I shouted at the receiver. "Mine ended up in a ditch. It had a puncture."

"Haven't you got a spare?" he countered, burping loudly.

"Yes, but-"

I ended the conversation as, with a sigh of baffled fury, I smashed the receiver back onto its rest and slammed the telephone box door. After promising the earth by way of the government and a long drawn-out promissory note, I was able to drive the car, but it was after one o'clock before I could make a start. Another worry became apparent when I checked the petrol gauge; it showed half-full and I had to go back to my room to raid the bank.

I pulled a face in the driving mirror, for every time the engine missed a beat my heart did also. After each jump of my system, I instantly thought, petrol! That is how car and driver struggled on in unison and uncertainty through London's winding streets, with me praying for a little more mileage and hardly daring to touch the accelerator. There was a thin film of perspiration on my brow as I frequently cast worried looks into the mirror, waiting and hoping for a miracle to happen.

As I neared my flat the familiar shopping area came into view, and my hopes soared to new heights until I turned the corner into my road and pulled up outside the building where I lived. I say 'lived' because my front door was hanging from one hinge and the façade of the building was a mass of bricks, plaster and dust.

CHAPTER TWENTY-EIGHT

I knew what had happened instantly. Branden or one of his henchmen had planted a device and the result was chaos. I thanked my lucky stars I had not been at home at the time. It left me with nowhere to stay, which is what was invading my thoughts when Jeannie made an appearance.

"They certainly made a mess of things," she said with a shallow smile. "You'll just have to come and stay with me."

Jeannie got into my car and we filled up at the nearest petrol station just around the corner.

Jeannie produced a key and entered her flat. She dangled a leg over the side of a low slung settee and took out a packet of cigarettes. She didn't offer me one as I didn't smoke.

"Did you get anywhere at the seaside?" she asked.

"No luck, Branden got clean away," I replied, shaking my head and dropping down to sit beside her, "after I lost them in Kent. They just up and vanished into thin air."

I burst a frustrated knot of air from my lungs and, with a deep sigh, closed my eyes.

"Did you call Lawrence?"

I shook my head and opened my eyes.

"I did, but no soap."

"Did you ask him?"

"I didn't give him a chance to talk. You know what he's like. Ignorant bastard wouldn't give me a car."

"What's your next move?" Jeannie enquired.

"I've got to find out where the next arms dump is."

"Perhaps he has gone to Frog Island light-"

"Where's that?" I interjected.

"It's a lighthouse on the south coast, I think."

I was all ears. Jeannie hadn't mentioned anything about a lighthouse before, and no one else had spoken of it.

"Whereabouts on the south coast," I quizzed her.

"I'm not sure," she said, wrinkling her brow. "My friend in Wandsworth will know."

The warden at Wandsworth eyed us both and almost baulked when he knew what we wanted.

"It's highly irregular," he said, fussing and shuffling papers on his desk. "I know it is official business, but it's still highly irregular. She's not allowed visitors. She is a dangerous member of the IRA."

He rang a bell on his desk and waited, drumming his fingertips on the hard wooden surface of the desk top. The office door opened and a man in a blue uniform entered.

"Take them to twenty-four will you, Watson."

We passed through several iron doors, the officer leading the way. Shortly he stopped before a matching iron door that he unlocked with a huge key. He waited until we were inside before slamming the door shut behind us. Jeannie threw her arms around the neck of the woman sitting on the bed, whispering into her ear as she did so. After they had finished cuddling each other they turned to me.

"This is Bill, Ellen, the one I've told you about." Jeannie came over to me and held my arm. "He's come here to ask you where the lighthouse is located."

Ellen was older than Jeannie. I'd say she was approaching sixty. She looked me square in the eyes, unflinching.

"Did you say you would help if I give you the thing you need?"

I stood there meeting her gaze, liking what I saw.

"I'll do all I can to get you out of here," I answered truthfully. "I've heard all about you, so there's no call to be frightened of me. I desperately need to know the location of the Frog Island light. You know all about Branden and his gang of cut-throats, so you see I'm doing it for the good of the country to get rid of men like him."

She looked hard at me, deep into my eyes without blinking.

"Please," I pleaded, returning the look, "you're my last hope. Don't let your country down."

Ellen tore her eyes away with just a small tear starting to appear at the corner of her eye. She gazed at Jeannie as she whispered.

"Very well, I'll do as you ask. Just be true with me as I am with you."

I caught my breath as she revealed the location of the Frog Island lighthouse.

"It's on the Goodwin Sands at Deal in Kent," she said,

her voice husky with emotion. "It's on a small island in the bay, on a rock shaped like a frog. It was abandoned, so it was taken over by the army. Branden uses it to store contraband goods and it's also an arsenal for a massive stockpile of arms and ammunition, all with the same method of destruction should it be penetrated by an outsider." She paused to look at Jeannie before continuing. "I have had time to reflect on my involvement with the army. I've also been doing a lot of thinking about how I have given my life to it. I bitterly regret many of the things I had to do in the name of the army. Now I have the means to right some of them by revealing where the arms are hidden. That is why I'm doing it, Jeannie, just pure and utter conscience, nothing more."

Jeannie smiled at the older woman and took her in her arms.

"I know exactly how you feel, Ellen," she whispered. "That is why I'm doing it as well."

"Now, that is one great lady. She had the sense to get out while the getting out was good. If only the others were as understanding," I said, on the way back to Jeannie's flat.

I knew my first duty was to inform Lawrence without delay, but because of my recent brush with the boss I was reluctant to confide in the fat fool. I was keen to go it alone and see if the lighthouse was all it was cracked up to be. True, I had the location of the sixth arms dump and by rights should call for back-up, but I had to see for myself. I had to make sure the plum was right for the picking. Branden and I also had to resume where we had left off. I still had to settle old scores with regard to the bomb to which he had tied me, and I relished the thought of having one last go at the terrorist.

I then had a stroke of luck. I was leaving Jeannie's when I happened to bump into a rat faced individual. I instantly recognised the shifty face as being that of Soames, the erstwhile park official. He caught sight of me at the same time and tried to dodge aside to avoid me. Quick as a flash I grabbed him by the throat and held him in a tight grip.

"Well, well, who have we here? " I said triumphantly. "I'll be jiggered if it ain't Mr Soames!" I continued with mock surprise.

I tightened the grip on his throat, digging my fingers into the delicate flesh of his airway. His whitened face blanched a shade paler as my fingertips squeezed, shutting off the air supply to his lungs.

"Well, Mr Soames, good to meet you again. What did you say? Speak up, I can't hear you!" I relaxed my grip on his throat and waited as he gasped in precious oxygen. "Well now, that's better." I pulled out my automatic and waved it in his face. "Now, Mr Soames, a few queries. Where's Branden?" I grated.

I waited as his heavy breathing eased and subsided before I spoke again.

"Quickly now, or it will be your last lungful of air. Where's Branden?"

"Go to hell!" Soames yelled, and then screamed as the barrel of my gun bounced off the bridge of his nose. "You broke my nose," he snuffled as the blood started to flow.

"It'll be your neck if you don't come up with the right kind of answers."

"I don't know," he said through blood and tears.

"Who bombed my flat?"

"Me and another guy called Devlin. We acted on Branden's orders. Devlin set the bomb – I had nothing to do with it."

Soames was panting from the force of his confession, dabbing at the wreck of his nose and swallowing blood as it slowly oozed out of the wound. He gazed at me with incredulity as I related all I knew about the arms dump at the lighthouse.

"Now there's just one more missing," I rasped. "I need to know the location of arms dump number seven and you are going to tell me, aren't you?" I waved the gun in his face and he turned a few shades paler as he looked down the barrel of my gun. "Aren't you?" I persisted, and lowered the automatic, aiming at his feet.

I squeezed the trigger, the gun emitted a small report and the bullet struck the ground an inch from his big right toe. He yelled and stepped back, watching as I drew a bead on his left foot and waited for his reaction. It wasn't slow in coming for he screamed in fright.

"All right, I'll tell you. It's in the wall of the foot tunnel at Greenwich. We had the job of repairing it after the bombing during the Second World War. We did it during the time it took to do the repairs. We also moved the arms in during that time."

"How do I know you are telling me the truth? How do I find the position of the arms dump?"

"Honest, mister, I'm being straight. The place where the room is located is found by a different sized tile. A difference of just an inch so it wouldn't be noticed, that's all."

I greeted his words with jubilation. It looked like my search for the arms dump was at an end. I celebrated by clubbing him over the skull with the gun. More blood, but this time it gushed out from a gash in his head as he hit the deck. It spread in a widening pool, staining the ground near his head.

Several horrified bystanders witnessed the scene. I treated them to a casual wave as I stepped over Soames' prostrate form and strode away.

In less than an hour my car was nosing into a car park in riverside Greenwich, and within minutes the bulbous shape of a glazed cupola broke the skyline.

We entered the lift and waited as the slow descent started. The floor of the tunnel came up to meet us and the lift doors opened. At first sight the tunnel was impressive; sloping away in a blaze of light and glittering tiles, and disappearing into the seemingly endless distance and infinity.

"Looks like we walk from here," I grated.

With Jeannie following behind, I set out to walk the distance to the exit in North London, treading from one pool of light to the next, sniffing the close air and listening to our footfalls echoing about us as we moved. About three-quarters of the way there I noticed that the tunnel had narrowed, so slowed down to examine the tiles around me. The search was slow and painstaking. The job was endless, or seemed to be. The tunnel stretched away into the distance with light reflections bouncing off the walls. Our shadows danced around us as we moved, flickering and twisting to the insistence of the overhead lighting.

Several other people went by, treating us to curious stares.

"Is it leaking?" one jovial soul quipped.

We went on looking, ignoring the stares, searching for the tile with the inch overhang. Suddenly we found it, or rather Jeannie did.

"I've got it!" she announced excitedly. "Or rather I think I have."

One inch bigger than the others... I measured it with the tape just to make sure. It was hardly noticeable, but it was there.

"No wonder it escaped detection all these years," I said. "No one noticed the difference." I picked at my lip in thought. "Lawrence will have to keep the public out while we examine the walls. If the dump is there we will need tools to get at the room behind."

Lawrence was informed and we were given permission to do it. We looked at the tile and wondered just where we were to run if the damned thing did explode.

"Well, let's get on with it," I said through pursed lips.

I picked up the drill and switched it on. The machine echoed through the tunnel in a rending crash, tearing at the tiles and entering the tunnel lining behind. Suddenly the drill was banging on steel as a heavy metal door was exposed. Bit by bit steel nuts came into view as the false wall was uncovered. It was just a thin layer of cement and sand, meant to fool everybody. I changed the drill for a shifting spanner and attacked the nuts. Surprisingly they came off easily, leaving the steel plate hanging on the bolts. I cautiously eased off the plate, standing it aside with care. There was the usual gap before the inner plate, with the hand hole for a hand to be inserted to stop the explosive mechanism.

Realising it was Jeannie's turn to try her luck I turned to her with a tight grin.

"It's your turn, sweetheart, good luck and don't make too much of a bang."

She laughed nervously and stepped inside as I stepped out, giving me another half-hearted grin.

"Let's hope I don't," she said in a husky voice. Slowly, but deliberately, she put her hand into the hole. "I can feel the bottle – it's awkward – been tipped over... I've got it – no I haven't – it's slipped. I'll try again. I've got it – it's coming now. Now, easy does it – eeaassyy! Ha!" She brought the bottle to light dangling the thing from between her fingers right before my eyes. "I've got the sodding thing!" she exclaimed.

I sensed her joy and kissed her, letting her put the bottle down safely on the tunnel floor.

"What about the other things?"

"You mean the arms and ammunition?"

"That's what I meant, sweetheart. What are we going to do about the guns?" I asked.

"Leave them there. There's no danger now. Leave it to the back-up team to clear up. Give them something to do."

I laughed loudly at Jeannie's summing up of the situation and, getting into the spirit of the occasion, she echoed my laughter with a sigh of relief and a laugh of her own. Sweat was running down her forehead and dripped off her nose; testament to the strain she had been under. I decided to put that right without further delay.

"Would you like to join me in getting something to eat, I'm starving?"

Her response was instant.

"Me too, my stomach thinks my throat's been cut!"

We left the tools, room and guns to whoever was coming after us and headed for the nearest restaurant where we quickly ordered two huge platefuls of steaming hot eggs and chips. We attacked the food and drink with amazing gusto for about ten minutes. I finished by draining my cup of the remaining dregs and ended my meal by emitting a loud and self-satisfied belch.

"I really enjoyed that, I think you did too," Jeannie said, giggling.

The conversation clouded as she spoke about Branden and of her friend languishing in jail.

"Let's hope your boss, Lawrence, will speak up for Ellen and of the way she has helped against Branden," she finished off.

"I'm sure he will," I agreed. "I'll try to keep him to his word, I promise."

We headed for the car and, as it was nearly dark, I switched on the headlights. I was about to drive away when I saw a faint shadow detach itself from a clump of close-meshing shrubs. I was instantly alerted to the danger of reprisals.

"Get out, Jeannie – get out quick!"

Jeannie, taken aback, hesitated.

"Get out *now!*" I shouted, pushing her towards the car door.

She fumbled with the lock and tumbled out of the car, cursing me as she fell. I wrenched the driver's door open and rolled out, calling her to follow as I headed for the car park fence. I dropped behind a solid looking tree and pulled her down with me, covering her face with my arm.

Suddenly the car exploded with an ear-shattering bang that echoed around the car park and surrounding countryside. We crouched behind the tree, sheltering from the shower of missiles that rained down on us. Things subsided as the smoke began to clear so regaining my feet I helped Jeannie up.

"Sorry about that," she apologised.

She was talking to thin air as I shot from the trees heading for the spot where I had noticed the shadow in the bushes. As things settled down the car creaked in its death throes and I realised he had vanished as I knew he would. As I stood undecided, Jeannie's hand stole into mine, squeezing with a gentle pressure that was designed to convey comfort and love. I could see the vehicle was heading for the scrapheap, which was obvious. I resigned myself to the fact that I would have to do a lot of walking, which was also obvious.

"Got any money?" I asked.

We both searched our pockets producing only five pounds, thirty pence, not enough for the train fare, but just enough to call Lawrence, which I did right away. Lawrence was missing and his underling, a man called Walker, answered instead. He appeared sympathetic to our situation, listening to me rather than blustering like his boss.

"I'll send someone to pick you up," he said at the end of our conversation.

Imagine Lawrence doing that, I thought.

We arrived home and went to bed.

I was awakened by the phone ringing its head off. Jeannie answered it and could hardly speak as the receiver constantly crackled in her ear.

"What's wrong?" I enquired, perturbed by her manner.

Ashen faced she sat down on the bed, staring straight ahead as she related all that had been said.

"It's Ellen, she's been found poisoned. She had a visitor, they said. It was then the fatal dose was administered."

Jeannie's eyes were brimming over and she refused any offer of compassion I ventured.

"If she hadn't helped you she would be alive today," she said, speaking in a whisper as though talking to herself. "She was just like a mother to me. She brought me up from the age of ten; washed me, fed me and sent me to school, although I was almost out of control. She even gave me her own bed to sleep in, that's what kind of woman she was. I will miss her terribly," she said, lapsing into inconsolable sobs.

I could have added that Ellen had passed on her prejudices and hates, even belonging to an organisation that was ensconced in terrorism to the extreme and specialised in killing innocent people, bombing dumb animals and destroying homes and churches. I could have said these things, but didn't, because of the effect it would have had on her. Instead, I waited for the crying to subside, trying to understand her feelings of regret.

Rightfully, I can expect no help from her now, I thought. If I was going to carry on I would have to do it without Jeannie. The realisation depressed me, but I had to continue, so I shook off my melancholy state, said a one-sided goodbye and set out to get myself another car.

The vehicle cost me three hundred pounds, which I withdrew from the bank, plus another hundred quid for insurance. I also purchased a map of Kent that showed the area around Deal. I studied it for awhile, especially where it showed anything to do with the Goodwin Sands.

I spent an uncomfortable night in the back of the car and was glad to see the sunrise push red rays through the glass window. The car had a tank full of petrol, so there was no problem about fuel. With that in mind I twisted the ignition key around and started the engine. It opened up, sweet as a bird, humming and singing as the gas pedal was pushed. I turned on the radio and whistled to the tune coming over the airwaves. I slipped into gear and the car slid away from the kerb.

With all due certainty, I was on my way at last – on my way to the final showdown with Branden. I was heading for the confrontation and it cheered me up, to the extent that it made me laugh at the thought. I whistled even louder. The red rays glinted in my eyes and the car gathered speed. The tyres sang a song of retribution, which is what I had in mind.

The open fields of Kent rolled by, helping me to focus my thoughts. I had to square up to Branden at the lighthouse, and he knew it. That was why he was making preparations to quit; running scared before the authorities caught him. He was frightened because he knew his number was up, and alarmed that his privileged life was coming to an end. He was running because he knew he had done wrong, but most of all because he was head of an organisation that advocated and openly encouraged terrorism.

Returning to reality, I wrestled my thoughts back to the present and watched the road as it rolled under the wheels. The roads were full, but not overfull. The morning was cold with a thin mist clearing as the weak sun got to work on it. I was tearing down the A2 past Rochester, Faversham and then on to Canterbury where I called a halt. I stopped at a small roadside café, wolfing down a bacon sandwich and coffee before resuming my journey.

The sun was up and overhead before Deal came over the horizon. I pulled up and sat on a patch of grass just looking at the place. It was classed as a market town with close associations with the Royal Marines, it being a garrison town. It was also close to the notorious Goodwin Sands, the area of shifting sand shelves that constantly changed with the ebb and flow of the tides.

I first saw the lighthouse in the distance as I drew closer. The bay was littered with exposed shipwrecks and light vessels that strained at anchor. The sand stretched for miles, glittering in the sunlight, but I was not interested in the geography of the place, my interest centred solely on the lighthouse and its position in the scenario affecting me. The tower was supported by a huge rock that closely resembled a crouching frog. It extended high into the air and exhibited weather-beaten brickwork telling of the violent storms that affected the area. A single dirt track tied the lighthouse to the shore.

I headed north, keeping the image of the lighthouse in my windscreen as it shifted from left to right. I steered through the outskirts of Deal proper until the tower appeared gigantic and awesome then stopped the car in the shelter of a deserted cottage close by. I got out and was able to observe the obelisk and all it revealed, from behind the corner of the cottage. The tower seemed innocent enough, showing signs of being deserted. The absence of any human agency seemed to add to its general air of neglect and abandonment. I peered out from behind a bush, making sure of my ground, searching for any sign of movement. There was none, so I relaxed and hid the car from sight behind the cottage, waiting for nightfall.

It was just getting dark when the hum of an engine disturbed the evening air. A carefully light-shielded lorry appeared out of the gloom, heading for the tower. There was little noise as it made for the causeway connecting the lighthouse to the shore, showing no evidence of what it contained or from where it had come. It approached the tower and was lost to view in the gathering dusk. It was then that I earnestly yearned for the back-up I had ignored and wondered if I was right in confronting the gang on my own. Shrugging, I dismissed the thought from my mind and waited for the tide to turn before thinking of my next move.

I had noticed a small dinghy moored to the jetty by the causeway and I earmarked it to convey me to the seaward side of the island. I consulted my luminious watch, deciding it was now or never. I checked my gun and the several spare clips of ammunition I was carrying before I set out, making for the boat. It was ancient, but seaworthy, and also hard to shift. As I untied it the tide was coming in under the planking, beginning to exert lift. I waited as the water provided buoyancy before I pushed out into open water.

The sea was calm with only little wavelets rocking the boat, producing a calming motion. I dug in the oars and splashed them awkwardly, prompting me to say under my breath:

"This won't do."

So thinking, I carefully eased the paddles into the water trying to avoid splashing. Slowly, hugging the shoreline of the causeway, I laboured at the unaccustomed dipping and rowing, pausing now and again to listen for any unusual sound. There was none. The light wind trod on the furrowing waves, smoothing out the undulating ripples into a series of gently heaving hollows. I slowly moved into the bay, approaching the seaward side of the lighthouse with gentle sweeps of the oars.

Very soon the black hulk of the island appeared out of the darkness and I gently eased the dinghy into a small rocky inlet, pulling the craft away from the waterline as far as I was able. I crunched on sand and shingle, then onto solid rock, and used tufts of coarse grass growing in rocky clefts as handholds. I pulled myself upwards, constantly keeping the lighthouse tower in view. The building was as black as night and showed not a glimmer of light, for all the world seeming deserted as it was meant to be. I forced a wry grin at this contradiction, recalling the lorry and its driver. I heaved my bulk over a large piece of Frog Island and found myself at the beginning of a stretch of wildly tangled coarse grass and seaweed that ran to and ended at the foot of the tower.

Slowly and softly, keeping the observation window of the lighthouse under intense scrutiny, I threaded my way through the obstacles, stumbling over hidden rocks at every yard. Painfully I finally extricated my feet from the last bit of clinging vegetation and was able to stand at the base of the tower, ears attuned for any danger, ready for any intervention.

CHAPTER TWENTY-NINE

The gentle dark closed in around me. There was no noise except a distant foghorn from the Goodwin Sands lightship, periodically blaring its forlorn message to the unwary. With the sound came the brilliant sweep of the light sending its rays across the dangerous waters of the sands. Once in every period it bathed the power in its dazzling light, then left it to wallow in intense gloom until the next ray reached it.

I had to gain access to the tower, so I gradually eased my body around the curve, during the blackness, slipping and sliding on the seaweed and flotsam brought in by the tide. I was in the process of dodging the light when I heard voices; male and female, faint, but audible. I froze instantly, pressing hard against the discoloured skin of the concrete rendering, my hand immediately going for the gun in my pocket. Hardly daring to breathe, I edged closer to the voices trying to see to whom they belonged. I gripped my gun until the steel hurt my fingers. The voices slowly faded away, leaving me sweating profusely and blowing with relief. I waited until silence had reigned for a minute before I continued my sliding actions.

A lorry, the one I had witnessed earlier, loomed up before me. I was tempted to look inside, but was put off by a tightly lashed canvas sheet fixed to the metal framework. I turned my attention to a yawning opening at the base of the tower. It led into a huge room running to the extreme sides of the tower and big enough to house several vehicles. I stepped inside, my gun ready to fire, finger just poised on the trigger. The silence disturbed me after the sound of the voices. I felt vaguely agitated, as I wanted to get to Branden and finish the job. Waiting was alien to me as was the silence.

I trod the first step of a flight of stone steps leading upwards, circling the tower with soft footfalls that hardly disturbed the countless years of neglect and dust. I went through a trapdoor to the first floor and entered a wooden-floored room that had a passageway with several rooms running off it. I pushed on one door and met with the silence of an empty room. I was just about to enter the second room when the door opened outwards, framing a fat man who was, to say the least, shocked to his socks. His jaw dropped and his eyes protruded with surprise. He saw my levelled gun pointing at his flabby belly and started to tremble with fear. I backed him into the room by prodding him with the barrel.

There was also another man in the room, who stared at the suddenness of my appearance. He suddenly sprang for a pistol that was lying on a polished table. I shot him easily, and waited as the smoke snaked up into the atmosphere of the room then watched him slump to the floor. I eyed the first man with a look of intense malevolence, murder in my eyes.

"I'm not armed," he said, quaking with fear. "Don't shoot me, mister, please."

The man on the floor twitched and was still, blood issuing from his chest and mouth.

"Where's Branden?" I snarled.

"I don't know," he replied, eyeing the body on the floor. "We're alone here and-"

I hit him in the face with the gun barrel.

""Don't lie to me, I know different. Where's the woman?" I rasped.

He was spitting out blood and teeth. He whined with pain and fright.

"She's upstairs," he blurted out. "She's cooking supper for the two of us – well, me."

He was looking at his dead mate and trying to stop the flow from his own wound with a ragged tea towel. I patted his pockets looking for guns.

"If you want to live," I growled, "just do exactly what I tell you to do, you understand?"

He nodded, spitting out more blood.

"Don't kill me, Mr Cox," he stammered. "I was just doing my job."

"So you know my name?"

"We have been told to expect you," he said, snuffling through broken teeth. "We got the know-how from Ellen in prison. She said she told you about this place."

"And now I'm right here right now," I finished for him, "just in time to catch you lot scarpering." I prodded with the gun barrel and my mood changed to a threatening one. "Now, you do as I tell you and you'll be OK."

He nodded, dribbling watery blood and staring at me. I strode to the door and looked out in both directions before nodding to him. I repeated the action at the head of the second floor, pushing him in front of me. He led the way into a small kitchen where a blonde-haired woman was in the act of breaking an egg into a pan. She gazed at me, fascinated by the gun and the wounded man, equally spellbound by the damage to his features. Using a length of clothes line I found in the kitchen, I tied them to each other.

"Now, that will shut you up for awhile," I said with a thin smile, and waited for Branden to show up, reloading the gun with fresh ammunition.

Half an hour later, Branden did show up surrounded by a dozen men, all armed to the teeth with handguns and automatic weapons. He smirked as he called to me from the shelter of his vehicle.

"Cox, you are advised to give up. You are outnumbered. I promise you'll go free if you give up now."

"I've got two of your gang with me. I could kill them," I shouted back from the kitchen window.

Branden gave a hoarse laugh.

"Go ahead, they're expendable."

"Don't think I won't," I vowed, ducking out of sight as a bullet smacked against the tower wall. "You had your chance to give up, but you blew it," I yelled. "Now it's fifty years in jail for you and those who follow you."

"I don't think so. You know why? Well, I have insurance. You know what kind of insurance?" he asked, laughing again.

"I don't want to know about your insurance," I bellowed, dodging another bullet.

He laughed once more, but louder.

"You will when I show you my kind of insurance."

A struggling figure was pulled to the front of the group and a rag gag was roughly removed. I gave a gasp of horror as the familiar features of Jeannie stared back at me. Branden continued in a cold voice.

"I told you I have my insurance. You wouldn't listen. All right, I give you just five minutes to think it over then we shoot Jeannie. Is that clear?"

My heart sank. Branden had the whip hand and he knew it. There was no alternative. I had to give in for Jeannie's sake and he also knew that. I ground my teeth together in abject rage.

He tried to hurry things along.

"You have just one minute remaining."

As the seconds ticked by I thought about shooting him from a distance. I brushed the thought aside as he guessed my plan by stepping behind his hostage. As for his threat to kill Jeannie, he had nothing to lose. He was ruthless enough to do it. Sadly I was out-fought and I realised as much by shouting:

"I'm coming down."

I freed my own prisoners and made my way to the ground floor, giving up my weapon to the waiting gang as they crowded around. Branden laughed in my face as he prevented one of the gang from finishing me off with a bullet.

"Save that for later, I want him to suffer a bit first," he said.

We were bundled up the tower steps and locked in the first room I had discovered.

"Well, well," I said, grinning down at Jeannie, "back to square one. It seems like we are always locked up together."

Jeannie showed her teeth as she copied my smile.

"It's all my fault," she said frowning. "If I hadn't been so pig-headed and tried to blame you for everything, none of this would have happened."

I tried to reassure her by cupping her face in my hands and kissing her.

"It's not your fault, love," I said. "They killed Ellen and will pay dearly for it, I can promise you that."

"Well, what about us? They mean to kill us too before leaving."

"I've heard that one before," I sneered.

Jeannie turned away, smiling at my attempt to be belligerent, knowing full well I was a gentle soul really."

"Even you with your phenomenal luck and fortitude are no match for a dozen men with guns. They would soon overwhelm and kill you, even use torture."

I drew in a big sigh.

"We will see, shall we? I've been threatened before, but nothing came of it."

I circled the room, eyeing the windowless walls and locked door.

"Nothing to use against them in an emergency," I said, "not even a chair."

Just then the door opened and swung aside. Branden stood in the doorway for awhile, filling it with his bulk, then entered with several men who gripped us tightly by the arms. He confronted me and I stared back at him as he leered into my face.

"Payback time, Cox, time to pay you back for all those arms places you stole from me and all the damage you caused. I assure you it won't be all that pleasant."

Branden nodded to his men, who tied our arms tightly behind our backs and gagged us with rags. He inspected the bonds and, with a nod of satisfaction, jerked his head in the direction of the door. They lead us downstairs, Jeannie stumbling on the uneven steps. They hauled us aboard the lorry and sat us on the cold floor, the men scowling at us. The engine started, jerking us forwards. I felt the tyres over rough ground and heard bushes slap against the canvas sides of the lorry.

I tested my restraints and groaned inwardly. The ropes gave no sign of any slack, so I tried reaching the knots, which I realised was impossible. There was no give and the rope was rubbing my chest raw. We rode for about half an hour before the lorry slowed to a halt, throwing us forwards. The men who had travelled in the back climbed over the tailboard, only pausing to grab us by the ropes and heave us off the vehicle.

Branden, who had sat in the front, led the way to a wooden shed that had a secure-looking padlock dangling from a metal hasp. Swinging the wooden door open wide, he roughly pulled me inside and pushed me to the floor with a kick to my leg that was meant to mean I was to sit. I dropped to the hay strewn floor and sat down. The shed had cracks in the panelling, enabling me to watch as Branden went out and pulled the door closed. The padlock rattled as they locked the door, leaving me in the semi-darkness, blinking as the hayseed dust motes rode on the shafts of weak sunlight.

I tried pulling at the ropes again. This time there was a

little slack, so I renewed my efforts and drew in a big breath as the ropes sawed at my skin. The ropes were as tight as ever, so I turned my attention to the gag. I worked it loose by twisting my head left and right. Now I could breathe more easily, which made the task less difficult. I stopped working at my bonds when I saw a glint in the strewn hay. I looked closer and saw a four-inch nail. Unable to believe my luck, I wriggled over to it and, turning, gripped it between my fingers, dropping it a couple of times before holding it securely. The sharp point dug into my skin several times and I reckoned the blood was flowing. I also stopped a few times to ease my aching hands.

I was able to twist my wrist a little after my efforts, or was I kidding myself? The encouragement of feeling a little free movement pushed me on to greater achievement. I was using the point to work against the coarse material, cutting one strand at a time, and within half an hour of constant struggle I was partially free. I tugged at the remaining restraints around my arms, pulling the rope loops free of my arms and wrists. I kicked them aside, exhausted.

I had no weapon except the nail and I examined it ruefully. I searched the shed for a stout stick and ended up with a length of wood two feet long. I used the rope to tie the nail to the stick and then tested my short spear by throwing it at the door. To my delight it penetrated the wood and quivered there. Now I had a weapon of sorts, which made me feel better. I retrieved the homemade weapon and gripped the shaft between my fingers, waiting for the first person to enter.

My second idea of the day occurred to me. I removed my shirt and stuffed it with hay, wrapping the rope ends around the dummy to give the impression of a bound figure. Standing at the edge of the door, I waited for someone to enter, heart pounding and nerves tingling. There was a noise as someone unlocked the padlock and I held the weapon before me, waiting for the door to open.

A figure stood in the doorway for a few seconds, checking the supposed prisoner. Evidently he was satisfied because he strode into the shed – the biggest mistake of his life. He stepped back in surprise, pulling the slung gun off his shoulder just as the four-inch nail penetrated his kidney. I scooped up the AK87 that he had let slide from trembling fingers and, holding the gun at the ready, leaped through the open doorway. I shot the first man in sight, running until I found a dense clump of trees and shrubs into which I immediately dived. Behind me all hell was breaking loose as the discovery of my escape was broadcast.

As I heard the general alarm I knew my immediate job was to rescue Jeannie. I racked my brains to search for the answer and it came in the shape of Branden, who was leading his men. He stood near the shed where I had been imprisoned, directing the men, and was temporarily alone as the gang followed his orders. I wasn't slow in seizing the opportunity and, quitting my hiding place, crept up and poked the gun in his back.

"One wrong move, Branden, and it'll be you last," I snarled.

I felt him stiffen.

"Well, not you *again*, Cox. You're getting to be a real thorn in my side. I meant what I said; the girl gets it if you don't surrender," he said.

"*Me* surrender? It looks like the boot is on the other foot. I've got a gun in your back, mate. If you don't do as I say I'll kill you – right away, *now*."

The gang members drifted back, eyeing their leader and the gun in his back. Undecided, they pointed guns at me, listening whilst Branden urged them to kill me, but I said I would kill him first. He berated them, calling them cowards and other such names. I shoved the gun into his back, so they could see I was not bluffing. It was no use threatening Branden, for he was still shouting for them to do something. I yelled for them to bring the woman out, and underlined it by firing into the air. Reluctantly they brought Jeannie out and stood by as the tables were turned.

Jeannie was shaken up, but managed to smile. With her behind me, I backed away from the gang still covering Branden whom I pulled by the belt. I could sense his impotent rage at the treatment. He was still raging at his men, who stood around in a circle, hearing him, but doing nothing because they knew I had the upper hand. I could have killed the master terrorist right where he stood, but I stilled my hand. I wanted the world to see him for what he was – a cold-hearted killer of people, who would stop at nothing to achieve his foul ends.

If anyone was to stop him, now was the time. I guess I was elected to do the job. If there was an odious man I was born to hate, it was Branden. He got under my skin and filled me with an itch to kill him. He was the type of man who, with his in-built arrogance, made it hard for me to finish him there, once and for all. I had to let him go. I had to care for Jeannie, so I pushed him hard with the tip of the gun.

"I'm letting you go this time," I snarled threateningly.

The push jerked him forwards. The gun barrel dug into his back and caused him to grunt with pain. He turned and treated me to a malevolent look full of hatred. I gave him another push.

"Go now, before I change my mind."

Branden sneered at me and held Jeannie in a cold stare.

"Next time you won't be so lucky, Jeannie," he said.

He was about to add something else, but I dug the gun barrel in hard, making him whoosh out a breath of air. He thought further about saying it and, turning on his heel, strode away. I watched him go, still scolding his men with a heavy tongue that had them cowering before him. Before they could collect themselves we jumped into the lorry, pressing the self-starter. At the sound of the engine they instantly came alive, surging onwards to stop us, firing as they advanced. Bullets ripped through the canvas back and rebounded off the wheels. The lorry sprang into life and shot forwards as I wrestled with the steering wheel.

Pure luck and divine providence were with us. The vehicle just kept on going, dodging the missiles with mechanical impunity, putting distance between us and our pursuers. Our luck ran out when the truck laboured for an instant then died, stopping at the edge of a dense wood. We hurriedly scrambled out, listened to the chase getting closer with each second then dived into a thick cluster of bushes. We breathed a thankful sigh of relief and wondered why they had not followed the road as we had done. We had outfoxed them - that was obvious.

We returned to the lorry, but realised that it was useless. The engine had copped a stray bullet in the radiator and the water was draining out. I saw the drops dripping into a widening pool beneath the vehicle.

CHAPTER THIRTY

I was aware that we were near Deal, but how far we had travelled with Branden was unknown. We were also unfamiliar with our immediate surroundings, in fact we were lost. We backtracked, following the tyre marks to a deserted main road. We pushed on until the sea came into sight and with it the lighthouse. My heart lifted at the sight and I made for the tower, meaning to continue the fight.

"He'll be preparing to scarper. We should let Lawrence know about it," Jeannie warned, obviously against my idea.

I knew she was right, so I asked her to do the phoning. I was continuing the fight under my own terms though. I kissed her once and set out, leaving her to find a telephone. The dinghy was out, as it was daylight and they would be watchful. I scanned the area from the shelter of a few bushes, deciding my next move. I had a gun and wondered about the ammunition. I broke open the box and counted the shells. There were nine, barely enough if I was about to start a war. Branden would have guns and plenty of ammunition. The trouble was it was all inside the lighthouse.

I was in a quandary. I was in two minds whether to wait for the back-up I knew would be arriving, but if I did, would it be too late to stop Branden? He was obviously preparing to flee the country. If I was to wait until dark, would that also be too late? The alternatives buzzed around in my head.

My questions were answered by the sight of the opening of the ground floor door. There was movement then a light shone from the open doorway, which widened as I looked. The rats were stirring and preparing to flee the nest while they had the chance. I had to stop them before they had time to escape, but what could I do? I could not count on luck for the second time. I had to rely on myself. As I had repeatedly told myself, any results are up to you. I was standing by as they were escaping, getting away with all the crimes they had committed, and with the blessing of Branden and his kind. They were going scot-free without anyone to stop them – no one but me.

The memory of nine rounds of ammo clouded my thoughts. They were capable of firing thousands of bullets at me to my nine. It made me laugh at my puny efforts. Time was running out and I was gazing at the gang, undecided, but they were really choosing for me, being instrumental in forcing my hand. I gripped the gun and stepped out from my hiding place.

When they saw who I was the guns opened up, pinging on the surrounding rock and ripping it to shale. I dropped behind an outcrop of rock and loosed off one of my precious rounds. I was rewarded by a cry as it hit one of the men. I was instantly overjoyed at the result and mentally counted it as number one. They kept under cover after that and the battle had begun. I relaxed, realising that nobody was going anywhere. I had them pinned down and they knew it.

Ten minutes or so passed before they made their first move. They were using a mobile lorry as cover to shield them from my fire. I expended another bullet to deter them and it glanced off the metal engine cover. Now, this is getting serious, I thought. They were about a hundred yards distant and inexorably closing the gap with each minute. I tried another round and hit nothing when suddenly the shape of a descending helicopter shot out of the sky. It dropped down to the island and hovered above it with a deafening roar before rising and heading towards the shore. I felt like cheering and almost exposed my position before realising it.

The marines had landed. Jeannie had managed to contact Lawrence and my back-up was on its way. This turn of events had to make some sort of difference to the odds, and it did. The lorry stopped in its tracks and figures were seen running towards the tower leaving the vehicle abandoned. Excited voices drifting on the wind spoke of the panic the sight of the helicopter had invoked. Now they had to make their move, I decided. Branden had to break out while the marines were in the process of moving in.

I skipped from rock to rock, keeping a low profile, all the time getting closer to the abandoned vehicle. As the gang prepared to leave, I quit a final rock and ran over open ground expecting a bullet, but getting none. I slid around the side of the lorry expecting trouble, but finding none. The gang had retreated to the safety of the lighthouse and was deciding on its next action. I used the lull to make some decisions of my own. I deliberately avoided the line of the upstairs windows, dodging around the vehicle until the last moment.

I threw myself forwards, avoiding a bullet that smashed into the ground. I landed on both knees, cradling the gun. The door was closed as I expected it to be. I paused undecided, looking for a way in, all the time keeping a low profile and sliding around the wall. Once again I was forestalled – another glitch to my plans. Frustrated, I was about to give up when the door opened and a voice called to me.

"Cox, I'll give you anything you ask if you will only let us go."

I recognised the oily voice of the master murderer himself.

"*Anything*," I asked from the cover of the wall, "anything at all?"

"Anything you want," Branden said, encouraged by my change of voice."You have only to ask and it is yours."

"How about doing fifty years in jail?" I said.

I mentally saw him grinding his teeth in rage, and wondered what he would do next. The answer was not long in coming, for the men spewed out of the tower in a burst of fury, fanning out and surrounding the entire lighthouse, capturing me at the same time. Branden's shriek of ecstasy greeted my demise. He ran to my side brandishing a gun aimed at my chest.

"Now, Cox, at long last," he said in triumph. "I'm going to finish you this time."

He levelled his automatic and I closed my eyes waiting for the bullet. Immediately a barrage of small arms opened up from the end of the causeway, bringing down three of his henchmen. My relief knew no bounds as I mentally cheered with relief. My back-up had arrived in force and was running up the causeway. Branden gave me a look of pure hatred and dashed into the lower room of the lighthouse, instantly followed by the remainder of his gang. I was blowing with relief at my untimely deliverance from death.

I waited as the first of the khaki-clad men arrived, shaking the hand of the first officer on the scene. I pointed to the closed door.

"You'll have to blast your way in," I shouted.

"No bother," he said, and called to a sergeant who was carrying a bazooka rocket launcher. "Knock that door down, sergeant, will you."

The blast cut a huge hole in the metal door. I waited until the smoke cleared away before leaping for the hole, jumping over dead men who had just been killed in the explosion. I dodged around the blazing wreck of the lorry before treading up the steps. Several bullets nicked the wall around me as I rushed upwards. The access flap was thrown down as I reached it. I shot the lock with the gun I had retrieved and then blasted through the remains. There was no opposition on the floor, so I let the marines catch up with me as I was out of breath from the force of my efforts.

"They're holed up in the lamp house," I said, "Branden and a few of his men."

The troops poured up, searching the rooms and taking defensive positions on the second floor. Surprise, surprise, Lawrence made an appearance then, puffing his way through the access flap to stand by my side. I had difficulty concealing my astonishment.

"Mr Lawrence, what a surprise. If I had known you would be here I'd have taken Branden prisoner," I said, with a trace of irony in my voice.

Lawrence chose to ignore the remark.

"Don't be facetious, Cox, where is Branden?"

"Upstairs, holed up in the lamp house," I answered.

"I'll take charge," he said, dismissing me from his mind and addressing the officer. "We'll try a full frontal attack on the lamp house, you with your men and me from the helicopter, all right?"

The officer nodded to Lawrence and then turned to me.

"Is that OK with you?" he asked.

I shook my head.

"You do that and he'll blow the lot up," I retorted, with some feeling. "Look, he has arms and ammunition stored up there with him. If you allow him to blow it and himself to kingdom come he'll be a martyr to his cause. He'll be a hero to his people instead of the bloodthirsty murderer whom we all know him to be. You may set law and order back another thirty years if you do."

The officer furrowed his brow in thought.

"You could be right," he said, after looking at Lawrence and me then the trapdoor, calculating the odds.

"We could try Cox's way," Lawrence conceded, trying not to look at me. "Branden might just blow it all up he's that type of man. All right then, easy does it. We just let him alone and negotiate."

The officer was relieved to have come to some sort of understanding. I looked at the trapdoor above us then at the officer and his men, venturing to offer advise.

"If I was you, mate, I'd clear out now while you've got the chance. He may still consider it, blowing it up I mean."

The officer did consider it and called his men to accompany him outside.

"Now what, Cox?" Lawrence leered as the men filed down the steps. "You can't negotiate with scum like Branden."

"Nevertheless, that's what we do," I insisted. "I know you can't really reason with a man like him; he thinks he's right and nothing will shift his beliefs."

I was looking at Lawrence with what I hoped was determination on my face. He was duly impressed with what he saw and smiled.

"Good to see your loyalty. It's very little used in this day and age."

I gave him a thin smile and, gripping my gun tightly to my waist, stepped onto the first stair. Instantly, as if it was alarmed, a voice that I took to be the master terrorist's, rang out.

"The lamp house is wired to explode. All I have to do is press a button and we all go up."

"Branden," I said, approaching the trapdoor, "this is Cox. Give yourself up and you go free." I corrected myself. "That is everyone *except* you."

Branden's hoarse laugh echoed through the trapdoor panelling, but his laughter turned to anger as he argued with his men about the surrender terms. They were not as dedicated as their leader and said so. Branden's voice could be heard above all the others as he lambasted all and sundry with his whiplashing tongue. Suddenly there was silence as the altercation ceased, the lock rasped in it's housing with a squeal and the flap opened.

"We're coming out," said a gruff voice, and a thick-set individual lowered his body through the hole.

I aimed my gun at him, but when I saw his raised hands I let him go past. Seven gang members were handcuffed and led away by the military, leaving the leader, Branden, remaining. He had slammed the trapdoor shut as his followers left.

"It's all up to you," I said through the wooden panelling. "Give up now and I'll see you get a fair trial."

Branden's laughter once more filtered through the wood.

"*Me* in a prison cell. I don't think so. I'm used to better places than that."

"That's all I can offer you."

"I might accept your terms," he said."I might accept your terms on one condition."

"And what's that?" I asked, with some suspicion.

"You let me serve my time in an Irish prison."

"That's not up to me," I said.

"If you mean Lawrence," Branden grated, "I'll abide by his rules, but only if it's in Ireland."

"OK, I'll see what he says, but... I can't promise anything."

With that parting reminder I clomped down the steps and out to the causeway. Lawrence was at the end, overseeing things, so I went to him to talk. He listened as I related all that Branden had said, shaking his head as I talked, his fat jowls wobbling as he did so.

"That's impossible," he said. "He's wanted in this country for the many crimes he's committed here. He-"

He was interrupted by an explosion that whooshed up the causeway in a blinding crash of eye-searing light. It echoed from the distant rooftops and surrounding hills then died away on the horizon. The top of the lighthouse had completely disappeared and stood there, a smoking stump of twisted metal and collapsed stonework.

So died Branden, the terrorist and Britain's premier enemy.

I returned to live with Jeannie and we were married a few months later.

ISBN 142511472-5